Who says you can't live the rock and roll life after forty? You just need a lot more vitamins and a bigger bottle of aspirin.

SEMI-PSYCHIC LIFE

Valerie Costa is pretty sure she's rocking her forties. She has an amazing coffee shop, two cool teenagers, and a new superpower that gives her insight into any random object she touches.

Okay, she's not thrilled about that last one.

For the past year, ever since she and her two best friends drove their car off the edge and into Glimmer Lake, Val has struggled with her new abilities. She's not exactly sure she wants to be psychic, she could live without her newfound glove addiction, and honestly, no one wants to know that much about their teenage sons.

But when Val's ex-husband goes missing and the police show up at her door with questions she can't answer, Val, Robin, and Monica are going to have to use their sudden psychic abilities to solve a mystery none of them saw coming.

Semi-Psychic Life is a standalone paranormal women's fiction novel in the Glimmer Lake series by *USA Today* best seller Elizabeth Hunter, author of the Elemental Mysteries and the Irin Chronicles.

...the 2nd book in the series is genuinely superb. I adored SUDDENLY PSYCHIC but SEMI-PSYCHIC LIFE was even better.

I love everything about this series! The small town setting, the close-knit friendships, the dialogue and the psychic powers.

SEMI-PSYCHIC LIFE

GLIMMER LAKE BOOK TWO

ELIZABETH HUNTER

Cover: Damonza
Content Editor: Amy Cissell, Cissell Ink
Line Editor: Anne Victory
Proofreader: Victory Editing

Recurve Press LLC
PO Box 4034
Visalia, California 93278
USA

To the introverts!
That's right, I'm dedicating this book to everyone who's been
socially isolating long before it was cool.
We always knew we were right.
Let's hang out.
Separately.
In our own houses.

CHAPTER 1

*V*al was battling a headache that had been brewing since she'd woken up that morning. It was just her luck that Americano Asshole handed her a refillable coffee cup. One that might hold traces of psychic energy. And one that he hadn't rinsed out. Of course.

"The usual," he said brusquely.

"Got it," Val said under her breath. "Anything else?"

Scattered on the counter were baskets of fresh lemon scones, homemade energy bars, and decadent blueberry muffins that her baker, Honey, had made fresh that morning, but he ignored them all.

He was staring at his phone and fingering the zipper pull on his Patagonia vest. "Nothing. Just my usual."

The usual for Americano Asshole was a café Americano diluted with so much milk and sugar that it would be impossible to detect the subtleties of flavor between espresso and the regular brewed coffee Val had sitting on the counter.

There was a valued place in the coffee world for the café

Americano, but not when you drank it like Americano Asshole. That's why he had his name.

"Café Americano, heavy cream, three sugars," Val said, ringing up the customer. He had a name, it was Allan Anderson, but nobody at Misfit Mountain Coffee Shop used it. He was Americano Asshole or AA for a reason.

Val reached for the silver coffee mug on the counter. She didn't notice the tiny hole in her glove until the flashing image of a woman pouring coffee into the mug filled her mind. The woman was wearing nothing but Americano Asshole's button-down shirt. The woman was also not AA's wife.

"Shit." She sucked in a breath and AA looked up.

"Problem?"

Val knew the woman was not his wife because Americano Asshole was married to a genuinely lovely woman named Savannah who came into Misfit every other Tuesday night with her book club.

The unexpected vision hit her fast. It was as if Val had been plopped in the room with AA and his sidepiece for a split second, then yanked out.

"I said"—he spoke slowly—"is there a problem?"

She plastered on a smile and swallowed the ream of curses she wanted to throw at him. "It's fine. Let me just rinse this out."

She adjusted her glove to shift the hole to the back of her finger before she slipped up again. Then she turned to rinse out AA's coffee mug so she could get back to the growing line.

It had been over a year since she'd experienced the car crash and near-death experience that had triggered her weird psychic abilities, and Val was still struggling.

Most days she was able to live normally. Thank God she only reacted to objects, not people. When she was home, her life was manageable.

She didn't hear random voices or see ghosts like her friend Robin. She didn't have scary premonitions or graphic dreams like her friend Monica. Val wore gloves at work and while doing chores around the house, and she could handle it.

Most of the time.

She handed the rinsed cup to her barista Eve and turned back to the register to get AA's money for his Americano.

"Two seventy-five," Val said, worrying the hole in her glove. She'd learned the hard way that touching money without gloves could be a nightmare.

AA noticed her glove and smirked. "You'd think with what you charge for coffee you could afford new gloves."

Eve sucked in an audible breath, and behind AA, the next customer's eyes went wide.

Val wasn't bothered. They called him Americano Asshole for a reason. "I try to coast on the wealth I've built from twenty-five-cent tips like yours, but the struggle is real."

Ramon, her cook, barked a laugh from the kitchen behind her, and AA's eyes went cold.

"I'd give anything for a decent coffee shop in this shithole town."

Eve handed her the Americano, and Val passed it over with a smile, along with the quarter AA usually left in the tip jar.

"But instead you're stuck with us. Bite me! And have a nice day."

He turned without dropping the quarter in the jar, and

Val flipped off his back before she turned to the next customer.

"Hey, Mom."

Marie Costa pursed her lips. "Honey, you really shouldn't treat customers that way."

"You worry too much. Where else is he going to go? There's not another coffee shop until Bridger City." She handed her mom a coffee cup. "Besides, that guy's always in a bad mood. Dad coming in?"

"He's parking the car."

Val handed over another cup and pointed to the counter. "The counter is yours. You want your usual?"

"Please."

Ramon yelled from the back, "You got it, Mama Marie!"

Val couldn't hide her smile. "Grab some stools."

"Thank you, Valerie." She pulled out her wallet and took out twenty dollars even though Val never took her money. "Thank you, Ramon!"

Val refused to let her parents pay for their weekly coffee shop breakfast when they'd been the ones to loan her the start-up money to begin with. So Marie, knowing Val wouldn't take her money, put it in the tip jar every week.

"And this is why my employees love you more than they love me."

"They're the ones cooking for me," Marie said. "Not you."

"And be grateful for that."

Ramon shouted, "Marie, you better grab one of those lemon scones Honey made before they're gone."

"Oh, that sounds delicious." Marie's eyes lit up. "I do love Honey's scones."

"She's trying to make me fat." Ramon was thin and wiry, the kind of guy who ran marathons and couldn't put on weight to save his life. He was married to Honey, who was as sweet as her name and carried all the curves in the family.

"Likely story," Val said. "If Honey didn't feed you sugar, you'd blow away in a breeze."

"Bite me." Ramon winked at her. "Get back to work, slacker."

Val had grabbed three more coffee orders and passed them to Eve before there was a break in the line. Two more tables had seated themselves, and her server Max was already getting them set up with coffee.

Long before she'd been a mom or a psychic, Valerie Costa had dreamed of being a rock star. Having zero musical ability had made her realistic about her chances with that, so being a rock star turned into having a place where rock stars hung out.

Unfortunately, she'd never taken more than a few administration courses at the community college in Bridger City. She'd married her high school sweetheart and spent her twenties partying up and down California with Josh, living for the next concert or road trip. Josh fixed cars, and Val got jobs at whatever office was hiring and didn't mind her multicolored hair and tattoos.

Val wasn't a purist. She tried lots of jobs. She worked in restaurant kitchens and accountants' offices. She worked as a landscaper for a while, then at a big coffee chain in her late twenties just to get medical benefits.

It was during Val's coffee stint that she got pregnant with her oldest son, Jackson. Faced with the inevitability of raising a brand-new person, she started to realize that while punk rock life was fun, having a house and a retirement account might be kind of necessary.

At first Josh was thrilled about the baby. He made all the right noises and dressed their newborn son in Metallica onesies, combing his fine baby hair into a Mohawk.

They were going to be different kinds of parents. Cool parents. Punk rock parents.

Life got more tense when kid number two rolled around. Val had to work, and she couldn't do it without her parents' help. They moved from Bridger City back to Glimmer Lake, which Josh absolutely hated.

"We're moving backward, not forward," he'd said.

Secretly, Val was relieved to be back. She was close to her parents and close to Monica and Robin, who could reassure her that she wasn't a bad mother because she wasn't a fan of baby talk or Wiggles CDs or fluffy blue diaper bags.

Val might not have been the average mom, but she adored her boys. And while Josh liked the fun stuff about being a dad, he didn't do well with changing diapers, balancing work and parenthood, or losing his nights to crying babies.

Josh started to stay out later and later. He didn't show up for school meetings, and more and more of his paycheck started going missing. By the time Jackson was seven and Andy was three, Val knew he was fooling around. She confronted him. He denied it; then he walked out.

And that was that.

Val was a single mother of two with no college degree, no steady job, and no resources except great friends and family.

She could work with that.

Val decided that if punk rock life was out of reach in Glimmer Lake, then she'd make her own oasis of punk in the woods. Her mother and father loaned her the money to start Misfit Mountain Coffee Stand. Val stuffed herself and her boys into the tiny coffee outpost while she figured out how to make better coffee than the chain where she'd worked. She stumbled and messed up a lot along the way, but she had a few things working in her favor.

Everyone in Glimmer Lake liked her, even if they didn't get her. She was the weird mom who accidentally dropped f-bombs at the park, but her kids were cute and surprisingly well behaved. Plus she was Marie and Vincent Costa's daughter. She made great coffee, she spoke her mind, but she always made you laugh.

The drive-through coffee stand turned into a café. Then Val met Ramon and Honey. Ramon was a kick-ass cook, and Honey was a baker. They'd grown up in Glimmer Lake but moved to the East Bay to work in the restaurant business, where they'd been blissfully happy. Then Honey's mom got sick and there was no one else to take care of her.

Ramon and Honey had been the spark that started the coffee shop. They weren't a full-service restaurant; the menu was limited to what Ramon could get delivered and what he felt like cooking that day. Honey's baked goods became legendary. Along with Val's personality and coffee skills, they'd been making it work for about three years, but they weren't out of the woods yet.

Of course, it was Glimmer Lake. They'd never really be out of the woods.

And Josh?

Val's ex was around, but he wasn't. He flitted in and out of her boys' lives like a punk rock fairy godfather, missing for months, only to show up with brand-new iPads for everyone or drunkenly professing his eternal love for Val after he'd broken up with yet another girlfriend.

Val ignored him. She had two kick-ass kids, amazing parents, and the two best friends anyone could ask for. She had her coffee shop, a good tattoo artist, and was paying her own bills. Just barely, but she was making it.

Okay, and now she had weird psychic abilities that were kind of complicating her life, but she'd figure out how to handle that eventually.

Or she'd go insane. Some days she really thought it could go either way.

JUST AFTER TEN O'CLOCK, Val's two favorite people in the world walked into Misfit.

Robin, Monica, and Val were as different as three best friends could be. If they hadn't all been put in Mrs. Cowell's advanced reader group in fourth grade, they might never have been friends. But that reading group had turned into a lifeline in junior high, then a united and unbreakable front in high school.

Val was the crazy and slightly dangerous one. Monica was the nurturing big sister of the group, and Robin was the planner with the heart of an artist. They'd seen each other through marriage, pregnancy and miscarriage, crying babies, hormonal teenagers, divorce, and death.

Monica waved Val over to their table. She handed the register over to Eve and walked to the corner table where Robin already had some notebooks spread out.

"I have fifteen minutes," Val said. "That's it."

"We can work with fifteen minutes." Robin spread her hands on the notebooks as if she was bracing herself. "What do you think about opening a mini version of Misfit at Russell House?"

Val blinked. "That's sudden."

"Kind of, but you've already had a coffee stand."

"A drive-through coffee stand is not Russell House."

Russell House was Robin's family home that they'd de-ghosted the year before. Robin's grandfather had been haunting her grandmother, and there'd been another ghost involved, the man her grandfather had murdered, and it was a whole thing.

But then they got rid of Grandpa Murderer Ghost, Grandma Helen passed peacefully, and Robin's mom and uncle were left with a giant house that neither knew what to do with, so Robin's mom and Monica had gone into business to turn the old mansion into a boutique hotel and event venue.

The first events had been hosted, but they were still working out the kinks of having real hotel guests.

"Hear me out, because this is not a stretch," Monica said. "We've already nailed down baked goods from Honey. She'll be doing an exclusive Russell House scone for the room bakery boxes every morning. But then we were thinking, do we want to have coffee makers in all the rooms? Or would it be better to have an espresso bar in the lobby and do in-room deliveries?"

Robin said, "It would basically be a coffee stand like you started out with. The hotel would just be paying you a certain amount to make coffee in the morning. Anything above that would be yours."

Hmmm. Could be interesting.

Monica said, "We're doing a lot of business day-conference things since Jake finished building the ropes course. You know you could make extra money during events like that."

Val perched on a chair. "I like the idea, but I just went through that whole expansion drama last year that didn't work out, so I'm feeling a little wary, and also—no offense—but I want to make sure I don't cannibalize my business here, you know?"

"Makes total sense." Robin slid a folder across the table. "I put a couple of ideas and numbers together for you to look at."

Val took the folder. "Of course you did."

"It's just some thoughts about how you could make it work if you wanted to." She drummed her fingers on the table. "I had time."

Monica and Val exchanged a look.

"How's life without Emma?" Monica asked.

Robin's youngest had shipped off to university in Washington State the previous fall, leaving Robin and her husband Mark official empty nesters.

"It's good." Robin nodded. "It was nice to see her and Austin over the holidays, but... it's also nice to have the house back to ourselves again, you know?"

Monica whispered loudly, "They're having freaky sex in whatever room they want now."

Val whispered back, "That's what I figured too."

Robin rolled her eyes. "Listen, weirdos, this is me and Mark, not..." Robin's eyes lifted when the bell over the door rang. "So, speaking of freaky sex..."

Val whipped her head around, only to see Sullivan

Wescott, sheriff of Glimmer Lake and a partial source of Val's headache, walking into the coffee shop.

She immediately spun around. "Shut up, Robin."

"I didn't say anything!"

"You were thinking it."

Monica raised her hand. "No, that was me, actually. I was the one suspecting you and Sully of having freaky sex."

Val hissed, "In what universe do I have the time to have freaky sex with anyone?"

"That wasn't a denial." Robin held her fist out to Monica, who bumped her knuckles. "We were right."

"You're both ridiculous." Val glanced at her watch. "And your time is up."

Monica leaned over to Robin. "She's leaving us so she can get his order."

"Of course she is," Robin said quietly. "I mean, who else is going to make flirty eyes at Sully? She can't have Eve doing it. She's young enough to be his daughter."

Val turned, flipped both her best friends off, then walked back to the register.

CHAPTER 2

*V*al made it to the register just as Sully stepped to the front of the line. Val was tall, but Sully towered over her at well over six feet. He was wearing his uniform, along with his old-fashioned felt Stetson, which was dusted with snow. His sandy-brown hair was getting long in back and fell over his jacket collar.

"Hey, Sully." Val kept her voice even. "What can I get you?"

"Large coffee." His blue eyes were on her. "How's your day going?"

"It's going." Val got a paper cup out. "To go?"

"Yeah."

People liked Sully. He was considered trustworthy and the kind of man who didn't need to shout to get attention, both qualities that fostered confidence in old-fashioned Glimmer Lake. Also, he was a massive guy. He looked and talked like someone who worked in timber, which made the old logging guys in the county vote for him.

Instead of just handing the paper cup over like she did

with most customers, Val filled it, then added the amount of cream he liked before she put the lid on. "Here you go."

Down-home, trustworthy sheriffs who walked grandmothers across the street and marshaled Christmas parades were not Val's type.

"Thanks." Sully reached for the cup and their fingers brushed, sending a thrill up her arm and reminding her too much of a stolen night and unwise decisions from a year and a half ago.

He might not be her type, but Sully was incredibly attractive. Not that Val would call him handsome. His jaw was square, and his mouth was a flat line across a usually serious face. His nose had been broken when he was playing football in college, and he looked like he was perpetually scowling.

To be honest, the scowl might have been the most attractive thing about him. Val constantly wanted to needle him just to see if she could make him laugh.

His eyes were the only soft thing about him, a brilliant sky blue that made Val think of a summer day on the lake. His beard looked pretty soft too, but he only wore that in the winter, so she didn't have firsthand knowledge.

"How're your boys doing?"

"Good." She finally looked up. "Your parents?"

"Dad's complaining about the weather, and Mom's talking about planting bulbs."

"So normal then."

A slight smile touched the corner of his mouth. "Pretty much."

"Two bucks," Val said.

"For a coffee?"

"No, for fucking awesome coffee."

"Oh, in that case..."

She could tell he wanted to roll his eyes, but instead he slid two bucks from his wallet and handed them over before he dropped a dollar in the tip jar.

Sully had lived in Los Angeles and worked there before moving back, as so many of their old classmates did, to be closer to aging parents. He'd run for sheriff in their rural mountain county twice now and won both times. He was divorced, no kids, and the one time they'd had sex had been way better than Val had anticipated.

Way, *way* better.

But who had time for that?

She realized she'd been staring. "Okay. Have a good one."

The corner of his mouth lifted a little more, and he tipped his hat. "See ya, Valerie."

Her lips parted, and she was grateful he walked away when he did. She didn't want him to see her reaction.

Dating did not fit in her life. Men did not fit in her life, period, unless it was the ex she was forced to occasionally deal with or the two mini-men she was trying to raise. Which was why—when Sully asked her out after their one night together—she'd said no.

He'd been pissed.

Not that she'd turned him down, but all the reasons she listed.

"You know, you're allowed to have a life."

"It's so obvious you don't have kids, Sully."

He had walked back in his bedroom and shut the door, and Val snuck out of the house, hoping no one saw her walking back to her car where she'd left it at Chaco's. It was early, but there were always nosy people around in Glimmer Lake.

And now they mostly ignored each other. Mostly. Every now and then—like he had last night—Sully would text her.

Come over.

I can't.

I'll make it worth your time.

I have no time.

And that would be it. Val would lie awake in bed, thinking about all the ways she wanted to say yes and cursing how she wasn't living her life. This wasn't what she'd planned when she was young. She hadn't really made any plans past the next concert or the next road trip, but she knew her life wasn't supposed to be like this.

But she was the one—the only one—doing All the Things for her kids and her parents and her employees.

So she would ignore Sully, and he would go silent for a few months. Until he picked a random night to mess up her sleep and make her wish her life were different.

She watched him walk out the door and get into the green pickup parked at the curb.

"Val?"

"Huh?" She turned to Eve.

Eve leaned over. "You were staring."

Val winced. "Sorry."

"It's understandable. He has a really great ass. And I'm not a uniform person."

"You're also young enough to be his daughter."

"So?" Eve shrugged. "Doesn't mean I don't have eyes."

SHE ARRIVED home about fifteen minutes before her kids. When they'd been younger, it was the only thing that allowed her to keep her sanity, those fifteen minutes of silence. Now, as they got older and retreated into their rooms and their phones and their individual social lives, Val dreaded the quiet.

It was all going too fast. Her oldest had earned his license in November. Now Jackson drove to the library to study, to his father's house when Josh had time for a visit, out with his friends on weekends. Jackson even drove Andy to school, leaving Val feeling particularly useless.

She walked to the kitchen and grabbed the giant bottle of aspirin that lived by the microwave before she went to the shower to wash the pervasive smell of coffee and kitchen grease from her skin.

She'd done it to herself. She'd raised Jackson to be an independent kid, and he was. How was she supposed to know that one day she'd wish he was a clinger?

The front door slammed shut as Val was getting out of the shower, her skin exposed to the world like a raw nerve.

Unless she was doing chores, she tried to keep from wearing her gloves at home. She didn't want the boys to notice and wonder about her turning into a germophobe or anything that might cause questions. She definitely needed them if she cleaned their room, but for the most part, her own small home provoked nothing but good memories. Those she could deal with.

Andy's cheerful voice echoed down the hall. "Hey, Mom!"

"Hey, kiddo!" She rubbed a towel through her hair and

thought about cutting it again. She needed a trim. She'd shaved the sides and back a couple of years before and never looked back. She kept the top long, but her hair was insanely thick and pin straight. Having the sides shaved let her do some fun things with the style and gave her neck a break. It also highlighted the tattoo work she'd gotten done on her upper back and neck.

She squinted at the foggy mirror.

You still got it. You're still rock and roll.

Val reached in the medicine cabinet and grabbed a packet of the vitamins Monica had forced her to start taking when she hit forty. She downed the small handful in a single gulp. She was rock and roll. Headaches from not getting enough sleep and iron deficiency were not.

She pulled on a pair of yoga pants and an old concert T-shirt before she left the bathroom. She'd only been able to buy the house five years ago, and her parents had to cosign because she was self-employed, but she made every payment and it was hers.

Two bedrooms and one bath, it sat within walking distance of Misfit Mountain and the grocery store. It was more of a cabin than a house, but Val still loved it. She'd given her boys the larger room since they had to share and had taken the smallest room at the southwest corner for her own sanctuary.

"Hey, guys!"

Andy came barreling toward her. *"Hola, madre."*

Val grinned. "I see someone had Spanish today."

"Sí." Andy adored school. He adored learning anything new. He loved languages and had a list of them he wanted to learn so he could visit far-flung parts of the globe. He got

excited about group projects. He loved tests, for heaven's sake.

Andy was an alien.

Val thought that probably one of Robin's kids and hers got mixed up somehow, because neither she nor Josh were school people. Whatever. She wasn't giving him back. Andy was too wonderful.

Dark eyes shaded by a fall of thick brown hair met her gaze from down the small hallway. Ah yes. Jackson was Val's Mini-Me with his father's good looks.

"Hey, handsome."

Jackson cracked a smile. "Hey, Mom."

"Any news I need to know about?"

The look on his face said there *was* news and she wasn't going to like it.

"What's going on?" she asked.

Andy disappeared into his room—probably to read Tolstoy or Austen or Aristotle like the lovely alien he was—and Val walked toward her oldest.

Jackson sighed. "I got my chemistry paper back."

"And?"

His face said it all. "D."

"A D?" Val's heart fell. It was a huge project, and she knew it was a big part of his grade. She wasn't the strictest mom, and she had no illusions about Jackson getting straight As—he didn't like school and he'd always struggled—but he was also insanely smart and science was usually his strong suit.

"What happened?" She sat at the table. "I saw you working on it. Did you not—"

"Stupid shit," Jackson muttered. "It's not English class, so

I don't know why they're being so picky about grammar and shit."

"So what if it's not English?" Val said. "It's still a paper. Did you not format it correctly? Didn't you edit? You told me I didn't need to look at it because a friend was editing for you."

"She did, okay?" The guilty look on his face told a different story. "Don't be uncool. I guess she's not as good at editing as you. It's not her fault."

Val held out her hand. "Let me see."

A single touch of the science paper gave Val a flash of a very cute girl and her teenage son making out in a corner of the library. The paper sat on the table beside them.

Ew. No, thank you. Val dropped the paper.

This wasn't Jackson not understanding, this was him not doing the work. Val rubbed her temple, trying to wipe the image from her head. "What the heck, Jack?"

He rolled his eyes and Val came to her feet. "I don't think so. First off, lose the attitude."

"Mom, it's one paper. Don't overreact."

"It's your *grades*. It's your future. Next fall you start applying to colleges, and you cannot have Ds on your transcripts, kid. That's not the way it works. You know you have to get scholarships, Jackson."

"Or I go to community college. We're not rich, Mom. You know that's what's going to happen anyway."

"Not if you get scholarships!"

"Why do you care so much?"

"Because I don't want you to end up like me and your dad, okay!"

The look on Jackson's face killed her. "You think I'm like Dad?"

Why couldn't anything they argued about be easy anymore? Val looked to the heavens and bit her lip hard before she responded. "You know that's not what I mean."

"'Cause"—he was clearly pissed off—"I'm the one who picks Andy up from school and takes him to soccer practice and tells him about shaving and does all that shit. So like, I'm already doing better than Dad."

Val walked over and put both her hands on Jackson's face. "Look at me and take a breath." She could see the waves of hormones and anger rolling off him. He was sixteen and had been taking on adult roles since long before a kid should have to. "Deep breaths, Jack."

Her son inhaled and got himself under control.

"Listen to me," Val said quietly. "I am so proud of the man you're becoming. You're twice the man your father is, and the fact that you have any relationship with him at all is a testament to the man you are and not the man he is. Do you understand me?"

Jackson nodded.

"When I say I don't want you to end up like me and your dad, I meant the *options* you have. I didn't think school was important and so I blew it off, and when I needed some kind of foundation for being on my own, it wasn't there. I had no degree. I barely had a high school diploma. I worked, but I had to work twice as hard to prove myself."

"But you did," he mumbled.

"Eventually. Yeah. But why make life more difficult for yourself if you don't have to? And your dad? He's a brilliant mechanic. He is an absolute artist with bikes and cars. But he has no idea how to run a business, so he's always losing money. He didn't get the training he needed to be successful. I do not want that for you."

"You never rag on Andy—"

"Your brother is probably gonna be a professor or something and write textbooks and make us all look like idiots, okay?"

Jackson started to smile.

"School is like a walk in the park for Andy." Val let him go and took a step back. "I know it's not the same for you, because it wasn't that way for me either. It doesn't mean you're not as smart as he is, it means you have to work for it. And that's okay. That means you're gonna know how to work better than your brother does."

Jack crossed his arms over his chest. "Fine. I hear you."

She tapped her fingers on the paper. Quickly. She couldn't mention anything about Jackson and the girl, but this grade was clearly a result of her son not doing the work he needed to do. "There have to be consequences for this. You know there have to be."

"Am I going to lose car privileges?"

Her father had given Jackson his old, beat-up Ford pickup. It wasn't much to look at, but it ran and Jack loved it. It was freedom.

"No, you're not losing the car." She pointed to the paper. "Yet. Don't let something like this happen again or you will. I'll think of something. It will not be overly heinous, and in the meantime, ask Mrs. Fletcher if there's any extra credit you can do to make up for this."

"Okay."

"Do you understand me about your grades? Four-year

college. Bachelor's degree. That's your goal. Scholarships. Forging your own identity and finding amazing friends and doing all the cool stuff." She tossed the paper on the table. "I want you to have that. You deserve to have that. But you're not getting it unless you put the work in."

"I get it." He rolled his eyes. "I can't believe some of my friends think you're the cool mom."

Val blinked. "Your friends think I'm the cool mom?"

"Some!" Jackson held up his hand. "Seriously, don't embarrass me. Just chill. A couple. Like maybe one."

"Yes!" Val raised her hands and pumped the air, tossing her head back and forth like she was headbanging. "I. Am. The. Cool. *Moooooom!*"

Jackson put his hand over his eyes. "I've made a horrible mistake."

IT WAS after midnight and she still couldn't sleep. Val pressed the heels of her hands to her eyes and took deep breaths.

In. Out.

Clearing her mind.

Relaxing her body.

Clearing her mind.

Relaxing...

Relaxing, dammit.

She sat up and walked to the dresser in the corner, opening the drawer to take out the antianxiety medication her doctor had prescribed six months ago.

"Take it at night. It'll help you sleep."

The pills had helped her sleep, and they also did what she'd been hoping for. They dulled her clarity when she got visions. Her perception wasn't as fast or as clear.

She hated feeling dependent on them.

But Val never wanted superpowers. She hadn't asked for any of this. She never wanted to know that much about anyone. It was bad enough living in a tiny town where everyone was in each other's business all the time. Owning the town's only coffee shop meant she perceived too much as it was through her five normal senses.

So occasionally Val convinced herself that she could manage without her pills and stopped taking them.

The anxiety always came back. The sleeplessness returned.

Val could battle through it... but it had been three nights of poor sleep because her brain wouldn't turn off. It had been days of hair-trigger visions she didn't want.

She gave in and took the small white tablet, washed it down with a glass of water, and returned to bed. Just as she was about to close her eyes, she saw her phone buzz. Josh was texting her.

You awake?

Val rolled over and closed her eyes. Josh was a pest and she did not want to talk to him. She didn't have the time, patience, or energy for her ex. She ignored the text and the buzzing sound that told her he was calling. If it was important, he'd leave a voice mail and she could check it later.

Nothing her ex-husband had to say was urgent enough to answer the phone at one in the morning.

CHAPTER 3

*V*al was bleary-eyed and aching when her alarm went off. She reached for the bottle of water on her bedside table, downed the contents, and set it back down. Then she sat on the edge of the bed and tried to wake up.

She could already feel the effects of her medication like a fog in her mind. She reached for her test object on the bedside table, a pair of her mother's reading glasses she'd swiped from the house. As soon as she touched them, she got a vision of her mother reading a book in bed.

Shit.

She needed to keep taking her medication. After a week or so, it would take a little longer for the visions to come, and that was all Val wanted. If she could control the immediate and sudden results of touching objects, she'd be able to live her life a lot more easily. She could avoid visions like the one with Americano Asshole and his mistress.

She rubbed her eyes and stood, stretching one way and then the other. She stepped onto the small rug in her room and did a few lunges, warming up her hips and knees. She bent over, dangling her head down as far as she could to loosen her back.

Why didn't Glimmer Lake have a boxing gym? She'd love to have a good reason to hit things. It would benefit her health on so many levels, all while giving her a perfectly decent excuse to wear gloves.

I can think of better ways to loosen up your back.

She pressed her eyes closed. She didn't need to be thinking about Sully.

Her phone buzzed on the dresser. Shit. She'd forgotten about the call and text from Josh. But would Josh be up this early? That couldn't be right.

She absently noted a voice mail notification from her ex, but when she saw the number of her produce guy, she called him back immediately. "Hey, Don. What's going on?"

"I'm running late today. Probably won't get there until after breakfast."

"Shit." She squeezed her eyes shut. "Seriously, Don?"

"Can't help it. Roads are icy as hell and it's gonna be slow."

"I get it. I do. It's just that I heard the phrase 'dangerously low on onions' yesterday, and you know how Ramon feels about onions."

"I got 'em, they're just rolling up the hill a little late."

Val sighed and wondered how many onions she had in her fridge. "I'll let Ramon know. Thanks for the call."

She splashed water on her face, put on a heavy slather of lotion to combat the dry winter air, and tugged on fresh clothes. She was going to have a ton of laundry come Monday.

Her phone buzzed again. It was a text from her other barista, JoJo.

I can't come in today.

Fuuuuuuuck. Val groaned. She tapped out a quick text message. *Are you okay?*

Fight with Mom.

JoJo's home life was anything but simple. Their dad wasn't in the picture, and their mom always seemed one fight away from kicking JoJo out of the house. She constantly used the wrong pronouns with JoJo and blamed them for everything going wrong in her life. Ramon and Honey were surrogate parents and trying to figure out a different living situation, but until they did, Val knew it was better for JoJo to do whatever they needed in order to not make waves.

Are you safe? That was the most important thing.

JoJo called and whispered over the phone, "Yeah, I'm okay, but she was getting on me about not doing enough to help around the house, so I think I better stay here and work. If I cut some firewood and clean the kitchen and do her laundry, I think she'll leave me alone. If I leave for work, I'll probably find my stuff on the front porch when I get home."

"This is bullshit," Val said quietly. "I know you pay rent."

JoJo sighed. "She doesn't see it that way."

"We'll find you a room somewhere soon. I promise."

There was a long silence on the phone. "I'm all she has, Val."

It was an impossible situation. JoJo was trying to be a good kid to a horrible parent. "At some point, honey, you're going to have to take care of yourself first."

"I know. Can Eve fill in today?"

"She has class."

"I am so sorry."

Val could hear the guilt in their voice. "Don't worry about it. Lie low and I'll see you tomorrow, okay? Call one of us if you need help. That is an order. I'll figure something out."

"Thanks, Val."

She hung up and ran a fast brush over her hair before she knotted it behind her and tied on a bandanna.

No delivery.

No barista.

Val was going to have to serve double duty on the register and the coffee counter. Greeeeat. And she might need to send Ramon to the market for sad onions, which was going to piss him off.

The sun wasn't even over the mountains, so Val was surprised to hear the quiet tap on her door. She grabbed her phone, pulled on her gloves and went to answer it. Jackson was leaning against the doorjamb, still in his flannel sleep pants and a T-shirt.

"Morning." Val ruffled his bedhead. "What's up?"

"I forgot to tell you that Andy has a permission slip he needs signed." Jackson yawned and covered his mouth. "I put it on the table. Can you make sure you sign it?"

"Cool. What's it for?"

He squinted. "Observatory, I think?"

"Fun." Val sort of wished she could be the mom who went on the field trips—at least the cool ones—but that wasn't in the cards. "I'm surprised he forgot about it."

"He barely moved his nose out of that book last night. I don't think he was thinking about anything other than that."

"Right." Val glanced at her phone and noticed she'd missed another call from Don. "Go back to sleep, honey.

You boys want to come by Misfit for breakfast this morning?"

Jackson yawned again. "Dunno. I'll ask Andy when he wakes up."

"Good man," Val whispered. She leaned over and kissed his cheek. Her phone buzzed again. "Are you kidding me?" It was Rachel, Josh's girlfriend. Unbelievable.

"You know," Jackson said, "you don't have to do everything on your own."

"I know I don't." She walked out of her room, trying to scoot Jackson back toward his bed. "I have you."

"I'm talking about work stuff. You have employees."

Val sighed. "I know, but those employees have their own lives and I'm the boss. Unfortunately."

"Just think about delegating more." He turned and waved at her. "That's all I'm saying. It's not you against the world. And don't forget the permission slip."

Which she absolutely would have done. Probably. She detoured from her direct line to the front door and signed the school permission slip after a fast scan, all while trying not to think about the multiple texts someone was sending her, judging by the constant buzzing from the phone in her back pocket.

So help her, if Josh and Rachel were trying to increase his custody again...

All he had was every other weekend and he barely followed through on those visits, but if he got every weekend written into their custody agreement, then the money he had to pay for child support would decrease ever so slightly.

Jerk.

It left Val in the unenviable position of documenting

every call and every visit the boys had with their father, just so she had evidence in court that she had full custody. It was maddening and draining and exactly what Josh probably wanted. He knew that eventually she'd forget something and she'd kick herself.

You know, you don't have to do everything on your own.

Ha! It was a nice thought, but Jackson had no idea. No idea at all.

THE BOYS DID COME into the restaurant, but only long enough to grab egg sandwiches before they sped off to school. Ramon was at the grill, Val was at the register and the coffee station, and Max was doing his best to keep the plates going in and out.

Unfortunately, because Val was pulling double duty, her customers at the counter were a little neglected. "Sorry, Dad."

Vincent Costa waved a hand. "I'm fine. I got my coffee, and Philip here is keeping me company."

Val glanced up and saw Robin's dad sitting next to hers at the counter. "Hey, Mr. Lewis, how are you this morning?"

She didn't catch his answer because the phone started ringing.

Don't cry. There's no crying in baseball. Or restaurants.

She picked it up. "Misfit Mountain Coffee Shop. We do not take orders or reservations over the phone." Val found it best to start every phone call with disclaimers.

"It's Monica. I was wondering if you'd had time—"

Val started to laugh hysterically. "I haven't had time to

pee since seven a.m. JoJo called in, so I'm short a barista and a server."

"That sounds uncomfortable for everyone. Want me to come help?"

"Are you a barista?"

"No, but I can work a register and serve breakfast, smart-ass."

Good enough.

Val snapped, "You're hired. Be here an hour ago. I love you forever." She hung up when another customer walked up to the register. "Hey, what can I get you?"

Monica walked in fifteen minutes later.

"You're my best friend," Val shouted across the restaurant. "Robin lost her title."

"I thought we were both your best friends."

"Yeah, but she made me brownies last week, so she'd pulled ahead slightly."

"Brownies?" Monica stashed her purse under the counter. "You're a cheap date. Apron?"

Val ducked down and grabbed one, tossed it to Monica, and pointed to the counter. "These two plates are for Jeanie and her friend." She pointed to the two women at the end of the short counter. "You're on the register and taking care of the counter. You know how to use this kind of register?"

"Same one Robin has." Monica tied on the apron and walked behind the digital register, shoving Val to the side. "Go. Make coffee and write snarky comments on cups. I got this. Hi, Ramon!"

"Hey, Monica. You hungry?"

"Not yet, but I expect onion rings for lunch."

"I'll be happy to make some *when I get some damn onions.*"

"I can't help that Don still isn't here," Val snapped. "I told you to go to the market!"

"Have you seen the sad produce at Granger's?"

"Sad onions or no onions! I'm not a miracle worker." Val turned and saw Sully standing at the counter. "Hi."

He frowned. "Sad onions?"

She nodded to the kitchen. "Ask my prima donna cook back there. You need coffee?"

"And a pastrami sandwich."

Monica said, "Hey Sully! How are you? Did you come in just to talk to Val? Because I would not find that at all surprising."

Val froze, but bless him, Sully took it in stride. "I came in for coffee and pastrami." He glanced at Val. "I don't think either of those have onions."

Monica smiled. "If you want to hang around and visit with Val, I'm sure we could get some." She punched in the order, and Sully held out a card to pay.

"Shut up, Monica," Val said, sliding a coffee cup toward Sully. "Here you go."

He grabbed the empty cup and looked at it for a second. Then he looked back at Val. Then at Monica. "Right."

He turned abruptly and walked to the coffee station, leaving Val glaring at Monica.

You're the worst, she mouthed silently.

"I thought I was your best friend."

"You need to cut it out," she whispered. "Nothing is going to happen there."

Something already did happen, not that Monica or Robin needed to know the details.

Ramon made the sandwich, Sully grabbed it and walked out without another glance in Val's direction, and the morning sped by with hardly a second to catch her breath before eleven o'clock.

They took advantage of a lull and stepped out to the screened porch off the back of the restaurant to catch some fresh air. Val sat at the picnic table and flipped on the small space heater they kept for employee breaks.

The forest around them was blanketed in snow, and several feet of it were piled along the borders of the parking lot. They'd had a pretty average year for snow, but the temperatures had stayed frigid at night, which meant not much had melted since the last storm.

"Seriously?" Monica kicked her feet up. "You're not going to do anything about the detective with the pretty eyes?"

"Sully's a sheriff, not a detective. And no."

"You're an idiot."

"Thanks. I love you too." Val desperately wanted a cigarette in moments like this, but she'd quit when she was pregnant with Jackson.

Still miss them though.

"Why are you so determined to stay single?" Monica asked. "I know you don't like being alone."

"I know you don't either, but it's just not the right time. You know that better than anyone."

"My husband died less than three years ago, and you've been divorced for almost ten years. Not exactly the same thing."

"How long did people wait until they tried to set you up?"

"Three months."

"No!"

Monica made a face. "I did not react well."

"Understandable." Val leaned her chin on her hand. "Do you remember what it was like when I was married to Josh?"

"Not that I'm sticking up for him, but you only remember the bad stuff. You and Josh had good times too. You liked being married."

"Yeah, before the boys came. After that, he was like another kid. He was so much damn work and I didn't have the energy."

"But the boys are older now. You have your own business. You have a house—"

"And I still have a shit-ton to do!"

"And you always will. You can't let it prevent you from having a personal life."

"Honestly? All I remember about relationships is that they're work. A *lot* of work."

"Yeah, they are work." Monica leaned back against the wall and looked out the window. Val could see how much widowhood had taken out of her. She'd lost weight. She didn't look happy. The new project with Russell House was helping, but she still seemed lost without her other half.

Men. You literally can't live with them or without them. What the hell?

"Relationships *are* work," Monica continued, "but the right ones are help too. Someone who has your back. Someone to share the emotional load with. If you can find a real partner—"

"That would be the sticking point," Val said. "I'm not sure any men capable of real partnership are still single. Every one has been married off. Not that I blame their wives or anything, but the pickings are slim, my friend. Very, very slim."

"And Sully?"

She hadn't given him a chance. Not to be good or bad. "Monica, I just don't have the time." She looked at her watch. "And neither do we. Back to work."

"Fine, but before we go..." She looked around at the empty yard. "I had a dream last night."

"*Dream* dream or—"

"Vision dream." Monica's voice went soft. "Blood on the snow. A lot of it. I've had the same dream a couple of times now, and I don't know what it means."

Val and Robin had both learned they couldn't discount Monica's visions, but not everything was as ominous as it seemed. "Did you see anyone in the dream?"

"No, but I saw tracks. Not animal tracks. They were in the snow and they were parallel like... skis, I guess?"

"Blood and skiing." Val frowned. "That could be anything from a nosebleed at the slopes to something serious." Her phone buzzed again.

"I know. It's not very clear at this point."

Seriously? It was the fourth message from Rachel. The first had warned her that Josh wasn't going to make his visitation this weekend. Big surprise there. The second, third, and fourth just said "Call me" with no other explanation.

"Still, it felt serious."

Val looked up. "What did?"

"The vision." Monica frowned. "Are you all right?"

Val shrugged. "Just some bullshit from Josh and his little girlfriend." She put her phone away. "Okay. I'll keep the boys from hitting the slopes for a while. I don't know what else we can do. Did you warn Robin and Mark?"

"Not yet."

"They're the most regular skiers. I'd shoot her a text."

"Yeah, good idea." Monica got out her phone. "What about you? Did you go back on your pills yet?"

"Last night. I don't like the cloudy feeling, but I had a vision from Americano Asshole the other day that convinced me I needed that buffer again. Skin contact is too difficult to avoid completely."

Monica frowned. "Americano Asshole?"

"Haven't you heard that one before?" Val nudged Monica back into the restaurant. "You're working here now. We'll let you in on all the nicknames."

CHAPTER 4

*V*al stood on the back porch of the restaurant, tapping her foot and wishing desperately for a cigarette again. She held her phone to her ear and waited for it to ring. It went straight to Josh's voice mail. Again.

You know what you're looking for, so leave me a message.

His voice was effortlessly sexy, but the allure of it had worn off ages ago for Val.

Just before lunch, she'd remembered to check his voice mail from the night before. She was expecting the usual excuses about why he wouldn't be able to keep the boys that weekend, but instead he'd left her a choppy message she didn't really get that ended with a vague request to call him. It was so unlike his usual breezy tone, she'd called him back immediately, only to be sent to voice mail.

Two and a half hours later, he still hadn't called back, which was unlike him. That, combined with the strange texts from Rachel, prompted Val to call again.

Val waited for the beep. "Josh, it's me again. Seriously, you need to call me back and let me know what's going on.

Rachel keeps texting me. You're not answering your phone. Are the boys at your place this weekend or not? I just need to know." She took a breath. "Call me."

She did not call Rachel. The woman was Josh's girlfriend and had no official status in her children's life. They were living together, but they weren't engaged. She didn't talk to Josh's flavor-of-the-year; there had been too many of them.

She walked back through the restaurant and gave everything a once-over. JoJo had texted a little while ago and assured her they were doing fine. The produce delivery had squeaked in just before lunch, and Don made peace with Ramon by throwing some surprise zucchini into their order.

Surprise zucchini was not a joke but desperately wanted to be.

The coffee shop closed at two in the afternoon. No exceptions. After that, it was family only, and her boys tended to head home these days instead of stopping by for an afternoon snack like they had when they were younger.

"See ya, Ramon." Val waved as she headed out the door.

"Where you going?" Ramon was wiping down his grill.

"Up to Russell House." She lifted the folder Robin had prepared. "I owe Monica a couple of hours after this morning."

"She and Mrs. Lewis made a real nice deal with Honey," Ramon said. "She's real happy with it. Going to double her business during the high season."

"That's awesome."

Val hopped in her truck and drove the five miles along the lake road to Russell House, a grand mansion that sat on the shores of Glimmer Lake.

The cold, clear waters of the lake hid the remains of the

old town of Grimmer, which had been flooded over eighty years ago by a hydroelectric dam. Glimmer Lake was a sleepy mountain town that swelled to bursting in the summer when the lower elevations of the valley were sweltering hot and in the winter when the mountainsides were covered in dense snow. The holidays had come and gone, but the town was still flooded with skiers on the weekends, which made Monica's vision all the more troubling.

Sierra Slopes, their local ski resort, had recently undergone a renovation and tourism during the winter was higher than ever.

Val pulled into the long curving driveway that had been carefully cleared of snow and looked at the festive decorations Monica and Grace, Robin's mom, had left up on the lampposts. Swaths of evergreen and pine cones tied with midnight-blue ribbons gave Russell House a festive air even though the holiday season had passed.

Monica was waiting under the covered entryway held up by stone-clad pillars. She smiled and waved. The friendly greeting and lively decorations helped Val shake off the automatic chill that ran down her spine when she saw the facade of the house.

Russell House was a showpiece of a home built by Robin's grandfather, Gordon Russell, to display his wealth and power. After Grandpa Russell died, he'd decided to hang around and oppress his family, who had lived with the weight of his secrets shadowing their lives.

Val had never liked the house when she'd been a child. They'd come to visit Robin's grandmother regularly to swim in the lake, go boating, or play in the snow. But no one ever lingered inside. It was only after Val, Robin, and Monica had banished Gordon Russell's ghost and cleansed the house that Val felt comfortable wandering around.

She parked her truck and walked up the steps. "It's looking good."

Monica smiled. As an empty-nester mom, she'd been looking for a new direction. Russell House was the perfect idea for someone with Monica's skills as a homemaker and hostess. She'd transformed the old home into a chic and comfortable mountain retreat. Now, instead of looking after four unruly kids, she was looking after business groups and bridal parties.

"We've had a lot of advance bookings," Monica said. "We're already booked solid for next Christmas."

"Are you serious?"

Monica nodded. "I knew it was going to work."

Val threw her arm around Monica's shoulders and walked inside. "Sometimes having psychic powers comes in handy."

"Luckily, I don't have them thrown in my face every hour of every day." Monica squeezed her gloved hand. "How was the rest of today?"

"Okay. Josh isn't answering his phone, so I have to assume he's bailing on the boys this weekend. I already texted Jackson."

Monica shook her head. "I will never understand that man."

"He's killing his relationship with his kids, but he's doing it to himself." Val surveyed the grand entryway of the house. "Enough about irresponsible men. What are you thinking for a coffee stand?"

"Come this way." Monica gestured toward the formal living room. "And let's talk about bars."

VAL WAS CHATTING with Eve at the espresso maker the next morning after the breakfast rush had slowed to the midmorning trickle. JoJo buzzed happily around the tables, and Ramon was singing oldies in the kitchen while he prepped for lunch.

Her staff was present and accounted for, the meat truck had arrived on time, and all was right in Val's world.

"There was an existing bar in the house," Val told Eve. "Old Mr. Russell did like his scotch. But they're expanding that to a wine bar for the afternoon, along with evening cocktails. That sort of thing. But before two o'clock, that area is just empty. What Monica is thinking is we set up a coffee bar there. Misfit would create a signature espresso drink for Russell House—"

"Probably a cold and a hot," Eve said. "To have summer covered."

"Good idea. So we do a signature coffee, and then all the usual menu. Guests preorder their coffees when they check in, and the staff delivers them in the morning with their pastry baskets. Russell House would pay us a flat fee for each morning, and the rest of the time we're just selling coffee like normal."

"So anyone can come inside and have a coffee and pastry at Russell House?" Eve asked.

"I think that's the idea."

Eve looked thoughtful. "You know, that might attract a lot

of tourists who can't afford to stay there, you know? 'Cause I know it's gonna be superexpensive. But if you just want to see the place and have a drink, that's pretty cheap."

"I think that's the idea." Val quickly rang up a customer and passed the order to Eve. "Monica threw out the idea of doing an afternoon tea, but I nixed it. Afternoon tea is not our brand."

Eve pursed her lips and looked around Misfit, from the blood-red ceiling to the skiing and snowboarding stickers plastered over the walls. "Is Russell House our brand?"

"Not really, but Monica called us a 'Glimmer Lake institution.'"

Eve laughed. "Meaning we're the only game in town?"

"Pretty much, yeah." The corner of Val's mouth lifted. "And they don't want it to be too stuffy up there. The Lodge has stuffy covered. They want sleek and sophisticated and just a little edgy. Younger patrons, not older."

"We serve everyone," Eve pulled a shot of espresso and gently added the milk. "You'll need another barista. At least?"

"I think one person will be enough most of the time." Val took the cappuccino from Eve and handed it across the counter. "We'll have to see if there are rush times. If there are —maybe on weekend mornings—we might be able to snag one of Monica's people to fill in."

"That could work. But we'll definitely have to train another barista."

"Unless we can find someone new in town, yeah."

Eve nodded. "But we have a couple of months."

"They're not officially open except for events until May."

"That gives us time."

"I thought so." Val glanced up and saw Sully enter the coffee shop. She instinctively reached for a large cup and wrote his name on it.

Eve asked, "Did Monica mention anything about signage for Russell House?"

"Nothing on the front of the house, but we can put something on the road to direct—"

"Val." Sully nudged aside two snowboarders at the front of the line to reach her. "You have a minute?"

Eve and Val exchanged a look.

"What's up?" she asked.

"I'm not here for coffee," Sully said. "I need to talk to you."

His face was grim and his mouth was set in a flat line. This was not a flirtatious visit or a coffee visit. This felt... official.

Val felt the blood drain from her face. "My boys—?"

"Are fine. As are your parents. I'm not here about..." He grew frustrated. "Can we just go to the back please?"

The snowboarders were watching with wide eyes and open mouths while Eve shoved Val toward the back.

"I'll cover the front," Eve said. "Go. I'll bring you back some coffee in a minute."

Val felt frozen as she walked down the hall. She tugged at her gloves, unsure of whether she should take them off or not. What was going on? What was happening? Why wouldn't Sully say anything?

He reached around her and opened the door to the back porch, then ushered her into the covered area and flipped on the heater before he turned to her. "I don't want you to panic. Your immediate family is fine."

"My *immediate* family?"

Sully took off his hat and set it on the table, running a hand through the shaggy brown hair that covered his collar.

"You need a haircut," Val said absently.

"I know. I've just been busy, and honestly, it's fucking cold and I can't be bothered."

She focused on his hat, crossing her arms and staring at the light brown Stetson. He was such a mountain man. Flannel and leather and cowboy hats. And she shaved her head and had a million tattoos and rarely dressed in anything but black. No one would put them together in a million years. What a weird idea.

"Val, look at me."

She glanced at him, then looked away. "You're going to tell me something bad."

"No one is dead, okay? It's Josh."

One name was enough to snap her out of her frozen panic. "Josh?" She uncrossed her arms and fisted them on her hips. *"Josh?"*

"Yeah, it's about Josh."

She let out a long string of curses. "You fucking had me in knots, Sully! What the fuck did Josh do?"

"Well..." He huffed. "It's not good. There's a warrant out for his arrest in Bridger, and no one can find him."

"His arrest? For what?" Josh was a dumbass, but he wasn't a criminal. He'd grown some pot when they were younger, but that was the extent of his nefarious ways. And pot was legal these days. "What's going on?"

"You know he was working for Luxury Pro Autoworks, right?"

Val snorted. "Yeah."

Sully got out his notebook. "Do you know why he left West's garage?"

"'Cause he's an idiot?"

Sully just waited.

She rolled her eyes. "Everyone knows. He slept with West's wife. I can't hardly blame the guy for kicking him out."

"Yeah, so apparently he was about to be fired from Luxury Pro Autoworks too. Not for sleeping with anyone"— he answered Val's question before she could ask it—"but because he was moonlighting. Offering cut rates to Luxury's customers to work on their cars in their own garages. You know he has that truck."

"Yeah. He was talking about starting something on his own a couple of years ago and found the money for the truck." Not that he could find the money to pay child support that summer, but *that* was another story. "He's an idiot. What's the warrant about though?"

"So he was working on some guy's Mercedes in Pheasant Creek off the books. This guy is claiming he gave Josh ten grand to buy parts and Josh took off with the money."

Val frowned. "Someone is claiming Josh stole ten grand from them?"

"Yeah." Sully's hand was poised over his notebook. "Sound like something he'd do?"

"No." Val shrugged. "You know I'm not of a fan of my ex, but that doesn't sound like Josh at all. Sleep with someone's wife? Sure. Moonlight if he thought a garage was taking too big a cut? Sure. But just flat out steal from a customer? No way. And especially not a rich one."

"Why not?"

"Because if you ask him, he'll tell you rich dudes rarely know how to drive the cars they buy."

Sully looked confused. "But why—?"

"They're the best customers," Val said. "They buy fancy cars and don't care how much it costs to fix them. They usually buy high-performance vehicles that can't be driven like Mom's minivan, but a lot of these guys don't really know how to drive, so they have to take their cars in a lot. He was constantly working on high-end sports cars when he was at West's."

Sully put a hand on his hip and slid the notebook into his front shirt pocket. "So you don't think he'd pull a stunt like this?"

"No way. The dude is lying. Don't know why, but he is."

"What if the guy was an asshole to him for some reason?"

"Then Josh just wouldn't work with him," Val said. "There's not many mechanics in the mountains as good as Josh. So if he told you no, you'd have to go a hundred miles to find anyone willing to work on a really high-performance engine. Unless this guy was an idiot, he wouldn't start a petty fight with the best specialty mechanic in the area."

Sully had his hands on his hips, mirroring Val's stance. He stared intently at her. Intent to the point of Val actually wanting to move out of his line of vision. "So you think the guy is lying."

"Yeah. That's what the warrant is about?"

"Yeah. Bridger PD has been trying to find him, and no one is answering. He's not at home. His girlfriend says he hasn't been around for about three days."

Val blinked. Three days? That would have been around the time he'd called her and asked her to call him back.

"Val?" Sully's blue eyes were lasered on her. "Has he called you?"

"Kind of? He called about three days ago and left a voice mail asking me to call him." Val shrugged. "It was the middle of the night. And it was kind of broken up."

"You didn't call him back?"

"I did the next day. I don't answer calls or texts from Josh in the middle of the night unless the boys are with him. It went to voice mail. He hasn't called back."

Sully blinked.

It took a second for Val to realize what she'd inadvertently revealed. *That's right, I will answer a text from you at midnight, Sully. Don't read too much into it.*

"Okay." He cleared his throat and reached for his hat. Val reached it before he did, deliberately allowing her wrist to brush against the rim.

In the split second before she turned to hand Sully his hat, she saw him sitting in his office, speaking to someone on the phone.

"Is foul play suspected?" This could be bad. Really bad. And it was the last thing Val needed on her plate. If she was ever going to give him a chance—

Not the time, Sully.

"We're asking around, but Mason wasn't exactly a choir-boy. He may not have a record, but he's had complaints. The girlfriend is lying about something. If you want my guess, he's in Vegas right now, trying to double his money. Seems like the type. Anderson is making all kinds of noise though, so we're not gonna get any rest until we find him and bring him in."

"What do you need on my end?"

"Talk to the ex. Sometimes they know more than the girlfriend, you know? They got kids together?"

"Yeah. They're teenagers."

"Check their phones if you can get permission from the mother. Gotta be careful with kids. This guy's a lowlife."

"Val?"

She blinked and shook her head, holding Sully's hat in her hands. "Sorry. This is just... not what I expected today, you know? It was actually an easy day for once." She handed him his hat.

"I know." Sully put a hand on her shoulder. "I don't know what to tell you. There's no sign that someone hurt Josh or that he's in any danger. What are the chances he's just lying low somewhere?"

"Where is he going to go? His vacation house at the beach?" She shook her head. "I don't know what to tell you, Sully. I guarantee he knows nothing about the warrant though."

"Why do you say that?"

"Because there is nothing Josh Mason loves more than defending himself against accusations he thinks are unfair. Trust me. I have the legal bills to prove it."

CHAPTER 5

he sat next to Andy on the couch, Jackson sitting in the chair across from her.

"So..." Jackson was clearly confused. "Dad is missing?"

"I don't think—" Val stopped herself. "I don't know what to think. There's no reason to think he's been hurt or that he's in any danger. It's possible he took off with some friends or he and Rachel had a fight or something."

Andy's voice was shaky. "We need to find him though. I don't think he'd do that, Mom. We talk every day. Almost every day. He would tell me if he was going away."

It *was* weird that Josh hadn't told Andy where he was going. Her youngest son had taken it upon himself to call his dad every day after school to give Josh updates about his day and chat about whatever he was doing.

To Josh's credit, he did enjoy the calls and if he wasn't working, he'd talk to Andy as long as Andy wanted, which was sometimes hours.

Jackson was suspicious. "What do the police say he did?"

"They're saying that he took cash from a client and then took off."

Jackson was no apologist for his father, but even he seemed skeptical. "That doesn't sound like him."

"I know. It was some rich guy in Pheasant Creek."

"What car?"

"I don't know, Jackson."

Her oldest didn't look satisfied by that answer. "What are the cops doing? This guy is lying about Dad. But why?"

"Right now I think they're just asking around. Talking with Rachel. With his friends."

Jackson snorted. "What friends? He pissed everyone off when he slept with West's wife. None of his friends are talking to him."

Andy sat up straight. "He did what?"

"Never mind, buddy." Jackson mussed Andy's hair. "It's not important. Don't worry about Dad. He'll show up."

"I think there's something wrong." Andy turned to Val. "What can we do, Mom? We have to do something. Can we make flyers or something and put those up?"

"Buddy, I don't think—"

"You guys both hate Dad." Andy stood, his face red and his eyes shining. "But he doesn't hate you. He loves you both. He loves all of us, and he wouldn't just ignore my calls if he was okay." Andy stomped off down the hall, leaving Val on the couch by herself.

She covered her eyes with her hand and willed back the headache that had been pressing against her temples since she touched Sully's hat that afternoon.

"I can't do anything right," she said. "I can't tell him that his dad might have just said to hell with everything

49

and taken off. I can't tell him that it'll all work out or that the police will find him. I can't tell him it's going to be okay."

"Mom, Dad and Rachel fight a lot."

"I know they do, but I figured that was just their dynamic or whatever." She looked through her fingers. "Did they fight in front of you guys?"

Jackson shrugged. "Not much. Just pissy comments more than anything, you know?"

"Do you think he took off to avoid stuff with Rachel?"

"I don't know. Maybe." Jackson didn't look like he believed it though. "Andy's right though. Dad always calls him back. Maybe not right away. But it's been over three days since Andy talked to him and Dad's voice mail is full. That's pretty weird."

"Are you worried?"

Jackson's expressions were usually more man than boy, but the look on his face was the youngest Val had seen in ages.

"I guess. Kinda. Why is this guy lying? Dad wouldn't steal his money. I mean... I can maybe see him taking off. But not stealing."

That's what had been bothering Val too. If Josh had just taken off, it would be one thing. He'd mused about doing that for years.

One of these days, Val. I'm not gonna be here for you to bitch at me. I'll just be gone.

"But," Jackson continued, "he takes off and then someone claims he stole something big? I want to know who this guy is."

"Agreed," Val said. "Tell you what. I'm going to ask Sully

tomorrow, but if no one has filed a formal missing-person report on your dad, I'll do that tomorrow."

"What does that do?"

"I have no idea, but it has to do something, right?"

Her phone buzzed. For once she was actually hoping it was Josh. It wasn't. Robin and Monica were asking how she was.

"Word travels fast," she muttered.

"Who is it?"

"Your Aunt Robin and Aunt Monica. They want to know what's going on. Want to know if we can come over to Aunt Robin and Uncle Mark's house." Val looked up. "She made lasagna." And Val hadn't cooked anything. "You better get Andy. Lasagna is better than ramen."

"You'd think having a mom with a restaurant would mean we ate better."

"I hire a chef for a reason, Jack."

"Why don't you go ahead?" Jackson looked down the hall. "I'll grab him in a little bit and we'll drive over. Give him a minute to cool down."

ROBIN'S HUSBAND Mark was the one who answered the door.

"This is bullshit," he said immediately after he gave Val a hug. "Josh is not a thief." He looked around her. "No boys?"

"Andy's pretty upset. Jackson's going to bring him over in a little bit. He's doing his big-brother magic right now."

"How are you doing?"

Val shrugged. "I don't know. My ex-husband is wanted

for theft, but maybe he's also missing? It doesn't even feel real."

"It really doesn't." Mark took Val's coat and hung it in the entryway by the winter boots and hats. "What did Sully say?"

"Well, what he said and what I saw are two different things."

Mark was the only one aside from Robin, Val, and Monica who knew that all three had developed psychic abilities after Robin's car went into Glimmer Lake and they'd almost drowned.

"What did you touch?" Mark raised a hand. "I didn't mean for that to sound dirty."

"You're so much more polite than your wife and Monica."

"We heard that!" Monica shouted from the kitchen. "Why don't you have the boys?"

"Jackson wanted to drive. They'll be here in a little bit." Val perched on a barstool at the kitchen island and watched Robin prepare a salad. "So what Sully said was that Bridger PD was looking for Josh and are asking around. What I saw in his head though tells me Bridger police think he just skipped town. They think he's not in any danger and he's probably in Vegas right now with a bunch of money." Val folded her hands. "They're not going to do anything except arrest him if he falls in their lap."

"So what do you want to do?" Mark got her a wineglass and poured half a glass of white into it. "White, right?"

"Robin, what have you been training your husband with?" Val narrowed her eyes at Robin. "He's being very thoughtful. I'm suspicious."

The corner of Robin's mouth turned up, telling Val that whatever Robin was doing with Mark, she was having just as much fun.

"Okay, never mind, let's talk about my scummy ex and his problems again."

"Well, we have to do something," Monica said.

"Why?" Val took a long sip of wine. "Why do we have to do anything?"

"Your boys love their dad," Robin said. "We have to find him for Jack and Andy."

"Josh doesn't deserve this many people worrying about him," Mark muttered.

"Thank you." Val reached over and clinked his glass with her own. "I agree."

"But we should definitely do something," he continued. "Sorry, Val, I have to agree with Robin. Your boys deserve to know what's going on."

Val let her head fall back and groaned. "I hate him so much and he's making my life impossible even now!"

"I know, but you know we're right," Monica said. "We can help and we should."

"The police—"

"The police don't know Josh like we do," Monica said. "And they don't really have any motivation to look for him. They think he's just another thief."

Mark raised his hand. "Guy's opinion here: There's a woman involved in this somehow."

"Why do you think that?" Robin asked.

Val and Mark spoke at the same time. "Because it's Josh."

Monica nodded. "I'd agree with that. Val, have you talked to the girlfriend?"

"No. She kept texting me, and I ignored her." She curled her lip. "Do I have to?"

"Yes." Monica walked behind Val and grabbed her phone from her back pocket. "Call her. Now."

Val glanced at the clock and guessed that Jackson and Andy wouldn't be on the road yet. "Fine." She scrolled through her contacts, found Rachel's number, and called. "But I'm putting her on speakerphone just so you all can share in the joy."

Robin set the salad to the side and grabbed a notebook and pencil.

The phone rang twice before a bored voice picked up. "It's about time."

"Hello, Rachel. Nice to hear your voice too. The sheriff came and talked to me today. Have you heard from him?"

"Would I be calling you if I did?"

Val bit her lip. Hard. "Okay, the last I heard from Josh was about three nights ago. He left me a voice mail in the middle of the night. How about you?"

"Did he say where he was?"

"No. Did he tell you where he was going?"

"No."

Val saw Robin scribbling. She held up a question.

Ask her when was the last time she saw him.

Val nodded. "Hey Rachel, when was the last time you actually *saw* Josh?"

There was silence, followed by a slight hiccuping sound. "We had a fight. It's been five days. I went to my friend's house and the last thing I said to him was really mean and what if something happened to him and that was the last thing I told him, something mean?" Rachel's voice was trailing off into panic by the end.

"Rachel, take a breath." Val rolled her eyes. The girl was way too melodramatic. "So you and Josh had a fight five days ago? But the police said he's been missing for three days. Do you know who else saw him?"

"I don't know. And we were texting until Tuesday."

"Okay. But he didn't say anything about leaving town or anything like that?"

"No."

"Did he mention any friends recently? Maybe people out of town he might have gone to visit?"

"I knew he was talking to West because I'm pretty sure that fancy new garage was going to fire him. He was super worried about that."

"Why?"

"He said something about them being pissed he was working a side job, but is that even legal? I mean, I work two jobs."

"Does your second job involve working for customers from the first job?"

"But he was giving them a better deal," Rachel said. "I mean, if he could do the work from his truck and not have to use the garage, he could charge them way less."

"Yeah, that's kind of the problem. Legally, I mean."

Monica closed her eyes. Robin wrote: *Is she really that stupid?*

Val nodded.

"I don't see what the big deal is," Rachel said.

"If he was doing work for customers he met at Luxury

Pro Autoworks and taking business away from them, do you see how they wouldn't like that?"

"But they were Josh's customers."

Val didn't want to argue with her about it. Rachel clearly wasn't the brightest bulb in the box. "Rachel, do you know which customer is accusing him of stealing? Do you know where he was working?"

"It was a guy in Pheasant Creek, but I don't know his name."

"Do you know what car it was?" It was possible one of the boys would know who the customer was if they could identify the car.

"Some waaaay expensive car that started with an *M*."

"Mercedes?"

"No, not like a normal one I remember hearing. It was a weird name. Foreign."

Val looked around the room. *Ideas?* she mouthed.

Mark reached for the writing pad. *Maybach?*

"Maybach?" Val asked. "Was it a Mercedes-Maybach?"

"No."

Mark wrote again. *McLaren.*

"McLaren?"

"No, I told you, like a foreign name."

Val wracked her brain. "Maserati?"

"Oh yeah! That one. It was a black Maserati."

Monica reached for the pad of paper and scribbled a question. *What was their fight about?*

"Hey Rachel. I know you're shook up, but what was the fight about? Did Josh maybe go to a friend's to cool off because he was upset?"

Rachel snorted. "Him upset? I'm not the one cheating on him."

Around the room, Robin and Monica both made exaggerated shocked faces and Val rolled her eyes.

"You think he was cheating on you?" It took everything in Val to make her voice sound concerned and slightly surprised.

For the record, she was neither.

"Yeah, I'm like *sure* he was cheating on me," Rachel said. "The bastard. And it's not like I couldn't have cheated on him like a hundred times. He's super old."

"Hey," Mark said quietly. "Josh is younger than me."

"What was that?"

Val jumped in. "Just the TV. So cheating? No way. That totally sucks." Her eyes weren't going to roll back into their original position after this phone call. "Could he be at this chick's house? Do you know where it is?"

"No, but I don't think he'd be there anyway. I'm pretty sure she was married."

Of course she was. Josh found the challenge of married women way more fun, and they usually never tried to make anything permanent. "Okay, well the boys are really worried, so if you hear anything, let me know, okay?"

"Okay." She sniffed. "Do you think he's all right?"

"Honestly? I have no idea."

The girl sounded on the verge of tears. "I mean, we were fighting, but I love him so much. And I was so angry with him and—"

"I think you're breaking up." If Val had to listen to any more of Rachel's weeping, over Josh of all people, she might puke. "Rachel, are you there?" She pulled the phone away from her mouth. "Sorry, the reception here is so bad."

"Oh, do you want me to try to—"

"Rachel?" Val hung up. "There. I called her and we don't actually know anything more."

"Wrong," Robin said, holding up the notepad. "We know he was working for someone in Pheasant Creek who owned a Maserati. There can't be too many of those. We know he was cheating on Rachel with a probably married woman."

"That would fit his pattern."

Mark said, "And we know he was worried about his job if he was talking to West."

"And all this adds up to—?" Val cut herself off when she heard the knock at the front door. "Boys are here." She reached for the notebook. "Something else. For now, we talk about anything other than Josh."

CHAPTER 6

*V*al knocked on the door loudly before she cracked it open. "Mom!"

She opened the door to her parents' house and nudged it wide with her knee. She was carrying a box of Honey's pastries in one hand and a beverage holder with coffee in the other. "Mom Marie, I'm here with coffee."

She'd slipped out of the coffee shop for a midmorning break once the morning rush died down. It had been a few days since she'd seen her parents, and she knew it was because of the weather.

A cold snap had hit the mountains, turning the roads icy and no doubt making her dad's knees hurt. Her parents were in excellent health, but they were still in their seventies.

"Valerie?" Her mother was in a snuggly house jacket and a pair of leggings. "You brought us pastries? How lovely. Thank you. Vincent!"

"What?"

"Valerie is here."

"Does she have the boys?"

"No, it's a school day."

"Oh. That's right."

Val walked back into the kitchen of her parents' old log house and set the pink box on the counter. She gave her mother a one-armed hug and handed over the coffee. "Eve made your latte with half and half."

"Oh, how decadent." Marie's eyes lit up.

Her mother was so thin Val had a hard time not worrying about her. All the women in her family were built like birds, but her mother was extra dainty and had only gotten more so with age. Val was always looking for things to fatten her mom up.

"Okay, where's the laptop?"

Marie waved her over to the table. "I promise I didn't do any of the things you told me not to."

"It might just need to be updated." Val sat at the end of the table as her father came in from the heated back porch where he built detailed birdhouses Robin sold for a small fortune at her shop. "Hey, Dad."

"Hi, sweetie." His eyes were worried. "How are the boys?"

"They seem fine." She'd told her parents the bare bones about the situation with Josh but hadn't gotten into details. Like the fact that there was a warrant out for his arrest. "They're both in school today."

"Has there been any news?"

"No." Val paused while the computer downloaded the update it needed. "I'm going into the station today to formally file a missing-person report since I don't think anyone has yet."

"Can't the police just tell where he is from his phone?"

Marie said. Her mother had a tendency to think technology was a powerful and mostly benevolent overseer. "Can't you?"

"He's not on our family plan," Val said. "So I can't track him like I can with the boys. And Dad knows how many dead spots there are in the mountains. The police won't be able to see his phone if he's out of range."

Vincent mostly knew about dead spots because he was addicted to sports radio and country music, which he listened to while he fished. He had to know which spots to avoid if a game was on live.

Her father frowned. "So all the spots where you can't call out or get a signal... if he was in one of those areas, the police wouldn't find him?"

"Nope."

Marie frowned. "I thought it was all about the satellites. Aren't our phones connected to satellites?"

Val smiled. "Only satellite phones are connected that way. Our regular old phones just use the towers all over the place. That's why they're putting that new one up over by Russell House. You know, the one that looks like a fake pine tree?"

"Oh, that's right." Marie grabbed her newspaper and sat down next to Val. "Well, it's all very confusing. I hope they find Josh soon. I'm sure the boys are worried sick."

The boys *were* worried sick, but Val didn't have the heart to tell her parents that the police thought Josh was living it up in Vegas.

She waited for the update to finish and restarted the computer.

Her father was studying her.

"What?" she asked.

"Are you and the girls thinking to do anything to find Josh?" Vincent's face was grim.

"I don't know, Dad." She glanced at Marie. "I don't know what we can do other than file a report."

"You're resourceful girls," he said. "And you know more about that man than the police. I'm sure you've talked about it."

Val shrugged. "We got together last night."

"And?"

"I don't know."

"He's the boys' father."

"Dad, I know." She looked up. "Trust me, I know."

"She doesn't have to do anything." Marie's voice was sharper than Val expected.

"Marie."

"No, Vincent. I told you to leave things be." Marie's cheeks were red. "You know I love Josh. I will always consider him a member of our family, but... Well, we both know he didn't treat Val well and he's disappointed Jackson and Andy over and over."

Val said, "I honestly don't know what I can do other than file a report, Mom."

"All I'm saying"—Marie looked at her pointedly—"is that *that* is all you need to do. Focus on your boys. Josh has made his own bed over and over. You don't have to sleep in it. It's far past time for everyone to stop expecting you to clean up his messes."

Marie's fiery proclamation soothed a wound in Val's heart she hadn't even realized was there. She'd been frustrated with her parents more than once for their steady hope that Josh would eventually get his act together and he and Val could be a family again. Her parents were traditional and very, very Catholic.

She understood her mom and understood what her parents thought she was losing with the divorce. They adored each other and had been joined at the hip for over fifty years. One of the hardest parts of her divorce was feeling like she'd disappointed them.

But Josh was not her father. And she was not her mother.

"Thanks, Mom." She managed to force the words out. "I know he's not my problem. But he is the boys' father. Whether I like it or not, we are still family." The rebellious, contrary part of her mind snarled a little, then lay down and settled. "I'm not sure what Robin and Monica and I can do to help, but we'll do what we can." She looked at her dad. "Okay?"

Vincent nodded. "That's all you can do. But you'll be angry with yourself if you don't."

"I know." She glanced at the computer and the log-in screen had popped up. "I think I fixed it."

"Oh, that's good." Vincent lowered the reading glasses that were sitting on his head and angled the computer. He typed in his password and the home screen jumped on the monitor. "Look at that. What a genius our girl is."

"Time for bear claws." Marie opened the box. "Oh, and turnovers. That's nice, isn't it?"

All Val had done was load and install the updates that had been slowing things down, but she'd take it. Especially if it netted her good-daughter points and a bear claw.

She walked into the sheriff's office a little after three o'clock, then leaned on the counter until a deputy came up to help her. It was Jarrod Richardson, who'd been a few years behind her in school.

"Hey, Val." His smile was unnecessarily cheerful. "How are you? What can I help you with?"

"I need to file a missing-person report for my ex-husband," Val said. "Other than that, I'm doing okay. How about you?"

Jarrod's smile fell. "A what?"

"Missing person. Joshua Mason. Has a warrant out in Bridger City?"

Jarrod's eyes were the size of coffee saucers. "Sorry?"

"Richardson," a voice barked. "Send Val back, will you?"

Jarrod lifted the flip-up counter and waved Val in. "You know where his office is?"

"Yep."

Val walked through the main room of the sheriff's department in Glimmer Lake. It wasn't a large building because the county seat was in Koso Junction, but since Glimmer Lake had the most tourists and the most activity, Sully spent the most time at the lake.

His office was tucked into the back corner of an old building that had been expanded in the 1970s when the ski resort was built. It was hardly the stuff of grandeur or television drama. The only window was no more than a foot across, and it was covered in spiderwebs from the outside. It smelled like pine air freshener and coffee. Half a dozen certificates were framed on the wall behind the desk, but Val didn't bother to read them. She sat across from Sully in the red-upholstered armchairs with cigarette burns on the arms.

"Hey," he said. "You want to file a missing-person report?"

"Yes."

Sully rocked back in his seat, watching her with suspicious eyes. His hair still needed to be cut, and she was pretty sure he had a grease stain on his collar, but his blue eyes were intent on Val. "Why?"

"Because it's not like him to be out of contact for this long," she said. "He is missing."

"He's an adult and he's your ex-husband. It's not illegal for him not to return your calls."

"He missed his weekend visit with our sons."

"And he's never done that before?"

Val looked away and shook her head. "You know he has."

"Does your ex-husband have any friends he might be visiting? Does he normally inform you of his movements?"

"No."

"But you think he's missing."

"I know he is. And his girlfriend thinks the same thing. This isn't like him."

"What is he like? Dependable? Responsible?" Sully's eyes never left her face. "Punctual?"

"No, but—"

"Do you have reason to think he is injured or hurt in some way?"

"No."

"Does he have any medical or cognitive dysfunction that would put him at risk?"

"No." She felt her jaw pop from clenching it so hard.

"Does he have friends or family in areas outside this community?

"Yes, but—"

"When was the last time you saw your ex-husband, Ms. Costa?" Sully leaned forward and appeared to be taking notes on a yellow legal pad. "Was it before or after he stole ten thousand dollars from a client?"

Val looked out the window and tried not to scream. "Do you think I enjoy this?"

"It's unnecessary," Sully said under his breath. "Bridger City already has multiple officers looking into—"

"Don't lie to me," she snapped. "You and I both know Bridger PD thinks Josh is a lowlife who left town to avoid a client he robbed. We both know they think he's in Las Vegas right now."

A muscle in Sully's jaw popped. "How—?"

"They're not going to do anything to find him." Val sat up straight. "Meanwhile, I'm fielding calls from his girlfriend, who thinks he's cheating on her—she's probably right—which means there could be an angry woman or an angry significant other out there."

"Val, if you think you have information—"

"I don't have information. I have suspicions and two boys who are wondering where their dad is and why he's not answering their calls. Because if there's one thing that Andy knows, it's that his dad may be irresponsible but he loves him, because who on earth wouldn't love Andy? Josh always calls Andy back within a day." She leaned forward. "Are you hearing me? Even when he goes to Canada for that bike rally every summer. If Andy calls, Josh calls back. If he was in Vegas, he'd call Andy back even if the police were looking for him. So yeah, Sully. I think something bad happened to my ex."

"Josh a gambler?"

"Other than the odd bet on the Super Bowl, no."

"Does he have any friends in the Las Vegas metropolitan area?"

"None that I've ever heard of."

Sully leaned his chin in the palm of his hand and stared at her long and hard. "So why do you think Bridger City PD thinks Josh is in Vegas?"

Val opened her mouth. Closed it. She couldn't exactly tell Sully she knew because she read it on his hat the other day. "It's... a nearby city."

"Sacramento and San Francisco are closer."

"But not as friendly to lowlifes."

He cracked a smile. "Val, your ex's girlfriend filed a report this morning. You don't need to file another one."

"Okay." Val scrambled. "That's good. I mean... good. So you're saying they have people looking into it in Bridger?"

Sully leaned back in his chair and let out a long breath. "Probably not."

Val stood up. "Then what the hell, Sully? You and I both know—"

"We know nothing." Sully cleared his throat. "You haven't been married to the man for over nine years. I don't know him, and my jurisdiction is limited in Bridger. He's a grown man, Val. Maybe he just took off."

She raised a hand and pointed it in his direction. Then she lowered it. She would not lose her cool with Sully. She refused.

She also refused to drop it.

"Fine." Val kept her voice steady. "See ya." She walked

out of his office, flexing her hands as she went. She'd go. And she'd find out what happened to Josh.

"Val, don't do anything stupid," Sully shouted.

She looked over her shoulder. "What could I do?"

Sully narrowed his eyes. He looked like he was clenching his teeth. "Just... don't do anything stupid about Josh."

She met his eyes and held them. "Like I said, what could I possibly do?"

CHAPTER 7

She waited until she was out of the parking lot to call Robin. "We're finding my stupid, irresponsible ex. You in?"

"Yep. I'll let Mark know. When are we going into Bridger?"

"Tomorrow morning?"

"Sure. That works."

She hung up and called Monica. "We're going to find my asshole of an ex-husband. You in?"

"Do you promise to finally examine your feelings for Josh and the divorce and why you've been unwilling to move on to any new relationship in a meaningful way?"

Val rolled her eyes. "Fine. Sure, I guess so. After we find Josh so my boys aren't traumatized for the rest of their life because their dad disappeared, okay?"

"Of course. Priorities."

"Can you go into Bridger tomorrow morning with me and Robin?"

"We don't have any events this week at Russell House, so I should be clear, but let me call Jake just to check."

"Cool."

Val waited for Monica to end the call, then she called Ramon.

"Hey-yah, boss. What's up?"

"Would Honey be able to fill in for me tomorrow at the diner?"

"Let me check." He covered the phone and there was a muffled conversation in the background. "Yeah, she says she can cover you. This about the ex? There any news?"

"Not yet, but I'm hoping I can get some information tomorrow."

"Okay. I'll check with her, but I think Honey's schedule is pretty easy this week. She can probably help with stuff at the coffee shop if you need her to, not just tomorrow."

"You two are the absolute best." It would strain Val's bank account, but it had been four days since anyone had seen Josh. If she was going to get information about Josh and figure out what was going on, she needed to move fast. "I'll call tomorrow and confirm with her for the rest of the week, but maybe pencil that in."

"You got it. Good luck."

Val was nearly home when Monica called her back.

"Okay yes, I'm free tomorrow and most of this week, but end of next week we have two bridal showers and a corporate motivational retreat, so I'll be limited then."

"A corporate motivational retreat?"

"I know. I was confused at first too, but it seems like they mostly consist of managers giving speeches and then all the employees bitching behind other people's backs in small groups."

Why would anyone ever choose to work in an office? "Do they get to drink?"

"Nope."

"Don't sign me up."

"They're not so bad. I think—judging from the skin tone of a lot of these office workers—they just need to get outside." Monica cleared her throat. "Speaking of outside..."

"Yes?"

"Can we talk about what you said in the car?"

Val groaned. "For the hundredth time NO. We are not talking about what I said in the car!"

When Robin's car went into Glimmer Lake, they'd all thought they were going to die. They might have said otherwise, but Val thought she was a goner. For sure. And when you thought you were going to die, you sometimes said stupid things.

Very stupid things.

"You said you wished that we were lesbians so we could marry each other, but you weren't sure you'd like lesbian sex and really you were still in love with Josh, even though you hate him. And you said the sex was really good. I'm assuming you meant with Josh since apparently I will never know the sweet, sweet touch of the passion that could live between us."

Val pulled into the driveway and sat in her car with a hand covering her eyes. "How do you remember all this shit?"

"I had to hold four children accountable for bullshit—I have a very good memory."

"Also, I said I was *kinda* wishing I could marry you. Kinda. It wasn't a definite thing."

"Can we talk about you being in love with Josh?

"Can we not?"

"Val—"

"Okay, yes, I was hung up on Josh for a while. He was the first man I ever loved. And for a lot of years it was good. When you're lonely, it's really easy to forget all the shitty things about someone and remember just the good stuff, okay?"

"I get that. But what's changed?"

Well, there was Sully, but if she brought that up, Monica would just have more questions, not less. She'd told Monica and Robin she'd had a "thing" with Sully, but she'd kept them guessing as to the extent.

"Uhhhh..." She squeezed her eyes together. *Think. Think. Think.* "I got my powers," Val blurted out. "I mean, the psychic stuff just changed everything. Changed the way I see people. Changed the way I... see my path." Yeah. Paths sounded like something you'd talk about in therapy. Maybe Monica would think she was in therapy instead of pining over her ex. "You know, purpose. And vision."

Monica was quiet for a long time. "You are so full of shit."

"Listen, just know that I am *not* in love with Josh. Especially not after he pulled that custody bullshit last year."

"Oh right. I forgot about that."

Everyone had forgotten about it except Val, apparently. The whole process had required mounds of paperwork, and as soon as the judge ruled that there was no way Josh's custody would be increased, her ex had dropped it completely. Apparently he had no problem pushing Val into spending cash on a lawyer. He was probably happy about it.

Val said, "The only reason I want to find the asshole in the first place is for my boys."

Josh was a cheater and a dog and a tightfisted father. He avoided paying for anything he possibly could and he had no problem letting Val make all the decisions. Not because he respected her opinion but because he didn't want to take responsibility.

Why was she looking for him again?

Oh. Right. The boys loved him.

She rubbed her temple. There it was, another headache. "It sucks being a single mom, Monica."

Monica gave her a sympathetic sigh. "Yeah, it does. Unfortunately, I gotta tell you it sucks even when they're grown-ups."

"That's not making me feel better."

"Sorry."

Val massaged her temple again. "I forget you're a single mother now."

"It's not really the same," Monica said. "I wasn't alone raising them. But I think some things are the same. I hate it when the kids call me with good news and there's no one to get excited with since Gil is gone. He was always the one who would make a huge deal about their stuff, and now it's just me and I kinda feel like the second-choice parent."

"You know you're not, but I get what you're saying." Val would never forget the first time right after the divorce when she'd called Josh to share that Jackson aced a science test he'd been worried about.

Kid's gonna be a nerd like your fancy friends.

That was it. No joy. No pride. He'd said "it was a joke"

when she'd gotten upset, but it wasn't a joke. Not even a little bit. They both knew it.

"Josh is such a jerk." Val let out a long breath. "I still hope he's all right."

"Where do you want to start tomorrow?"

"Only one place to start."

West. She was going to see West.

THEY TOOK Monica's minivan even though Val knew it would cause endless ribbing from Josh's old garage buddies. The minivan had awesome legroom, a built-in cooler, and a full tank of gas. It was a no-brainer.

They parked on the curb in front of West's Custom Body Shop on the industrial east end of Bridger City. The shop was surrounded by auto body and repair shops, paint and customization places, and more than one bike shop. The foothills around Bridger were home to a couple of different bike clubs, and most of them got their work done at West's or across the street at Bridger Motosports.

At one point, Josh was building custom bikes for West and making good money. When the bike shop wasn't busy, he'd work on high-end sports cars and anything else West wanted him to do. Val and Josh spent holidays at West and his wife Georgia's home. Josh and West were as close as brothers.

Then Josh slept with Georgia. Because of course he did.

Monica and Robin eyed the garage. "What do you want us to do?" Robin asked.

"I'm not sure." She glanced at Monica. "You see anything familiar?"

Monica's visions would often come like dreams, long and elaborate clips like a movie scene taken out of context. She also had flashes of intuition that popped into her head. Those, she'd once explained, were harder to interpret. Who was to say what was a vision and what was normal imagination?

Monica squinted at the three-bay garage. "I can see him here, but I don't know if I'm projecting or seeing something important. He worked here for so long."

"Gotcha." Val kept her sunglasses on as she opened the minivan door. "Maybe just wander around. Robin might find someone to talk to."

Robin smiled. "Very possible. Let's see if any spirits thought West's garage was their happy or sad place."

According to Robin, spirits who didn't move on to... whatever the afterlife was tended to hang around in places they had a strong emotional connection to. A beloved home or the site of an untimely death were common hangouts, but ghosts could pop up in weird places too. Like an auto-repair shop.

Val sauntered toward the first bay, where she could see West leaning over the open hood of a car. He was wearing dark blue coveralls and heavy boots in the cold, and he'd grown out a full grey beard. She couldn't lie—if you were into the older, slightly seedy biker look, West was not hard on the eyes.

His hair was steel grey and clipped short, other than the beard. His tan skin was clearly friends with the sun, and years of squinting had left creases around his eyes. Colorful tattoos peeked over the collar of his coveralls and at his wrists.

Val knew his body was covered in them, but it worked on West.

Really worked.

West looked up when he heard her approach. "Can I help you?"

Val took off her sunglasses and smiled. "Really?"

West squinted his dark brown eyes. "Aw, hell. I hardly recognized you with the hair. What the fuck, Val?" He walked over, wiping his hands on a red rag before he gave her a hug. "Where ya been?" He looked her up and down with undisguised admiration. "You're looking hot as hell."

Val's thick hair was clipped short around the sides and back, the short sides dyed a purplish red, with the long fall of her natural dark brown skimming past her shoulders. She'd worn skinny jeans and a tall pair of boots to the garage along with her favorite shearling-lined black parka.

She was as punk as she could be in thirty-degree weather, and she knew her audience. West had always been attracted to her. Unlike Josh, however, she didn't fool around with married people, and West had never made a move.

"I've been around. Still in Glimmer Lake."

"You got a café or something, right?"

"It's just a coffee shop, West." She shifted and shoved her hands in her pockets. "We're not that fancy."

"How're the boys? Jackson graduating soon?"

"He's got a couple years yet," she said. "But he's doing good. Andy's a little genius. I don't know where he comes from."

West squinted. "Eh, his parents aren't too dim; I'm not surprised."

"His dad could be smarter."

West grimaced. "Being intelligent and being a dumbass aren't mutually exclusive. You know that as well as I do."

Val shook her head. "I was pissed to hear about Georgia. He's such an idiot."

"Yeah." He shrugged. "She made her bed. Took off. Somewhere down south now. Good riddance." He looked at her legs again. "You want to get a drink?"

"It's eleven in the morning."

The corner of his mouth turned up. "And?"

Val couldn't stop her smile. "Sure. You know I'm here to ask about Josh, right?"

"Yeah." He ushered her toward the small glass-walled office at the front of the garage. "Doesn't mean we can't enjoy ourselves."

"Are you hitting on me while I'm looking for the father of my children?"

"No." He held open the door. "I'm... comforting an old friend in her hour of need."

"Right." She reached for her phone and texted Monica.

Having a drink with West.

He's hot, she texted back. *Like TV biker hot.*

Too complicated.

We're getting a cup of coffee at this deli on the corner and walking around the neighborhood.

Val texted back, *I'll text you when we're done,* then put her phone away.

She walked into West's office and immediately remembered why Josh had always loved working for him. Despite his rough demeanor and devil-may-care attitude, West was meticulous. The office floor was immaculate and the parts desk was clear of clutter. His own desk was in the back corner, also ruthlessly organized.

He pulled over a chair and Val sat across from his desk. He poured two cups of coffee from the carafe on the counter, plopped down at his desk, then brought out a bottle of Johnny Walker from the bottom drawer. He poured a decent shot of whiskey in both glasses and shoved one toward her.

Val cautiously took off her gloves and reached for the mug. After all, if she was going to use her extra sense to search for Josh, she had to deal with the consequences.

The mug touched her skin. Nothing clear. The level of relief surprised her.

"To cheating exes." West raised his mug. "And not having to deal with their bullshit anymore."

"I hear that." Val clinked the edge of her mug against West's, then took a sip of coffee and almost burned her mouth. "Did it happen more than once with Georgia? It surprised me when I heard. Not Josh. He was a dog. I didn't think that about her though."

West frowned. "We were going through a rough patch when it happened. My dad had just died and I was being a prick. But she picked checking out and cheating as a way to deal. I'm not about that."

"I hear that." As far as Val knew, West was a straight arrow when it came to relationships. He couldn't stand a liar, and cheating was a lie. "Josh—"

"Josh..." West's eyes narrowed. "Josh should have known better. He didn't have respect. For you or any woman. The police made a call last week. I didn't have much to tell them."

"Do you think he did it?" She took a sip of coffee, and the whiskey made her eyes burn.

"Moonlighting?" West shrugged. "I wouldn't be shocked. In his defense, Luxury Pro Autoworks charges their customers up the ass and they pay their people shit. There's a reason the owner's office is that fucking fancy. So if Josh was moonlighting, it wouldn't surprise me. Don't know why the police care though."

"What about the money?"

"What money?"

She took another drink of coffee. The whiskey was warming her up. "That's why the police were asking about him. One of the customers he was moonlighting for says Josh took ten grand for parts and then didn't do the work. They think he took off."

"The fuck?" West shook his head. "No. That's not Josh."

"That's what I told them, but I guess this guy knows people or something. I don't know. Do you know anyone who owns a black Maserati in Pheasant Creek?"

He let out a low whistle. "No one around here is driving anything that nice. I'd notice. I can ask around. There can't be more than one or two in town, but Josh is definitely who you'd want working on a vehicle like that."

"Yeah."

West finished his coffee and looked out into the garage with his eyes narrowed. "If you find him... tell him I'll hire him back, same arrangement we had before."

"Seriously?"

"I don't have a wife for him to poach anymore, so... yeah, probably. I'd take a couple of swings at him first, but I'd hire him. Damn hard to find mechanics with the same touch Josh has."

"You're a peach, West." She set her coffee cup down,

already feeling her head swimming a little. She really wasn't used to drinking in the morning. "I'm trying to think where he'd take off to."

"He still seeing that girl? Does she know?"

Val rolled her eyes. "She doesn't know her ass from her elbow. No help there."

West grinned. "That's what you get for hooking up with a girl instead of a woman."

"I see what you're doing here, but it's not going to work."

"Don't tell me you're still hung up on the dumbass."

"No. I only want to find him for the boys." Val set her mug down and didn't know what to do with her hands. She dropped them on the arms of the chair and immediately got a flash of West in a compromising position with a woman she didn't recognize.

"Oh." She pulled her hands away and folded them in her lap. "Um..."

West frowned. "You okay?"

Her cheeks felt hot. She'd probably looked a second longer than was strictly necessary. Half a second. "I'm fine. Just not used to whiskey in the morning."

"Right." He was still frowning. "You drive yourself?"

"No. Remember Monica and Robin?"

"A little. They drove you?"

"Yeah, they were just going down to Gino's to get a coffee while we talked."

"I don't know what else I can tell you. If he shows up, I'll call you."

"When was the last time you talked to him?"

West scratched his beard. "Ya know, I actually got a call from him last week. Saw his name on my phone and ignored it. Wasn't in the mood. But I was going to call him back eventually. Then I heard about all this shit."

"You think he was involved in anything illegal?"

"Pshhht." West narrowed his eyes. "It's Josh. Half the guys out there? Yeah, they might get into something dirty. Josh wouldn't. Not on purpose, anyway. He wasn't a great father, but he loved your boys enough to keep his nose clean."

"Thanks." She had to keep remembering that. Josh loved the boys. He was a piss-poor example, but he did love them. "I probably needed that reminder. This isn't fun."

She was currently keeping her hands stuffed under her knees, trying to keep from accidentally touching anything else. *Not fun* was an understatement.

"Tell you what," West said. "I'm gonna find out whose car this is, and I'm gonna call you. Because I think there's something else going on. The boys don't need to be wondering about this shit."

"Thanks, West."

"No problem." He got to his feet. "I better get back to work."

Val stood and put on her gloves again. She wasn't risking touching anything else in the office. "Thanks for the time."

He put a hand on the small of her back and led her toward the door. "You got my number?"

"I think so."

"Call if you or the boys need anything."

"Sure." She wouldn't call. Not West anyway. He meant well, but he was Josh's friend first. "I'll call if I hear anything."

"Cool."

Val saw Robin and Monica waiting near the minivan. "That's my ride."

West squinted into the sun. "Who's the chick in the purple?"

"Monica?" Val looked at him from her corner of her eye. "That's Monica. She was married to Gilbert Vasquez."

"Was married?"

"Gil died a couple of years ago. Heart attack, really sudden."

"That's fucked up." He hadn't taken his eyes off Monica. "That minivan hers?"

Val waved a finger at West. "Don't disrespect the minivan. She loves the minivan."

"She needs to be driving a muscle car with curves like that," he said under his breath, his eyes still locked on Monica. "Take care, Val."

"You too. I'll call you."

Val walked toward Monica and Robin, hopping over the low shrubs near the sidewalk. "He doesn't know anything about Josh, but he's gonna ask around about the Maserati."

Monica said, "He's staring at my car. He better not be judging my van."

"Pretty sure he's staring at your ass, not your car." Val crawled into the second row. "Come on. Let's head back. I'll fill you in on the way."

CHAPTER 8

"Why would he be staring at my ass?" Monica started her car. "What's wrong with my ass?"

Robin said, "I'm pretty sure he thinks nothing is wrong with your ass."

"You mean he was... like, checking me out?" Her voice rose. "What?"

Val snorted. "Monica, you can't be serious."

"He's like TV-biker hot."

Robin shook her head. "False modesty doesn't suit you."

"I'm just saying I'm in jeans and a hoodie. It's not like I'm dressed up."

"Pretty sure your ass does not need dressing up to attract attention," Val said. "But getting back to Josh, did you guys find any leads?"

Robin said, "Monica, turn down that alley behind West's garage."

"Right."

"So you *did* find something?"

Robin looked over her shoulder. "Not exactly something. More like some*one*."

Monica drove past two porta-potties and stopped near a trio of large shipping containers across the alley from West's garage.

"What are we looking at?"

Robin rolled down her window, and the cold air rushed in. "Hey, Harry. You still around?"

Val's mouth formed an O, but she stayed silent. Now she knew what Robin was talking about. Someone might not be living, but that didn't mean they weren't a valuable source of information.

"Hey, Harry?"

Monica asked, "Did you bring your sketchbook?"

Robin shook her head. "I'll bring it tomorrow and we can try again. He's gone." She turned to Val. "Pretty sure Josh has been around here recently. I can't say for sure, but I think this ghost saw him around the shipping containers."

"The shipping containers?"

"Weird, right?"

Robin asked, "Did Josh keep anything in storage? Would he have used these?"

"I don't think so. I think these are West's."

"Interesting," Monica said. "Then why would Josh have been hanging around West's storage unit?"

"Are we sure he was?" Val asked. "How well do ghosts tell time? Could it have been years ago?"

"Completely possible," Robin said. "The best thing to do would be to ask about hairstyles or things like that, because ghosts are super bad at telling time as far as I can tell."

Monica continued through the alley. "Okay, so tomorrow

bring your sketchbook, but right now I think we better head out. It'll take us an hour to get back to Glimmer Lake."

"Where are we going tomorrow?" Robin said. "I can leave earlier tomorrow."

"I'd like to visit Luxury Pro Autoworks and take a look at Josh's house," Val said. "If we have the time."

"Do we need permission from what's her face?" Monica asked.

"Who? Rachel?" Val shrugged. "I'll call her, but I know where Josh left a key."

"He told you where he left a key to his place?"

"Yep. I'm still on his life insurance too."

"He has life insurance?"

"Weird, right? It's like the only responsible thing he ever did. He got a big-ass life insurance policy right when Jackson was born. He was racing bikes right around then, remember?"

"Oh, I do remember that," Monica said. "I think Gil was the one who harassed him into it. Glad he kept it up though."

"Me too." Val took a deep breath. "But I really, really hope I don't have to think about that anytime soon."

They pulled into Misfit to drop Val off just as she saw Americano Asshole pulling out of the parking lot at high speed. He was driving a silver-grey sports car Val didn't recognize instead of his usual blue BMW.

"That guy," she muttered. "He's such a jerk. Rich as hell and yet so cheap."

"That's annoying," Robin said. "Have you met his wife though? She's really sweet. She bought a dresser from me last month. Said it was for her new 'me room.' I thought she was so cute."

ELIZABETH HUNTER

Monica said, "And yet married to Allan Anderson."

"Yeah, she is. Poor thing."

Monica rested her hands on the steering wheel. "I heard he won a gold medal for something in the Olympics."

"Really?"

"I haven't heard that."

Monica nodded. "He's from some fancy family back east, but his wife is from Bridger City. That's why they moved to California."

"Well, he certainly acts like a complete snob," Val said. "What did he do in the Olympics? Is being an asshole an Olympic sport?"

Monica laughed. "I have no idea. Skiing maybe? They ski a lot."

"I think they're part owners of the ski resort," Robin said. "Either that or they have season passes. They're up there all the time."

Robin and Mark were the only two regular skiers in their group of friends. Though they only lived ten minutes from Sierra Slopes, Val had never enjoyed the sport, and Monica had only skied a couple of times a year when Gil wanted to go. She probably hadn't been at all since he died.

"I better go check in before it closes," Val said. "Leave at nine tomorrow?"

"Sure." Robin and Monica exchanged a look. "We can make that work."

Val walked into Misfit and was surprised to see Savannah Anderson, the wife of the Americano Asshole—should they switch it to Olympic Asshole? Maybe. She'd have to think about it.

Savannah was sitting in the corner of the coffee shop

nearest the counter, reading a book and drinking a coffee. Her cheeks were flushed, and she was looking down studiously at her book.

Val glanced at her but then headed toward the counter. Rich people's marriage problems were not her concern even though she wanted to shout "Run away!" very loudly.

Honey leaned on the counter, her voluminous bosom pressed against the varnished wood covered with snowboarding and watersports stickers. "Hey, baby."

"Hey, sweetie." Val smiled. She adored Honey. The woman was a killer baker and one of the coolest people in Glimmer Lake. Her thick brown hair was always highlighted with a different color, and intricate tattoos of flowers and vines decorated her light brown skin. Her nose was pierced, and while Val was tempted to get something similar, she figured her sons would give her too much shit for it.

But I am the cool mom...

"You been up to trouble," Honey said. "I can tell by the look on your face. You seeing ghosts?"

Ghosts? Val stopped short. "What?"

Honey often commented on the spooky atmosphere in Glimmer Lake. After all, the town was built on the shores of a lake that swallowed an entire town.

"Ghosts?" Honey asked again. "People from a past life? Exes and formers?"

"Oh." She slid through the pass. "Kind of. I was down in Bridger, asking around about Josh. They police still can't find him."

"That shit's strange."

"I know. He's not the most responsible, but it's not like

him to just disappear. He'd tell the boys if he was going on a trip or something. So I have no idea."

"You worried?"

Val took a deep breath. "Starting to be, yeah."

There were so few people in the café Val nearly jumped when Savannah Anderson came up to the counter behind her, her bag slung over her shoulder.

"Oh!" Val smiled. "Can we get you anything else?"

"No. I'm fine. My ride is here so..." The woman still looked upset. Her eyes were glassy and her cheeks were red. She had long blond hair that was usually pulled into a neat twist. Today it was down in a messy braid. "Let me just..." She pulled out a wad of cash and stuffed it in the tip jar.

Val reached out and touched her hand. "You don't have to do that."

Savannah nodded, still looking at the tip jar. "Yeah, I do." She looked up and met Val's eyes. "Sorry."

Honey was the one who spoke. "Ma'am, you do not have anything to apologize for."

"That's very kind of you to say." She glanced at Val again, then down. "Have a nice afternoon. Thank you again."

After Savannah walked out, Honey lowered her voice and said, "They were having some fight earlier."

Val looked out the windows. "You see who's picking her up?"

"I don't know. Maybe one of her book club friends? He took her car."

"That was her car?" Val's mouth dropped. "Asshole."

"Yup. I never see her with anyone but book club people or him. You think she really has a ride?"

"She wouldn't have left without one," Val said. "Pheasant Creek is twenty miles away at least."

"Yeah." Honey shook her head. "She needs to get out of that mess. I got a bad feeling about that man."

STEVE GARCIA WAS the owner of Luxury Pro Autoworks, and he looked exactly like the kind of guy you'd trust to work on your hundred-thousand-dollar vehicle. His teeth were white and fiercely straight, and his skin was a golden brown. His technicians were wearing immaculate coveralls, but Steve was in a sharp red polo shirt with a logo on the breast pocket that matched the Luxury Pro Autoworks sign.

Val'd had a feeling she'd be dealing with someone along Steve's lines, so she'd worn a simple pair of jeans and a flannel under her plum-colored parka. It was about as soccer mom as she could manage with a wardrobe that consisted of mostly black.

"I don't know how much I can tell you, Mrs. Mason—"

"It's Ms. Costa. Just Val. I'm Josh's ex-wife, and I'm honestly not here to cause problems. I'm just asking around because I'm worried. He's my boys' dad and they're worried, so I'm worried." She spotted a picture on the console table behind the desk. "You're a father, so I'm sure you understand."

The manicured smile flashed. "If your kids are unhappy, you're unhappy."

"Exactly."

She was sitting down for a friendly chat with the owner of Luxury Pro Autoworks while Robin and Monica did their best to get more information out of the ghost behind West's garage.

"That said," Val continued, "he's also my ex. I have no illusions about what a great guy Josh is." She shifted and flexed her ungloved hands on the arms of the chair.

Her medication was beginning to kick in, so the visions weren't as fast or as furious. But there were several scenes she'd gotten so far. All were a mixture of excitement and twisting embarrassment. Luxury Pro was going to fix your vehicle, but they'd charge through the nose for the privilege. The emotions felt in this chair were all about feeling taken advantage of by the man across the expensive desk.

To say Val felt uncomfortable was an understatement. The emotions leaked into her until she folded her hands in her lap. She had the urge to wash her hands. Get some hand sanitizer going. Something.

Steve said, "As I said before, I understand where you're coming from, but I'm just not sure I can tell you much that would be helpful."

From the glimpses of memory and emotion, Val knew she was dealing with a savvy and clever businessman. "Josh was moonlighting," she said. "How did you find out?"

There was a flash behind his eyes.

Oh, you don't like being cheated, do you? You want to be the one with the upper hand.

"Unfortunately, I only learned about it when the customer came to me with the accusations of theft." His tone turned to a carefully measured regret. "As I told him, that is why you hire a reputable company and not an independent operator. Especially not one who's lying to his boss."

"Did he have a noncompete clause in his contract?"

"All our technicians do."

"Do you have other guys who could do the work that Josh did?"

Steve's smile wavered only a second. "Josh had a very elevated opinion of himself. No one is irreplaceable."

"But he was working on the high-end side, correct? Someone told me the client had a Maserati. You don't find too many of those in Bridger City, right? Or many people who can work on them. Could Maserati parts run in the tens of thousands of dollars?"

Steve's smile was frozen. "Possibly."

"So why were the police so quick to jump to theft?"

"I believe it was because of the client."

"Who was the client?"

"I can't tell you that." Steve's genuine smile was back. He enjoyed keeping things from her. "Client confidentiality."

I'm going to find out who it is anyway, dickhead. "Sure, sure, of course. Did Josh *know* you knew about the moon-lighting?"

"I confronted him about it last week."

"So he knew you were going to fire him before he disappeared?"

Steve paused.

Oh. Interesting. Was Steve not going to fire him? Hmmm.

"Josh was on probation here at Luxury Pro. Our human resources department has a process."

A process? Or clients who needed Josh's expertise. "Was it just the one client that he was working for on the side?"

"As far as I know, but..." Steve spread his hands. "People who tell one lie often tell another."

"For sure!" She forced a sympathetic laugh, even though all this was rubbing her the wrong way. All of it. "Did Josh ever steal from you, Mr. Garcia?"

"He stole a client from my business."

"But otherwise?"

The frozen smile was back. "As far as I know, he did not. But as I said, a person who lies about one thing often—"

"Tells another." She smiled sweetly. "I know that better than anyone."

Steve chuckled and Val joined him, biting back the snarl that wanted to curl her lip.

"Well," Steve said, "if there's nothing else—"

"Actually, I was wondering about his toolbox," Val said. "Is it still here?"

Ah, hello again, frozen smile.

"It is."

You were hoping no one would ask about that, weren't you? "If it's all right, I'll have a friend come over and get it."

In addition to his work truck, Val knew Josh would have kept his professional toolbox wherever he was working. Not only would examining it be a wealth of information for Val, that toolbox was probably worth thirty-five or forty thousand dollars at minimum and represented two years of Val's own work at a particularly annoying accounting firm in Bridger.

She was not leaving the tools with Smiley Steve.

"I'm sorry," he said, "but as you're Josh's *ex*-wife, I'm not sure—"

"I can get my lawyer on it if you want." Val fixed a polite, don't-fuck-with-me smile on her face. "His girlfriend is... just a girlfriend. They're not engaged. He had that toolbox from when we were married and if something has happened to him, it'll belong to his boys. It's better if we take care of it, that way you don't have it hanging around."

Steve was mentally debating; she could see it.

"Like I said, I'd be happy to get my attorney working on it. Or I could call the police and see what they want to do about—"

"That's fine." Steve's smile fell. "You want it, you can have it. I want it gone by tomorrow, or I'll sell it to recover the losses your ex-husband caused me."

Oh hell no. Val rose, trying not to let the anger show on her face. She leaned on Steve's desk and put both her hands flat on the surface.

Gross. He was fucking his secretary. Grooooooooss. This man was a walking, talking stereotype.

"I don't think you want to threaten me, Steve." She kept her voice low and steady. "I've lived around here a long time and I know people. I know *things*. Like the affair you're having with the nice lady at the front desk. I don't think you want your pretty blond wife knowing about that, do you?"

Smiley Steve's face went pale.

Val smiled sweetly. "You aren't going to touch Josh's toolbox or anything inside it. Let's just part as friends, okay? I'm going to have someone come and pick up Josh's stuff just as soon as I can. Do we have an understanding?"

"Fine."

Smiley Steve really hated her. Val didn't have to be psychic to figure that out. She straightened and walked out of the office, dialing her phone as she walked and fighting back a wave of nausea.

"West? Hey. Remember you said to call me if I needed anything? I need a favor."

CHAPTER 9

*V*al walked to the nearest coffee shop to wait for Robin and Monica. She was frustrated. She was angry. And she had a giant bitch of a headache.

What was she doing? She was doing all this, going through all this mess for *Josh*? She'd tried so hard to restart her life—not the life she planned, but it was a good life—and he was still dragging her into his drama and bullshit.

Maybe he *was* off in Vegas, going to clubs, drinking with friends, and having a blast while she was back in Bridger City, cleaning up his mess.

Again.

Half an hour after she left Smiley Steve at Luxury Pro, her friends showed up, looking as frustrated as Val felt.

"Why do I feel like we're working backward?" Robin asked. "Harry was there, but today he said he didn't recognize Josh at all."

Monica sat down with a sigh. "Ghosts are the worst."

"Men are the worst," Val muttered. "We should go home and forget about all this."

Robin and Monica frowned. "What? Why?"

"Because this man is not my problem, okay!" Val bit her lower lip. "Why do I always have to be the responsible one? Why does that land on me? Maybe he just stays gone, and would that really be a bad thing?" She rested her face in her hands, covering her eyes as the headache began to batter her.

Monica rubbed her back. "I do not blame you for feeling that way. Not even a little bit."

"Do you need an aspirin?" Robin reached for her purse.

"It's not the headache—it's not *just* the headache. It's... my life." She felt her eyes get wet and she blinked hard. "Every time I think I'm getting ahead or I've hit my stride, my ex-husband pulls some bullshit like this and it drags me down. I'm looking for him right now instead of working. This is literally costing me money. I'm going to be behind on paying off my credit card next month because Josh went missing and my boys asked me to find him."

"Yeah," Monica said. "It's infuriating."

"And he won't appreciate any of it. He'll say nice things, but then if I ask him to chip in when it comes time to buy school clothes or pay for Andy's soccer gear, he'll make an excuse why he can't help out. Or he'll miss a child support payment and I'll have to wait for fucking tax season to get caught up." She wiped her eyes and took a deep breath. "And if I ignore all this—pretend like it's not my problem—my boys will never forgive me. Because Mom is the one who gets shit done."

Monica was still rubbing her back. "Yeah. She is."

Val blinked away the tears. "We get married and have these babies, and really our life doesn't belong to us anymore, does it? It belongs to them. And we don't get it back for a long time. Maybe never." She raised her hands. "And now I have this... thing. And I don't want it, but I can't lie that sometimes knowing things—things that other people don't know—it's kind of addictive. I spied on Jackson the other day because of a bad grade on a chemistry project. Is that ethical? Am I a bad mother for doing that? I don't know."

"Val, you're an awesome mother," Robin said. "You are amazing. You do so much and you have no one helping you."

She wiped her eyes. "You guys help. My mom and dad help. I'm in a lot better position than most single mothers."

"But it's still tiring," Monica said. "And this whole mess..." She sighed. "I will tell you, the boys may not say anything now, but one day they will realize who their hero is. And it's not the guy who donated sperm."

"But no matter what Josh does, they'll still love him." Val frowned. "And I don't want them to *not* love him. Maybe I just want them to love me a little more." She looked up. "See? Bad mom."

"Not a bad mom," Robin said. "I mean... we give birth to them. We cook their meals. We cleaned up so much poop."

"So very much."

"Dear Lord, there was so much poop."

Val sat for a moment in silent gratitude that diapers would never be part of her life again.

"Secretly," Robin continued, "we all want them to love us just a little bit more than they love their fathers."

Monica pursed her lips. "Okay, I've never admitted that before, but you're kind of right."

Val couldn't stop her smile. "I mean... we grew them in our bodies. I have permanent scarring from those boys." She pretended to claw her stomach. "It's like a mountain lion mauled my belly."

Robin nodded. "We hosted them for nine months. Like parasites."

"Adorable parasites," Monica said.

"Eh." Val shrugged. "You had cute, chubby babies. Mine were kind of thin and wiry. They got cute, but they were kind of funny-looking at first."

Monica snorted.

Robin narrowed her eyes. "You're right. Children ought to love their mothers more."

"Right?" Val looked between her friends. Her headache was a little better. Her nerves were a little less raw. "Fuck, I love those little monsters. I guess we should find their deadbeat father."

Monica bumped Val's knee with her own. "Yeah, we probably should."

Robin asked, "What happened at Luxury Pro?"

"I had to get mean with Smiley Steve about Josh's toolbox."

"Smiley Steve?"

Val rolled her eyes. "Josh's boss. He had one of those super-fake smiles, you know? And he used it like a weapon. He was weird."

"Do you think he had something to do with Josh disappearing?"

"No. But let's just say I understand why Josh was moonlighting. The guy is a jerk and West says he doesn't pay his guys well. Josh was proud about his work and he had a right to be." Val shook her head. "I can't understand why he never gets his shit together. Whatever. Not my problem."

"So did you get Josh's toolbox?"

"Oh no. It's huge; you actually need a tow truck to move the things. West said he could send a couple of guys over to pick it up tomorrow. One of them worked with Josh a long time, so he'll be able to see if anyone messed with it."

"Do you think this Steve guy is going to break anything? I remember how much you guys spent on Josh's tools."

"I don't think so." Val sipped her coffee. "I kind of threatened him."

"You threatened Smiley Steve?" Monica asked. "I want to be you when I grow up. Minus the disorganization and laundry issues."

"How did you threaten him?"

"I told him I knew about the affair he was having with his secretary."

Robin wrinkled her nose. "Gloves off in the office?"

"They'd been going at it right on the desk. Could he be any more of a middle-aged-male stereotype?"

Monica rolled her eyes. "I mean, if you're going to be a lying prick, at least be imaginative."

"I don't think imagination is in Smiley Steve's wheelhouse." She drummed her fingers on the table. "We've talked with West. We've talked with the current employer. We still don't know who the client is, but West says he's waiting to hear back from a couple of people."

"Do you still want to go to Rachel and Josh's house?"

"I don't think I can." She rubbed her temple. "Can we just go home? This headache is killing me. I had my gloves off in that office for like an hour and there was a lot of shit coming in. I think I'm going to need to be fresh for Josh's house."

"Let's go then." Robin rose. "I have aspirin in my purse."

"Thanks, Mom."

Val, Robin, and Monica walked out to the minivan, and Val got in the back seat, slid her glasses on, and leaned the bucket seat as far back as it could go. She felt her phone buzzing in her pocket, but she ignored it while she grabbed the water Monica handed her and the two aspirin from Robin's purse.

They were headed back to Glimmer Lake and her phone was ringing again. She kept ignoring it. If it was her boys, they'd be texting. She didn't feel like talking to her parents right now.

Robin's phone rang. "It's Sully." She touched the screen. "Hey."

Val opened her eyes. "What does he want?" She checked her phone. Yep. Sure enough, three missed calls from Sully. She sat up straight. "Is there news about Josh?"

Robin handed her the phone.

"Sully, did you hear something from—"

"Why aren't you answering your phone?"

"I have a headache. I put it on mute."

"Where are you?"

She narrowed her eyes. "Driving with Robin and Monica. Why?"

"Why are you harassing Josh's employer, Valerie?"

Shit.

Val put him on speakerphone. She couldn't handle the speaker that close to her ear when her head felt like this. "I'm not harassing anyone."

"Bridger PD is calling me, asking me why Mason's ex-wife is going around Bridger City, asking people about her ex.

Trying to get Josh's stuff. Did you threaten Steve Garcia? Do you know how many people on the city council he knows? He's neighbors with the mayor, for Christ's sake."

Robin's eyes went wide, but Val only waved a careless hand. "I don't give a shit. He threatened to sell Josh's toolbox. Do you know how many thousands of dollars Josh spent on that toolbox? Those tools are his professional *life*. It took him years to build. If something happened to him, they belong to his sons, and I'll be damned if some asshole who knows the mayor—"

"Did you threaten him?"

"What on earth am I going to threaten him with?" Her head was pounding. "Did he tell you? What? I'm going to beat up a guy six inches taller than me? How am I supposed to have threatened this guy? He's the one threatening *me*."

Sully was quiet for a moment. "Did he threaten you?"

"He threatened to sell Josh's tools."

"Did he threaten *you*, Val?"

"What difference does it make?" She pinched the bridge of her nose.

"Because if he threatened to sell some tools, that's one thing, but if he threatened you, then I'm going to have to drive down to Bridger City and find Steve Garcia and beat the shit out of him for threatening you, so tell me *did he threaten you, Valerie?*"

She could hear the simmering anger in his voice. She spoke calmly. "Sully, he did not threaten me personally. And I didn't threaten him."

Lie. She completely threatened him.

"I don't think he likes me very much," Val continued, "but I don't really give a shit about that. Tell the truth,

Bridger PD isn't doing jack about finding Josh, are they? They're not doing anything."

Sully was silent.

Val felt tears come to her eyes. She cleared her throat. "You know, just because he's not a rich guy with connections doesn't mean he's not worth looking for. He has two children who love him. He has friends. He has family. He's been missing for five days, and I haven't seen a single thing on the news. No one is looking for him except for me."

"Val—"

"So back off." She sniffed. "I need to do this. I can find answers. I know... I know things, okay?"

"No one is saying—"

"All of you are saying it." She pressed the heel of her hand to her eye. "Why are those women asking questions? Don't they know they're not the police? What do they think they're doing?"

"Valerie, you, Robin, and Monica are not trained investigators. If foul play was involved—"

"If foul play was involved and someone came after him, no one would know because they're not looking!" Val let out a choked laugh. "Are they? Are they looking, Sully? Are they treating him like a... a regular dad who went missing? Are they treating his case like they would if Steve Garcia went missing?"

Sully was still silent.

"Or are they assuming because he was a working-class guy with some debts who pissed off a rich man that he's a thief on the run?" She closed her eyes and leaned back. "Just tell me, Sully. Is *anyone* looking for him?"

"No."

"Then don't tell me what I should and shouldn't be doing to find my boys' daddy." She ended the call and pushed the phone forward into Robin's waiting hand. She stuffed her fist in her mouth and bit down hard to keep from screaming.

Josh, where are you?

What did you do?

Where did you go?

She was going to find out what happened. If it took her the rest of her life, she was going to find out what happened to Jackson and Andy's dad.

"Are you okay?" Robin asked. "Do you need more water?"

"I'll be okay."

"What happened between you and Sully?" Monica asked. "He just threatened to go beat the shit out of a guy he doesn't know if that guy threatened you. That is not casual and flirtatious behavior. That's 'I care a hell of a lot about this woman' behavior."

"I don't want to talk about it," Val said.

"Was it bad?"

"No. It wasn't bad." In fact, it was good. It was nice. And thinking about the cold walk home from Sully's house in the early-morning hours after she'd slipped away from his bed made her sad. She should have stayed. She should have given him a chance. She should have gotten out of her own head and tried.

But she didn't have time for that. She had a business and two kids to worry about. And now she had an ex-husband who was missing.

CHAPTER 10

*V*al was exhausted by the time they got home, but she was able to lie down for an hour before Jackson and Andy got out of school. She was up and making grilled cheese sandwiches for an afternoon snack when they came barreling through the door.

"Hey, Mom!" Andy the whirlwind burst into the kitchen, hugged her around the waist, and slung his backpack on the kitchen table before he ducked under her arm. "Grilled cheese! Is it ready?"

"Give me a minute." She ruffled his hair. "How was school, professor?"

"Great. We're building rockets in science class and I really think my group is going to do the best. There's a contest next week on Friday I think; can you come?"

"I have to check my schedule, but I'll try." She kissed the top of his head, realizing that she only had one or two more years before Andy's head, like Jackson's, would be well out of reach.

"Hey, Mom." Jackson's deep voice still surprised her. "Any news today?"

Val looked over her shoulder and shook her head. "Sorry. I talked to Sully, but nothing."

Jackson nodded. "Right."

"You want a grilled cheese?"

He smiled. "Yeah. That sounds good. Who's sick?"

She usually only made grilled cheese and tomato soup when one of them was sick. "This time it's me. I have a killer headache."

"You want me to make the sandwiches?" Jackson said. "You could go lie down."

Val smiled. Yes, he was an alien parasite, but he was her alien parasite and he was the best. "Thank you so much, but I better not. If I do, I'll fall asleep and I don't want to wake up at two a.m."

It wouldn't be the first time. When her powers first manifested and she didn't know what was going on, she ended most days curled into a ball in her bedroom. A year plus, and she was better. Between the gloves and the antianxiety medication, she was coping, but she still got tired easily.

"Cool." Jackson drummed his fingers on the door. "I was thinking of going to the library, but maybe I'll stay home."

"Could you?" Val knew Jackson wasn't going to the library to study. He was going to see the girl she wasn't supposed to know about. "I'd appreciate it."

It was the delicate dance of the mom and the teenage son. Jackson likely suspected that Val knew he was going to the library for reasons other than academic, but he didn't say anything, and Val would let the mild deception stand as long as Jackson didn't slack off around the house or let his grades drop. She knew from picking up his backpack his feelings about this girl were serious, but she had no way of knowing how the girl felt.

Who knew why he wasn't telling Val about her? Maybe her parents didn't allow her to date. Maybe she was shy. It could be any number of reasons. Val wasn't willing to push.

He's allowed to have a private life.

Kind of.

"Yeah." Jackson tugged on Andy's sweatshirt. "Hey, let's go wash some clothes while the grilled cheese is finishing. Mom'll call us when it's done."

"Laundry?" Andy groaned. "I don't need to do laundry."

Laundry was the first thing she'd put her foot down about after her powers hit. She could not handle going through her children's dirty clothes anymore. Just... no. On many levels.

Jackson said, "Dude, I can hardly walk on your side of the room. You need to do laundry."

"Fine." Andy sighed. It was the end of the world. Clearly.

She might have felt overwhelmed earlier, but Val really didn't know how she'd lucked out with her two boys. She wasn't going to question it—it was probably because of her parents anyway.

Jackson was far from perfect, but he knew how to take responsibility when he needed to. And Andy... he was still her sweetheart even if he'd inherited her hatred of folding clean clothes.

Val had just finished the last grilled cheese sandwich when she heard the knock on the door.

"Andy! Jack!" she shouted down the hall. "Sandwiches are ready."

She heard the clomp of footsteps on the hardwood as she opened the door. Sully was standing on the porch.

She closed the door and spun around.

Jackson was frowning. "Who was that?"

"Val!" He knocked on the door again. "Open the door please."

"It's the sheriff," Val said. "We kind of had a disagreement earlier in the day, and he's part of the reason I have a headache, so I don't want to talk to him.

"Valerie." Sully knocked again louder. "I'm not here to fight with you."

Jackson and Andy both looked confused.

"The sheriff's here?" Andy asked. "Why?"

"Yes."

"Why is he calling you Valerie?" Jackson asked. "Only Grandma calls you that."

"You're not going to talk to him?" Andy asked. "What if he knows something about Dad?" Andy started toward the door, but Val held him back.

"He would have told me on the phone earlier if he knew something about your dad." And if she didn't open the door, he'd have to go away. Eventually.

Probably.

Jackson was also looking skeptical. "But that was hours ago, maybe—"

"Val!" Sully knocked again. "Will you just open the door?"

Jackson started toward it and Val held up a hand. "You better not."

"I'm not here to talk to you," Sully said. "I need to talk to your boys."

Val's eyes went wide. She spun and yanked open the door. "You don't get to talk to my boys. You want to pry information about Josh out of them? You have a lot of nerve, Sullivan Wes—"

"I'll talk to you." Jackson spoke over her. "Come in."

Val looked at Jackson. "Kid, you may be closing in on adulthood, but this is not your house."

Andy was tugging on her arm. "Mom, I want to talk to the sheriff. It's like on the TV shows, you know? Maybe we know something that can help."

Val looked back at Sully, who was waiting with as neutral an expression as he could manage, but she could tell he was pissed.

"Mom, I want to talk to him."

"Me too."

Val gave in to their plaintive voices and widened the door to allow Sully to enter. "Boys, go grab your sandwiches and take them to the family room. Sully can talk to you there."

"Yes," Andy said under his breath. "Now we're getting somewhere."

Val's eyes never left Sully. "If you even breathe a word out of line—"

"I'm trying to help," he said quietly. "The little one is right. They may know something they don't even realize could help."

"Andy," Val said. "Andy is my younger boy."

"And the older one is Jackson," Sully said. "I didn't forget."

VAL LISTENED from the kitchen as Sully questioned her boys about their father.

"When was the last time you saw him?"

Jackson said, "It's been about four weeks, but he talks to Andy almost every day."

"That true?"

"Yeah." Andy's sweet voice chimed in. "Sometimes when I call him he can't talk, but he always calls me back later."

"So it's unusual for him to go this long without calling."

"Yeah," Jackson said. "Really weird. That's why we're sure something bad happened."

"He never takes off—like on a fishing trip or a road trip?"

"Sometimes," Andy said. "But he'll tell us about it. And this time he didn't."

"Andy... did you notice anything strange about your dad when you talked to him in the past couple of weeks?"

"No. Well... maybe."

Val paused with her hands in the soapy dishwater.

"What do you mean, maybe?"

"He was worried, and he wasn't happy with Rachel."

"Yeah," Jackson added. "I think he and Rachel were going to break up."

Sully said something Val couldn't quite hear.

"No," Jackson said. "I mean, Rachel's okay, but she doesn't really like us much. You can tell she thinks we're annoying. His girlfriend before Rachel was nice, but Rachel is... kind of whiny."

"Yeah. And she wants a lot of stuff," Andy added. "Like purses and a new car and that kind of stuff."

"Did your dad say anything about breaking up with Rachel?" Sully asked.

"No," Andy said. "Last time, when he broke up with Carrie, we didn't even know for like a month."

Val felt the hurt in Andy's voice like a spear to her heart.

Damn Josh and his flippant attitude to his children's feelings! Jackson was older and more jaded, but Andy had been attached to Josh's ex-girlfriend. He asked for weeks whether he could call Carrie even when Val told him it wasn't a good idea.

"So your dad and Rachel were having problems." Sully's tone shifted. Went deeper. "Jackson, did your dad talk to you about his work at all?"

Jackson was silent for a while. "I mean... I knew he was working outside of the garage. I didn't know it was illegal though."

"It's not illegal," Sully said. "A boss might fire you for doing something like that, but your dad didn't do anything *illegal*. If your dad's boss wanted to be a dick about it, he might have sued him, but probably he'd just fire him."

"So Dad can't get in trouble for that?"

"No. The police in Bridger are looking for him because there's a man who says your dad stole some money from him that was supposed to go to buying parts."

"I heard about that. It's bullshit." Jackson was angry. "My dad wouldn't have stolen from a customer. Who's saying he stole from him?"

"I can't tell you that."

"Why would someone say that?" Andy asked. "Did this guy not like Dad?"

Val was struck by the simple insight of Andy's obvious question. Why *had* this customer claimed Josh stole from him? Was it personal? A misunderstanding?

Jackson asked, "When does this guy say he gave Dad the money?"

"About a week and a half ago."

"But that's stupid," Jackson said.

"Why do you say that?"

"Because it can take at least that long to get parts in. Why did this guy assume my dad didn't just order the parts and they're taking a while?"

"I don't know that," Sully said.

"I mean, especially if it's specialty," Jackson said. "That stuff can take time."

"Did you work with your dad a lot?" Sully asked.

"In the summer, yeah. Not when I'm in school."

"So you know how he works."

"I'm not..." Jackson sighed audibly. "I know my dad isn't the most reliable person."

Andy said, "Jack, don't—"

"No, bud, be real, okay? Dad isn't a great father. He's always forgetting stuff, and he'd probably forget we existed if Andy didn't call and remind him. He loves us, but out of sight, out of mind for him, okay?"

Val closed her eyes. It was painful and true.

"But Dad isn't a thief," Jackson continued. "So this guy— whoever he is—had another issue with Dad. It wasn't about money."

It wasn't about money.

It wasn't.

Val blinked. Jackson was right. She'd been looking for the business reasons why Josh might have taken off, but if she believed Jackson and her own intuition, this wasn't about money. Not the charges. Not Josh's disappearance.

If it wasn't about money, what was it about?

Val closed her eyes and took a deep breath. Mark had said it days ago. Rachel had hinted at it.

"Guy's opinion here: There's a woman involved in this somehow."

"Him upset? I'm not the one cheating on him."

Why would a customer accuse Josh of stealing from him, especially if he knew it wasn't true? If Jackson was right, the parts for the job would show up eventually, and the police would be forced to drop the charges.

Maybe it wasn't money that Josh had stolen from this customer. Maybe Josh had been tuning up something way more delicate than a high-performance automobile. The possibility was not far-fetched.

The wash water had gone cold by the time Sully found her in the kitchen.

"Hey," he said. "I'm done talking with them."

Val could hear them back in their room, arguing about doing laundry.

She turned and wiped her hand on a towel, keeping her voice low. "Did you learn anything new?"

"Not much." Sully also kept his voice quiet. "That wasn't really why I came by."

Andy's voice was happier. Jackson's was more assured that she'd heard in days.

"You want them to feel like they helped."

"I didn't make them any promises," Sully said. "But if it were me and my dad was missing, I'd want to feel like I did something."

"That's a good idea." Val nodded. "You're a good guy."

"I try not to embarrass my parents. I guess that's all any of us can do."

She kept her eyes on his. "You're a good man."

"And you're a good mom. Your boys love you." He glanced down the hall. "I know I can't stop you from... doing your thing with your friends—whatever that is—but be careful. You have two young men who need you."

"I know."

He opened his mouth. Closed it. Then he pushed away from the kitchen counter. "I better go."

"See you."

"Yeah." The corner of his mouth turned up. "I'll see you around."

CHAPTER 11

*V*al had been battling a headache all morning while Monica drove her and Robin into Bridger City. It pounded in her temples and made the skin along her neck crawl.

"You doing okay back there?" Robin reached back and squeezed her knee.

"I want to hide in my room for a week," Val muttered. "I want a dark, cool room with no distractions and nothing that doesn't belong to me."

Her own possessions didn't trigger her. It was one of the reasons her bedroom was a sanctuary.

Her phone buzzed and she glanced at it. There was a message from West.

Boys got Josh's toolbox. All locked up. Think it's good.

She texted him back. *Thanks, West.*

What do you want me to do with it?

Can you just hold on to it for now?

You got it, babe.

Val ignored the *babe* and focused on the fact that there

was one less thing to worry about in all this mess. West had come through.

"We can go home," Monica said softly. "Just say the word."

"No, today it's been six days." She slipped her sunglasses on. "Six days since anyone has talked to him or he's reached out. I have to find out what happened."

"His and Rachel's house, right?"

"Yeah."

They kept the minivan quiet as they rolled down the mountain and into town. Robin and Monica spoke softly if they spoke at all. Val was dreading the confrontation with Rachel because she knew it was coming.

The girl's response to her text earlier in the day had been lackluster at best. *I don't know what you think you're going to find that the police didn't.*

They'd searched the house with a warrant, looking for the cash, Val guessed, but she wasn't looking for cash.

This isn't about the money. Forget the money. Look past the money.

The van pulled up to the curb in front of the tidy bungalow in a working-class neighborhood in Bridger City. The yards were neat and lined with chain link or picket fences. Dogs barked from porches, and children's toys were scattered across the neighbor's yard. Work trucks and vans were parked in the street.

"This the place?"

Val peered out the window. "Yep."

"She home?"

"I don't know. I told her I was coming, but I know where the spare key is."

Robin turned around. "Isn't that a little strange?"

Val shrugged. "Is it strange that he still calls me with questions on his taxes and I'm still his emergency medical contact? It's Josh. I'm the only truly responsible person he knows."

"Once you have babies with someone, they're your family forever," Monica muttered.

Val sat up and opened the door. "Let's get this over with."

She left her gloves in the car. Better to deal with stray images than Rachel's nosy questions. If she was home.

The curtain fluttered in the front window.

"She's home," Robin said.

"Caught that." Val stuck her hands in her front pockets and walked up to the front porch. Monica knocked on the door and they all waited for Rachel to answer.

The young woman opened the door and leaned against it, blocking their way into the house. She was wearing a velour tracksuit and a tank with the word BABY written in glitter across her boobs. Her hair was pulled up in a messy bun, but she had makeup on.

It was... a look.

"Hey," she said.

"Hello, Rachel." Val kept her sunglasses on. The winter morning was brutally bright. "Can we come in?"

"Have you heard from Josh?"

"No. Have you?"

"No." She sighed heavily and opened the door wider. "Come in, I guess. I don't know why we're doing this."

Val stepped into the small living area. She could see a breakfast nook in the back corner of the house and lights that probably led to a kitchen. There was a large television mounted to one wall, and a sectional sofa crowded the rest of the room. Josh's old recliner was in the corner closest to the television.

Val turned around, surveying the house. It was clean, but she could see Rachel's stress in the pile of mail by the door, the water rings on the otherwise spotless coffee table, and the scent of pine cleaner coming from the kitchen.

Monica put a hand on Rachel's shoulder. "How are you holding up?"

The girl blinked hard. "I don't know what to think. Everyone is acting like he just took off. But that's not Josh."

"No it isn't," Robin said. "That's why Val is looking."

"The police already came and searched—"

"They searched for money," Val said. "Obvious stuff. I was with Josh for seventeen years, Rachel. Just let me look around, okay?"

Robin said, "Do you have coffee? I don't know about you, but I'd love some coffee."

"I don't drink coffee, but I have this detox tea that's really good," Rachel said. "I can make some if you want. It's very cleansing."

"Detox tea?" Monica shuffled her to the kitchen. "That sounds great. What does it cleanse?"

As soon as Monica and Robin had Rachel in the kitchen, Val went to work. She looked for items she knew were Josh's and picked each one up in turn. Scattered visions of daily life. Josh bitching at Rachel. Rachel bitching at Josh. Some laughs. She walked to the recliner and sat, putting her hands where his would have rested.

Nothing but football. The man did love football and he was pissed at the 49ers. No surprise there.

She walked to the small desk in the corner, opened the drawer, and found two checkbooks. She bypassed the one with the scrolled leather cover and went for the simple navy-blue bank cover.

Bingo. She picked it up and immediately saw Josh writing checks, frowning. What was the frown about? She paged through but found no deposit for the ten thousand the police claimed he stole. She held it in her hands and tried to sense any emotion, but nothing came to her. There was no strong memory or vision. A vague sense of worry and stress, but that was everyone paying bills, right?

Val wandered from the living room to the bathroom. She hated to do it, but she snooped, trying to avoid anything that looked like it belonged to Rachel. She spotted Josh's favorite brand of deodorant. Touched the handle of each toothbrush. His hairbrush.

It was remarkable how superficial her ex-husband was. Or maybe everyone's hairbrush was accompanied by thoughts of how great they looked. Val didn't want to know.

She touched a bottle of cologne without thinking, and the flash of memory nearly brought her to her knees.

"I smelled it and thought about you. That's all."

"This is expensive stuff."

"If you don't want it—"

"I want it."

Val braced herself on the counter and stared at her own shocked expression in the mirror.

Wow. Okay. Hmm.

Of all the people she'd imagined seeing in Josh's memories, that one was a complete shock. She'd been expecting to see someone other than Rachel, but she hadn't been expecting Savannah Anderson.

Josh was sleeping with Americano Asshole's wife.

"Seriously?" Robin stared at Val back in the minivan.

Val was taking shelter in the third-row seat, which was the darkest. The blinding headache hit her hard ten minutes after she dropped Josh's cologne bottle. She'd forced herself to pick it up several times, getting a little more of Josh's memory with each touch.

"Savannah Anderson," Val said. "I saw her give him the cologne."

"Did you see... anything else?"

"No. They were somewhere drinking coffee I think. It was the middle of the day. I think it might have been the mall. There was a lot of background noise."

"So you don't know for sure that they're boinking?" Monica said.

"You think they're just coffee buddies?" Val asked. "Rachel thought he was cheating on her. Mark thought a woman was involved. Do you know of any woman who would get a random man cologne if she wasn't sleeping with him or thinking about it?"

Monica shrugged. "Probably not."

"If Josh was sleeping with Savannah, are we assuming that the customer accusing him of theft is Allan Anderson?" Robin asked. "Josh could have met her when he was working on her husband's car. I can imagine him having a Maserati."

"I'm going to text West real quick, but that makes

sense to me." Val got out her phone. *Does the name Allan Anderson sound familiar? Does he have a black Maserati?*

"We know he has a lot of money," Monica said, "but does anyone actually know what Allan Anderson does for a living?"

"I do!" Robin said. "I asked around after we saw him at the café earlier this week. Mark got to talking with one of the owners of Sierra Slopes. Anderson *is* one of the owners. He and a couple of his pro-skiing buddies bought the place. They're the ones fixing it up and modernizing it. They sank a bunch of money into the project. Not sure it's going to pay out."

"I hope it does," Monica muttered. "I wanted to talk to them about a room-and-ticket package for Russell House."

"Getting back to Josh and Savannah." Val watched her phone, waiting for West to text her back. "What do you guys think? Logically, the next person I should talk to is her, right? If they were having an affair—"

"Do we call Josh's random boinks affairs? Is that accurate?" Robin asked. "No offense."

"None taken. I know what you mean, but this..." The emotions that the cologne bottle stirred up were more shocking than the identity of Josh's lover. "I don't think she was a random for him."

"Really?" Monica glanced at her in the rearview mirror. "He had real feelings for her?"

"I mean..." Val replayed the vision in her mind. Surprise. Discomfort. Affection. Longing? "I think he really cares about her. I could feel what he was feeling, and it was a lot. None of it seemed superficial. And the emotions are... I don't want to say old, but he's known her for a while, I think. It's not new."

"So we need to talk to Savannah Anderson," Monica said. "Does anyone know where she lives? I know they're in Pheasant Creek, but I don't have any friends over there that I can call."

"We could wait for her to come into Misfit," Val said. "She's always in at least once a week."

Robin held up her phone. "Or we could ask Miranda to look up her address in our computer."

"You have her address?" Monica asked.

"Yeah. That dresser she bought?" Robin dialed and held the phone to her ear. "She wanted it delivered. I'm sure we still have the address."

"Robin knows everything," Monica said quietly.

"That's why she's the best on trivia night." Val saw a message pop up on her phone from West. *Let me call someone.*

"Miranda, do you have a minute?" Robin's voice was bright. She'd hired the girl a few months before and it was working out well. In addition to selling antiques, Miranda was also a ceramic artist and was expanding the local-art section of the store, including some of Robin's own paintings. "Yes, I need an address."

Val sat up straight and reached for her water bottle. She needed to wash down some aspirin if they were going to talk to Savannah. Her phone buzzed again. It was West.

Yep. Anderson, black Maserati. He's some big investor at the ski resort.

Thanks, West.

"It's him," Val said. "West just confirmed. Anderson owns a black Maserati. He says he bought it last year."

"Thank you, West," Monica said.

"Savannah Anderson," Robin said into the phone. "She should be in the system. We delivered a dresser to her about a month ago."

Robin scratched something down on a paper she'd grabbed from her purse. "Thanks, Miranda. I'll be in after lunch, okay? Great." She hung up and handed the paper to Monica. "We have an address."

"We have a client," Val said.

They were finally making progress.

PHEASANT CREEK WAS a planned development in the foothills between Glimmer Lake and Bridger City. It had been a ranch, but developers had bought it years ago, slowed the creek to a crawl to widen it, and sold lots for custom homes that soared in price. Homes in Pheasant Creek regularly sold for over a million dollars, which was nearly unheard of in the foothills.

Green lawns and manicured landscaping wound through granite-dotted hills. Pheasant Creek was just far enough down the mountain that snow fell, but it didn't stick around.

The cars switched from practical Fords and Hondas to Lexuses, BMWs, and Mercedes. Monica drove her minivan through the open gates and looked for the turnoff to the Anderson home.

"Do you think she'll even be home?" Monica asked. "And

how do we know Americano Asshole won't be home with her?"

"Good question," Val said. "We do not want to talk to Savannah when that guy is around."

Robin pulled out her phone again. "I have someone I can call. I bet you he's on the mountain today." She touched a number and held the phone to her ear. "Cassie? Hey! How's the snow looking today?"

Val listened as Robin made skiing small talk. They were talking about storms and snowpack. Lift lines and tour groups.

"Hey, is that Anderson guy on the mountain today?" Robin paused. "I have a friend who wanted to talk to someone about a promotion with her new hotel. Is he the guy to ask? I know he's an owner."

Monica whispered, "You know, she looks like such a soccer mom, but she's a frighteningly good liar."

Val whispered back, "I assume all soccer moms are masters at deception. No one enjoys going to peewee soccer games every Saturday for months on end."

Robin held her hand out and gave them a thumbs-up. "Oh, okay. I'll let her know. Thanks, Cass. Yeah, I think we're going up tomorrow. I'll see you." Robin turned off her phone. "She's one of the ski instructors and a school friend of Austin's. Anderson is on the mountain, so he will not be at his house." She turned to Monica. "But Charlie Gross is the one to talk to about promo stuff. Just so you know."

"Cool." Monica held her hand out, and Robin bumped her knuckles. "You're super useful. Thanks."

"Glad I could do something since the ghost thing is kind of a crapshoot this time."

"At least you're getting something. I haven't had a single vision that's not related to blood, snow, and skiing."

Of course, blood, snow, and skiing seemed a lot more ominous now that they knew Josh was sleeping with the wife of a former pro skier.

CHAPTER 12

The Anderson home was an attractive Californian adaptation of a Swiss chalet. Made of stone and exposed wooden logs, it stretched across a rise that overlooked the neighborhood and the valley below. A broad porch shaded the first of three stories.

"This is... large."

Robin squinted at it. "Kinda reminds me of Russell House."

"Let's hope this one isn't haunted too," Monica said. "I don't have any sage with me."

"We really need to start carrying some stuff," Val said. "For emergencies."

"Emergency sage?" Robin smiled. "That and salt guns."

"It wouldn't be a bad idea," Monica said. "Maybe I'll make up a kit."

"Okay, Ghostbusters, let's do this before the neighbors call the police." Val walked to the front door and pushed the doorbell. A cascade of chimes echoed through the house, and a blurry outline appeared in the frosted glass of the front door.

Savannah answered the door herself. "Hello." She recognized them and frowned. "Hi. Aren't you—?"

"I'm Valerie Costa." Val stepped forward. "And there is no way this is not going to be awkward, so I'm just going to spit it out. Josh Mason is my ex-husband—not sure if you knew that—and I know you guys are... close."

Savannah's already pale face went even paler. "You're—"

"It's fine. I don't need to know." Val held up a hand. "It's none of my business. The *only* reason I'm here is that I don't know if you realize he's missing." She waited for Savannah to jump in, but the woman was speechless. "Looking at your expression right now, I think you probably do know, and I wanted to ask if you knew anything about where he might have gone. If he mentioned anything to you. Or if you have any idea where—"

"Josh was my husband's mechanic." Savannah cut her off. Her face was pale, but her expression was frozen. "I met him, and I think I brought him a coffee once. But I don't know anything more about him. I'm sorry."

"Your husband has a black Maserati, right?"

"Yes." She started to close the door, and Val stuck her hand out.

"Please." Val stopped the door from closing. "Please, Savannah. I know Josh was more than your husband's mechanic. I know you got him a bottle of really nice cologne. And I know he cared about you a lot. I know..." She racked her brain for memories of the vision. "I know he... He was worried about you." She looked up and met Savannah's eyes.

"He was worried about you, Savannah. Why was he worried about you?"

When the woman spoke, it was barely over a whisper. "You need to leave."

"Why was Josh worried about you?" There was something delicate and sad in Savannah's expression. Something wistful that made Val angry. "Please. My friends and I can help if you—"

"You need to go." With a firm hand, Savannah shut the door in Val's face.

She turned and saw Robin and Monica staring at her, both wearing worried expressions.

"She's scared of something," Robin said.

"Yeah. Big time."

"Let's go." Val headed to the van, a knot of dread in her belly. "Whatever is going on, I don't want to make trouble for her."

SHE STARED at the door of the coffee shop, willing Savannah Anderson to walk through the door. Maybe she didn't want to talk at her house. Maybe they had staff who would report on her to her husband.

That was a frightening thought.

Imagine being so trapped that you didn't feel comfortable talking in your own home. Customers stepped up to the register, and she took their order by rote.

"Double-shot mocha with caramel."

"Refill on a brewed coffee."

"Regular latte with skim."

The ebb and flow of customers in the coffee shop was soothing. The bustle of school kids walking in and out, skiers on their way up the mountain, the year-round residents of Glimmer Lake greeting each other across the room.

This was her place. It was good. Misfit Mountain was for everyone. The weirdos and the punks and those who didn't fit in. And it was for the soccer moms and old ranchers and the kids. Val had wanted to make a place where everyone fit in because no one did.

That includes you, Savannah.

Val had taken the day off from investigating because she'd hit a dead end. She'd talked to everyone she could think of and didn't know where else to go. Robin hadn't found any spirits with insight, and she hadn't been able to summon the ghost behind West's garage again. Monica hadn't had any other visions except one where she saw Savannah driving through the mountains in her pretty silver sports car, which wasn't all that helpful.

Val was trying not to be discouraged, but it was hard. She'd taken days off work, and she still didn't have any solid leads. It had been a week since Josh went missing, and she was starting to think that maybe he did take off.

Maybe he didn't take the money like the police thought, but maybe he did just up and moved. Maybe he couldn't face his feelings for Savannah, didn't want to deal with breaking up with Rachel, and didn't feel like explaining himself.

It wasn't implausible. Josh was nothing if not an emotional coward.

He might be out there, completely oblivious to anyone being worried about him. Maybe the choppy voice mail he'd left explained what was going on, and she didn't get the message because the signal was crappy. Maybe he really was that asshole who didn't care that his kids worried about him.

All completely possible explanations.

At two, she turned the sign for the café around and locked the door. It had been quiet after the lunch rush, and there were no remaining customers to shoo out the door. JoJo and Max were cleaning the tables and chattering about the apartment they'd found. They had to find one more roommate willing to share the rent with them and they'd be good to go. Val could see the excitement on JoJo's face at the prospect of being out of their mom's house.

Honey and Ramon were happy. All her employees were happy. The café was busy and profits were increasing.

And her boys were worried and miserable.

You can do one thing well. You can either be a great mom or a great business owner. You don't get to have both.

She saw Sully's pickup truck in the distance, parking at Glimmer Lake Realty.

And you definitely don't get to have that.

She tossed the wrapped sandwich Ramon had made for her in the passenger side of her truck before getting in and warming up the engine, blowing on her hands to keep them from freezing. Another cold snap had dropped the night before, and Val could smell fresh snow in the air. She wanted to get home before the boys did, start a fire, and eat her lunch.

She didn't want to think about Josh. Or Savannah Anderson. Or blood on the snow.

She unwrapped her sandwich while she was waiting for the truck to heat up.

Pastrami and provolone. Damn, Ramon was good.

HER DARK MOOD bled over from her afternoon into her evening. The boys came home and were quieter than usual. Jackson didn't ask to go to the library. Andy put his head in a book as soon as his homework was finished. They didn't even fight about doing the laundry or the dishes.

At nine o'clock, both boys were in their room and ready for bed.

Val stuck her head in the doorway and caught Jackson's eye. "Hey."

He looked up from his phone. "Hey."

"I'm going out for a drink okay? I won't be long."

"Is it snowing?"

"Not supposed to come down until midnight. I won't be that late."

"Are you meeting Monica and Robin?"

"I'll text them." Which was not a yes. She would text them, but she didn't want to catch a drink with them. "I'll have my phone on me if you need anything."

"Okay, no problem." Jackson's shaggy hair fell in his eyes, and Val fought back the sharp urge to brush it away and kiss his forehead like she had when he was little.

"I'll see you later." Val closed the door, grabbed her keys, and slipped out of the house, taking long sharp breaths on the front porch while she surveyed the night sky. The snow was coming soon. She could smell it. She could feel the stillness in the air. By morning, there would be an extra foot of the stuff on the ground.

Walk or drive?

She didn't want to drive, but what was in walking

distance? Oh yes. Chaco's. She ducked back inside and wrapped an extra scarf around her neck before she grabbed her wallet and walked out the door again.

Chaco's was a local bar. It wasn't fancy, but it did attract the tourists. Hopefully none of them would be drinking on a weeknight in the middle of winter. Val shuffled down the sidewalk and toward the main drag with her hands stuffed in her pockets and her eyes on the road. She didn't worry about bears or mountain lions, but a tourist who didn't know how to navigate icy roads? Now that was a deadly predator.

Ten minutes after she left her house, she was sliding onto a barstool at Chaco's with her phone in hand. She waved at Sergio behind the bar, and he gave her a chin nod to tell her he'd be right with her.

Before he walked over, Val sent a text to Robin and Val. *At Chaco's. Do not need rescuing. What are u up to?*

Robin was the first to text back. *Movie with Mark.*

???

Social Network.

Good one.

"What'll you have, Val?" Sergio took a rag and wiped off the bar in front of her. "Anyone joining you?"

"Nope. And just a beer."

"805?"

"Sounds good."

Robin texted back, *You know, the movie's not over but I think Facebook is evil.*

Ur just figuring this out?

Monica joined in just as Sergio brought her beer. *I'm cleaning out the guest room.*

You wild woman.

Needed to be done.

Val typed, *This is why her house always looks better than ours do, R.*

You're not wrong.

Val reached for the bowl of nuts on the bar, only to be met with the abrupt image of a tourist wiping his nose and then reaching for them.

Ew. No.

She waved the dish at Sergio. "Can I get a fresh bowl?"

He walked over and leaned against the bar. "You think my nuts are dirty?"

This was Chaco's. She wasn't getting out of here without a few nut jokes. "Are you telling me that tourists have been in and out of here all day and they haven't put their fingers all over your nuts?"

The corner of Sergio's mustache twitched. "I keep my nuts fresh, tourists or no tourists."

Val tapped on the bowl, valiantly keeping a straight face. "Fresh nuts, please."

"You're lucky I like you." He swiped the small silver bowl from her hand. "Or I'd be offended by you insulting my nuts."

Val felt him before she heard him. Somehow she'd known he would show up that night.

"If the woman wants fresh nuts, give her fresh nuts." Sully sat on the barstool next to her. "And don't complain. It's not like anyone else in here is asking for your nuts."

Sergio smirked and walked across the bar to refill the tray.

Val looked up at Sully. "I never need to hear the word *nuts* again."

"Nuts." He reached for her beer. "I'm not keeping

count."

"Poacher." She watched him take a drink and remembered a summer night when they'd shared a beer. Then a bed. Unlike that night, Sully was wearing heavy winter gear. He'd taken off his uniform and was in the typical Glimmer Lake uniform of T-shirt with a flannel over it and a vest over that. He'd probably left his parka by the front door like Val had.

"How was your day?" she asked.

"I've had better. I've had worse." Sully nodded at Sergio when the man brought him a tall glass of gold brew and set the silver tray of nuts on the bar between them. "How was yours? You stay in town today?"

"Yeah. Kind of hit a wall."

He grunted. "I know how that feels."

"Still haven't heard from Josh." She grabbed a cashew from the bowl.

Sully took a long drink. "Just so you know, if you do"—he lowered his voice—"you don't have to tell me."

"I'm not trying to withhold anything because I don't think he stole that money. I think as soon as he shows up, we're gonna find out that he ordered parts with it. Or that he never had it to begin with."

"So why would Anderson lie?"

She raised her eyebrows. "Oh, are we sharing now?"

Val could tell Sully hadn't realized he let the name slip but also that he didn't care that much.

He shrugged. "Might as well. I'd be shocked if you hadn't figured that part out yet."

Val turned to Sully and squared her shoulders. "Fine. I'll show you mine if you show me yours."

CHAPTER 13

"*I*'m definitely not going to turn down that offer." Sully finished his beer in one long gulp and set the empty glass on the table. "Allan Anderson is an asshole—"

"At the coffee shop, we call him Americano Asshole. Really. That's his nickname."

Sully frowned. "Why?"

"Because he orders a café Americano with heavy cream and three sugars."

"And?"

"You know what that is? It's a sweet caffe latte. Only he's too cheap to pay the extra fifty cents to order a sweet latte. So he orders an Americano and he doesn't even have the decency to go to the milk-and-sugar station and put the milk in himself. He wants us to do it for him."

"So why don't you tell him to fuck off?"

"That's generally considered bad for business," Val said. "Also, he drives a BMW and leaves twenty-five cent tips. Americano Asshole."

"Yeah, even I know that's kind of shitty."

"It is. Which is just to say that yes, Anderson is an asshole. But apparently he's friends with the mayor in Bridger, so everyone listens to him."

A large group of skiers walked into the bar, raising the volume of the room. Val and Sully scooted closer together.

He shook his head. "It's not just the mayor. He's friends with God and everyone. The county commission sucked up to him and gave the ski resort all kinds of tax breaks to renovate because they figure it'll be good for businesses in the area."

"To be fair, it is. Sierra Slopes brings in a ton of business. I know all the hotels have had a lot more bookings this year since the renovations. Our business went up nearly thirty percent. Everyone in Glimmer Lake is happy about it."

"Agreed, but it also brings in more work for the police and sheriff's office. Do we complain about doing more on less tax dollars? No. It's fine. But then Anderson is on the phone with Bridger PD every fucking day."

"About Josh?"

"Yeah. This guy is obsessed with finding your ex."

"I've seen the man's house. I don't think ten grand is really obsession-worthy for him."

Sergio brought Sully another beer. "Agreed." Sully stared at her. "Which makes me think this isn't about the money."

Sergio broke in. "Just so you know, I'm gonna turn on the game. I'll try to keep the volume from getting crazy."

"Thanks, Serg," Sully said.

Val waited for the bartender to leave before she turned back to Sully. "Okay, I can't tell you *how* I know this, but I'm pretty positive Josh and Savannah Anderson were having an affair."

Sully's mouth firmed into a line. "How positive?"

"One hundred percent. I know they're having an affair."

"I *knew* it," he muttered. "I fucking knew it. Wait, *were* having an affair? They're not anymore?"

"I don't know if they still are. No idea about that part. I couldn't get her to talk to me."

Sully stared at his beer. "Do you think she knows where he is?"

"I didn't get the sense that she did. I think she's as confused as the rest of us. But I can tell you that she's afraid of something."

"Josh?"

"Wouldn't hurt a fly. Seriously, the man doesn't even like to kill spiders."

"So Anderson?"

Val raised and lowered her shoulders slowly. "Your guess is as good as mine. I can't tell you that. And I can't touch—tell...," Val stammered. "I can't tell how long it's been going on. Or, I mean, I don't know how serious. With her and Josh." She cleared her throat. "You might have better luck talking to her. She might not have talked to me because I'm his ex."

He was frowning, staring at her. Then he glanced at her hands. Val stuffed them in her pockets and tried to look nonchalant.

"Okay," Sully said. "I'll try talking to her. Bridger PD didn't question her. I know that. They're totally focused on the line Anderson fed them about your ex stealing the money. You're definitely sure about the affair?"

"Yeah. I'm sure. I still don't know why he took off, but I don't think it's about the money."

"I don't either." Sully's thumb flicked along the edge of his beard. "Would he be afraid of Anderson?"

"Josh? No. Maybe he should be, but he wouldn't be. He doesn't have the sense to be afraid. Also, he's too confident. He always thinks he can get out of any situation by bull-shitting."

Sully took a pull of his beer. "I'm starting to see why you two ended up divorced."

Val rolled her eyes. "It was a lot more than the bullshit, but that didn't help."

Sully looked at her. Looked away. "How are your boys doing?"

"They seem a little better since they talked to you."

"Good. I didn't sugarcoat anything for them. Didn't tell them I was bringing their dad home or any shit like that. Just so you know. I wouldn't do that. It wouldn't be fair."

"I know," she said. "I think just having someone in authority listen to them helped. That was thoughtful. I can tell you know kids."

"Well, I know boys anyway. I grew up in a house full of them. Kinda lost when it comes to girls, even though I have like five nieces."

"You're the oldest, right?"

"Four brothers." He popped an almond in his mouth and crunched it. "I remember being that age." He turned and raised an eyebrow. "It was a while ago, but I remember."

The volume of the football game increased, and Val leaned closer. "I was thinking earlier that work was going so well right now. The kitchen is running smooth. All my servers and baristas are happy, but... my kids are sad. So all the other stuff means crap. It seems like I either have a good business or I have happy kids. I never seem to manage both."

"You're a good mom, Valerie. Don't doubt that."

She leaned on the bar and let out a long breath. "Why do you call me Valerie? Why do you do that?"

Sully leaned so close she could feel his breath on her cheek. "Because your name is sweet and soft and I like thinking of you in my bed, sweet and soft and—"

She slapped a hand over his mouth. "We don't need to talk about that."

He shoved her hand away. "I don't agree."

Val narrowed her eyes at his sullen expression. "Are you pissed at me?"

"Kinda."

"Why?"

"Because you left." He scowled. "And part of me gets it. I really do. I know your life is hectic as shit. But the other part of me is pissed because I'm not asking for some huge commitment, okay?" He glanced around the bar. "I mean, if you want me to take you out, I'll take you out. If you wanted to meet my parents—"

"I could go to church on Sunday with my parents because they sit like two rows behind them?"

"Well yeah," he muttered. "I'm just saying that if you want that stuff, then we can do that. And if you wanted to just... hang out sometimes, I'm okay with that too."

Val blinked. Did Sully just volunteer to be her fuckbuddy? Did she want that? Did responsible adults have fuckbuddies? Was that an option? Was she even a responsible adult?

Those were all questions up for debate.

He was staring at her. "You're not saying anything."

"I don't know what to say."

"What do you want?" he asked. "That's all I'm wondering. Do you want a relationship or do you—?"

"No. I don't think so. Not right now." Val could tell he was disappointed, but she wanted to be honest. "Maybe when this is all over," she said. "Right now I can't think about anything other than figuring out what's best for my boys, you know? They have *one* responsible parent. Me. I'm it. Josh is just... He's the fun one. I'm the not-fun one."

"I think you're fun."

She lowered her voice. "Well, that's because you've had sex with me and I'm never going to nag you to do your homework."

The corner of his mouth turned up. "You could give me homework if you wanted to."

"Stop."

"Stop what?"

Being so damn attractive. Being nice. Being funny and making me feel special.

"Just stop bringing it up. I'm not saying no, okay? I'm just saying... not now."

He nodded slowly. "Okay. Not now. I can deal with that."

"And don't be pushy."

"I'm not some punk kid." He looked at her from the corner of his eye. "Have I been pushy?"

"No."

"Your friends are the pushy ones. I'm the one pretending not to hear the comments."

She closed her eyes. "And I appreciate that."

"Good." He nudged her glass toward her. "Finish your beer. I'll drive you home."

"I can walk."

He looked over his shoulder. "It's snowing. I'm not letting you walk home in the snow."

"Is it?" Damn, he was right. Tiny white flakes were falling in the glow of the parking lot lights. Val finished her beer. "I can walk. It's not far."

"Just let me drive you home. I got this one, by the way." He stood and put a twenty on the bar, enough for both their beers and a healthy tip. Sully walked to the jacket hooks by the door. "I will drive you home as a *friend*. Because it's cold."

"Okay. Thank you, *friend*." Val walked to the wall, carefully pulling on her gloves before she even reached for her jacket.

Clothes were one of the things that triggered her visions most strongly, and rifling through a mess of jackets would probably give her a seizure. She delicately picked through the jackets that had been piled on top of hers, careful not to let the fabric touch her skin.

"Gotta stop doing this," she said.

"Stop doing what?"

Leaving my clothes where they could get tangled up with someone else's. "Gotta stop going out for random drinks in the middle of the week."

"Why? You got a drinking problem with your"—he glanced back at the bar—"one beer and cashew habit?"

"Ha ha." They walked out to the parking lot, and Val spotted his lifted pickup parked on the far end. "Boy, you don't like taking the close parking space, do you?"

His breath huffed out in a cloud. "It's stupid, but it makes sense in my head."

"What does?"

He stopped and looked between the front door and the truck. "I can run to my truck and get to the road faster than I can drive through the parking lot if there was an emergency."

Val looked between the truck and the quickly dimming facade of Chaco's. "Huh. I wouldn't have thought about that."

"Sometimes minutes count." Sully put his hand on the small of her back and opened the door, making sure she was steady as she climbed on the running board.

Val sat in the truck and turned, waiting for him to close the door. He didn't. He just stood in the gently falling snow, looking at her.

"Can I kiss you?" he asked.

Yesssssss.

No.

Yes?

No.

"Better not," she said quietly.

His eyes drilled into her. "Okay." He nudged her knee. "Better scoot in. Watch your toes."

He walked around and Val had to hold back from banging her head on the window.

Not no, just not now.

Not no. But not now.

Not now was going to kill her. Her libido was not happy with her brain.

Sully hopped in the other side of the cab and started the

truck. He rubbed his hands together and glanced across the bench. "Gotta give her a second to warm up."

"Yeah."

"She's a diesel, so she takes her time."

"Mm-hmm." *Say nothing. Say. Nothing.*

"Nice thing about a diesel engine though, once you get her hot, she'll go for hours and—"

"Sully!"

His low laugh filled the truck.

Val could feel her cheeks getting warm. "You're an evil tormenter."

"Takes one to know one."

"I am not evil."

"Don't pretend like I haven't seen your tattoos, Valerie."

Okay, well there is that one...

"Can you please take me home now?"

"I will. As soon as the truck warms up."

"Right." Val stared at the dark forest in front of the dashboard.

Sully fiddled with the radio, tuning it to a classic country station before he said, "So did I ever tell you about the police psychic I worked with in LA?"

CHAPTER 14

*M*onica and Robin stared at her, openmouthed.

"Police psychic?" Robin asked.

"What does that mean?" Monica unfroze and started pacing in the kitchen of Glimmer Lake Curios, where they had met for lunch. "Does he know? How could he know?"

"I don't know." Val threw up her hands. "I didn't really say anything about it. He rambled a little bit about this lady in LA who worked with the police."

"What did you say?" Robin asked.

"Nothing! I just hmmed and said 'that's interesting' a couple of times and prayed that he'd stop." She unwrapped the roasted turkey on sourdough she'd brought for herself. She'd hardly gotten a wink of sleep the night before after Sully dropped her off. "I don't know what to think."

"How could he know?" Monica asked again. "Have you told him anything personal? Like... anything you'd have no reason to know?"

"No." She rifled through her memories. "At least, I don't

think so. I mean, I told him I knew about Josh's affair with Savannah, but I didn't tell him how I knew."

"What about when you guys..."

"I don't read people," Val said. "It doesn't work that way. I didn't pick up anything accidental from him, if that's what you're thinking. And even if I did, why would he bring that up now?"

Robin and Monica stared at her.

"I have no idea," Monica said.

"I don't know what you should do." Robin unwrapped her roast beef. "But this isn't good."

"I don't know," Val said. "I mean, as long as I don't confirm anything, he can think what he wants to think. It's not like he's going to accuse me of being a witch or something."

"And if he did, who would care?" Monica sat down at the table and reached for her chicken salad. "Anyway, witch is the least of the names people have called you."

"Exactly." Val took a large bite of turkey. "Maybe I should tell people I'm a witch. I bet the boys would love that."

"Teenagers have no sense of humor," Robin said. "Did I tell you about the time I picked Austin up from school in my Princess Leia outfit? He was a freshman. Didn't even laugh."

Monica frowned. "Out of curiosity, why?"

"Why Princess Leia?" Robin reached for her drink. "It was Halloween! We were going to a party. I wasn't wearing the bikini or anything. Just the white Princess Leia robe with the hair." She circled her finger around her ears. "I had the wig and everything."

"Awesome," Monica said. "We're just cooler than our kids want to admit."

"I do have the bikini though." Robin smiled. "Mark likes it."

Val snorted. "He's such a geek."

"Oh, he definitely is." Robin cocked her head. "You know, Mark likes Sully. I wonder if he'd vote for telling him." She picked up her phone. "I'm gonna ask."

"Why?" Monica said. "Telling Mark is one thing—he's your husband—but Sully isn't in the group."

"He could be." Robin glanced at Val. "I mean, he likes Val. He's part of the police—"

"Sheriff," Val said. "It's different."

"Not around here," Robin said. "Maybe he could help. And it would be nice if we didn't have to answer any weird questions in the future. He knows what happened to us last year."

Sully was the one who'd investigated the car crash that had dumped them into Glimmer Lake and triggered their psychic powers.

Monica tapped on her chin. "He did make a point of telling you about the police psychic. Maybe that was his way of telling you he's trustworthy?"

"Okay, yeah." Val put down her sandwich. "But that doesn't mean I need to tell him anything."

"Why don't you want to?" Robin held her phone up to her ear. "I mean, what can it hurt? He's clearly open to the possibility."

"Because he can suspect, but if I tell him the truth..." Val couldn't bring herself to say it.

He'll think I'm a freak.

That'll be the end of that.

There's no way he'd ever be with me if he knew.

Shit. She felt more for Sully than she'd been willing to admit. Otherwise, why did she care? She couldn't imagine even the most secure man being fine with dating a woman who could see though any story with a single touch.

Seeing visions like Monica? That was kinda sexy and dreamy. Seeing ghosts like Robin? That was cool, if a little creepy. But being able to pick up on visions by touch? No way. No one wanted to be around someone who could do that. That was why she was never telling her children. She could barely admit the scope of her power to Robin and Monica!

Tell Sully? No fucking way.

Robin was nodding on the phone. "Uh-huh." She looked at Val and mouthed, *Mark.* "You think?" She doodled in the corner of the notepad she constantly had with her. "Yeah. I'll tell her."

"Tell me what?" Val muttered to Monica.

"Probably that you should tell Sully," Monica said.

"Why? Because he's tired of being the only boy in the club?"

Monica snorted. "I have no opinion on this. I can see pluses and minuses to the idea."

"I don't know why anyone else thinks they get a vote." She finished off her turkey club and wiped her hands. "My life is not a democracy."

Robin hung up the phone and said, "Mark thinks you should tell Sully."

"I'm shocked," Val said. "So shocked."

"And not because he's the only boy in the clubhouse."

Robin smiled. "Did you think I couldn't hear you? He said Sully is a valuable resource for information, and since he brought it up to you, he clearly suspects something and he also clearly doesn't have a problem with the idea of psychic powers being real."

Val crossed her arms. "Did you tell him we were involved? And that we might... I don't know. Someday want to be involved again?"

Monica's eyebrows went up. "I thought you said it didn't work out."

"It didn't. But that's not saying that it'll *never* work out. When life isn't so complicated—"

"When is life going to not be complicated?" Robin asked. "Serious question."

Val said, "You know, I'm not one hundred percent certain, but I'm gonna say it'll probably be less complicated when *my ex-husband isn't wanted by the police and missing.*"

Monica raised her hand. "I'm going to agree with Val on this one. Can you imagine Mark being happy with your knowing literally everything about him just from touching his keys? Privacy is important in every relationship. I never knew all Gil's stuff; he never knew all mine. Sully knowing that Val has this kind of power could kill any chance they'd have of making romance work."

"Fine," Robin said. "I'm just passing a message along. You have to admit, he would be a good resource. And it would be nice to have one official-type person in our corner if we got caught... I don't know, breaking into the morgue to look at dead bodies or something."

"We only did that once," Monica said. "And hopefully we will never need to do it again."

"Also, we got away with it," Val said. "Just saying."

Val's phone buzzed in her pocket. She grabbed it, looked at the number, and answered. "Hey, Ramon. Everything cool?"

"Nothing going on over here," he said. "It's Tuesday, so it's all pretty chill. But Don called just a minute ago."

Val groaned. "Is he running late again? I don't want to have to stay late because the produce guy is kicking back and—"

"It's legit this time. They closed down the highway between here and Bridger for an hour or so. Guess someone went off the road near Sugar Pine Road."

Val winced. "That's not good."

"Search and rescue had to go down—they had the helicopter out—and they were dragging the car up the hill. So all the equipment blocked the road."

"Can't be mad at that," Val said. "Hope it's no one we know."

"Probably a tourist."

Val was certain Ramon was right. She was still going to check her Find My Phone app as soon as she hung up to make sure her kids were in school.

"I'm almost done here," she said. "So I can stay late. Tell Don to drive safe, and I'll tell the boys to just head to the shop after school."

"You got it. You want me to lock up?"

"No. I'm heading that way in a few minutes." She hung up and checked her boys, happy to see their electronic dots hovering around the Glimmer Lake middle and high school campus.

"What's going on?" Monica asked.

"Car went over the edge by Sugar Pine," Val said. "They had to get search and rescue out."

Robin gasped. "Someone Ramon knows?"

"No. The produce guy just called to tell us he's going to be late, so I told Ramon I'd stay to meet him."

"You're a nice boss." Robin wrapped up the remainder of her sandwich. "I should be nicer to my employee."

"She'll survive," Monica said. "Didn't you say she still mixes up vendors?"

"Constantly. But in the plus column, I told her about the shop ghost and she actually seemed excited about her. So there's that."

"Can't complain about an employee who's cool with the resident haunt." Val stood. "I'm out. Let me know if anyone has a helpful vision about where Josh's butt has disappeared to."

"Will do."

"Thanks."

SHE TURNED on the television for some white noise as she wiped down the tables and married the ketchup bottles in the dining room. The buzz of a local gardening show hummed in the background, and she nearly missed her phone ringing a few minutes after three thirty.

Val smiled when she picked up her phone. "Hey, kiddo."

"I got your message"—Jackson was talking with what sounded like a crowd in the background—"but do you mind if we head home? I've got a paper I need to work on and all my notes are at the house."

"Do you want to drop Andy off here?"

"Nah, he's okay. It was library day today. He won't get in my hair."

"Ah." Library day meant Andy with new books, which meant he'd be completely out of it until he read all his new finds. "Okay. Well, I guess if you don't want to hang out with your supercool mom, then you can just go home and be boring by yourself."

Jackson laughed. "Thanks, Mom."

"Hey, out of curiosity, if I picked you up at school wearing a Princess Leia costume, would you be too embarrassed to speak to me?"

"Which Princess Leia costume?"

"Just the regular white-robe one. Not the bikini."

"Good. If you wore the bikini, I'd have to deal with Carter drooling over you, which would just be gross."

Val blinked. "What?"

"Never mind. He's one of the guys who thinks you're cool. Don't wear a Princess Leia bikini, Mom. I gotta go. I'll see you at home."

"Okay, but tell—" The phone cut off and Val frowned. He'd never actually told her if he'd speak to her if she showed up in a Princess Leia costume. She was going to assume he would.

After all, she was the cool mom.

Ha!

She caught a familiar name being shouted on the television and turned to look.

"Sheriff Sullivan!" A reporter was chasing Sully's back. "Do you have any more information about the woman whose car went off the road today?"

They must have interrupted the gardening show to cover the accident that had shut down the road. In Glimmer Lake and Bridger City, things like that were huge news.

"She is alive and being transported to Bridger City right now. I don't have any more information that I can share with you at the moment." His expression was written with worry. "As you can imagine, we're still in the process of contacting family, so we're asking all the media"—he looked directly into the camera—"to please respect that. Even if you get a name, let's just hold off on reporting anything like that until we can be sure the family of this woman has been notified."

Val knew that he'd be heading up any accident notification. He took his job personally, and Glimmer Lake was his home.

"Is there any more you can share at this time?"

"I can tell you search and rescue did an incredible job and got the driver to the hospital in Bridger as quickly as they could." He looked up. "Especially in weather like this, we want to caution all drivers to slow down, be careful, and watch for ice. Even on sunny days, if you hit a shady spot in the road, the results can be tragic." He nodded at the camera. "Thanks, Kim. I can't say anything more right now."

The tapping on the door distracted her. "Val?"

It was Don. The produce delivery had finally arrived.

She waved him toward the back through the window and walked to the back porch to unlock the door. "Hey, Don!"

"Sorry about the time." The older man immediately began unloading his truck. "Bad scene on the highway."

"I just saw Sully on the TV." She reached for each crate and set them on the picnic table. "Did you see who it was?"

"I didn't see the accident, but I saw the car they pulled

out." Don finished unloading the full crates and reached for the pile of empty plastic lugs Ramon had set out from the previous week. "Some fancy little silver thing. Most likely a tourist. Can't imagine anyone around here driving a silver convertible in the winter."

"A silver convertible?" Val felt the blood in her face drain away. "Are you sure?"

"Yeah." Don frowned. "One of your friends drive something like that?"

She wasn't exactly a friend. But Val only knew one flashy silver convertible on the mountain, and it belonged to Savannah Anderson.

CHAPTER 15

*V*al drove home without checking the news. She made sure her phone ringer was on high and resisted the urge to call Sully. He would be busy. She was probably wrong. There were probably numerous people with silver cars who could have been heading up to Glimmer Lake.

She walked into the house and heard the news on high volume. "Boys?"

Following the noise led her to the cozy family room where the wood stove had already been lit and both her sons were sitting on the couch, staring wordlessly at the blaring television and the face of none other than Americano Asshole standing in front of the Bridger City hospital.

"My wife"—his brow was furrowed—"is an excellent driver. An experienced driver. She grew up here and isn't some tourist driving too fast. I expect a full and complete investigation from the police and the sheriff's department."

The reporter stuck a microphone even closer to his face.

"Mr. Anderson, are you claiming that some kind of foul play was involved in your wife's accident?"

Fuck. Fuck. Fuck.

Anderson's cold blue eyes looked directly into the camera. "I'm saying that Josh Mason—my former mechanic—has been wanted for weeks by the Bridger PD because he's a dishonest man who stole money from me. He worked on my car and my wife's. And now my wife is in the hospital after a mysterious accident. You're the reporter. You figure it out."

Oh no. No, no, no, no. Val looked at Jackson and Andy, whose pale faces were frozen in horror and disbelief.

"Change the channel." Val looked for the remote and saw it in Jackson's hand.

He wordlessly flipped to the next station.

"Mason, who was moonlighting from his legitimate job at a high-end auto shop here in Bridger City, reportedly stole over ten thousand dollars from the Andersons and has been missing ever since last week. Sources say—"

"Turn it off!" Val reached for the remote and Jackson snatched his hand away. "Jackson, turn—"

"It's on every channel." His voice was cold as he stood and flipped through the local news. "Dad's picture. Dad's name. These people. The lady in the hospital..."

Each screen was filled with pictures of Savannah Anderson with her angelic blond curls, Allan Anderson looking dashing in front of the ski resort, or Josh.

The news had managed to find the one scary-looking picture of Josh, which happened to be from his driver's license, but they'd cropped it to look more like a mug shot. He was staring into the camera without a smile, all charm and life stripped away.

Val looked at Andy. His eyes were filled with tears. "Mom, did Dad—?"

"Baby, he would *never*." She knelt in front of Andy and took her son's cheeks between her hands. "He would never do something like this. He would never hurt someone on purpose. That man is full of shit. He's accusing your father because something else is going on, and I'm going to figure it out." She forced Andy's eyes to hers. "Do you believe me?"

Andy's lip trembled, but he nodded.

"Good. You ignore all this, do you hear me? Ignore it. If someone says something at school, you tell me. Your father would never hurt someone on purpose. Never."

Her phone was buzzing in her pocket, but she paid it no attention as she reassured her younger son and ignored the stoic expression of the elder. Jackson had turned off the television, but he was glaring at his phone.

She'd just settled Andy into his room with a book and a mug of hot chocolate when she heard the knock at her front door.

"Shit." Would the local news have tracked her down that fast? Would they want to stare at Josh Mason's ex-wife and kids?

The knock came again, a bit louder. "Valerie, it's me!"

It was Sully. Before she could reach the door, Jackson was already there and yanking it open.

Jackson stared straight into Sully's face. "Did he do it?"

Sully blinked, but to his credit, he didn't flinch. "You know your dad better than me. What do you think?"

"I think he's a piece of shit, no matter what Mom says and Andy thinks." Jackson's face was red and angry. "And even if he didn't steal from those people, he was probably fooling around with that chick because she's totally his type, and now something bad happened to her."

Val's heart broke. "Jack—"

"No, Mom. You defend him *all the time*"—Jackson turned to her, blinking hard—"and you try to paint this nice picture for Andy, but we all know I'm right. He's a piece of shit. He cheated on you. He cheats on Rachel." Her son was nearly shaking with rage. "He's supposed to be an adult and he can't keep his dick in his pants. And he screws up everything he touches. I don't care if he did this or not. I don't want anything to do with him." Jackson looked between Sully and Val. "Nothing."

"He's your father," Val said. "I know he's not a good father, but he's the only—"

"I don't give a shit anymore!" Jackson had tears in his eyes. "He fucks everything up, Mom! I want nothing to do with him. *Nothing*." Jackson looked at Sully as if daring the man to challenge him.

Sully crossed his arms, looked at Val, then back at Jackson. "You're on the way to being a grown man," he said quietly. "You get to choose who you want in your life. That's part of being an adult."

"Yeah." Jackson tugged on his hair and spun around, hardly glancing at Val. "Exactly." He stomped off to his room, slamming the door behind him.

Val stared at the closed door, wondering how much Andy had heard, wondering what Jackson would say to his soft-hearted brother, and wondering if she should intervene.

"Leave it," Sully said. "They're brothers. They'll figure it out."

Val put a hand over her eyes. "He's so angry." She could feel the headache starting to pound in her temples.

"He's angry because someone who should be an adult isn't acting like one. Kid has a right to be angry."

Val turned and looked at Sully, her arms crossed in front of her. "Why did you come?"

"To see if you'd heard." He waved his hat at the hallway. "Question answered."

"Is Savannah alive?"

"She's in intensive care right now," he said. "That's all I know."

"He wouldn't have hurt her. He wouldn't have done that, Sully."

Sully took a deep breath and let it out slowly. "You know him better than I do."

Val motioned to the counter that overlooked the kitchen. "Sit. I'll make some coffee."

"Thanks. I have to drive back to Bridger tonight."

"Something was wrong with her car?"

"You know I'm not supposed to tell you anything, right?"

She glanced up after she'd ground the coffee beans. "You know I'm not going to say a word to anyone."

"Other than Monica and Robin?"

Val shrugged. "Obviously."

"I don't know the details—I don't know enough about cars, to be honest—but someone tampered with the brakes. I got that much in all the technical talk."

"Who's doing the investigation? Bridger?"

He shook his head. "Not their jurisdiction. Technically it's mine, and I called highway patrol. They're the experts."

"But now Josh is wanted for questioning about attempted

murder? Even though no one has seen him around here or in Bridger for over a week now?"

"Anderson is spewing in front of the news cameras. I have no idea why. He's saying Josh is around and in hiding. That this is all about revenge for him because Anderson complained about the missing money."

"That's bullshit, and you know it."

"Hey." He raked a hand through his hair. "I'm a lowly sheriff. No one listens to me. Unfortunately, even if no one has seen Josh, it doesn't look good."

As far as Val was concerned, there was one suspect in Savannah's case, and it was the man married to her. "No one is looking at the husband?"

"He's friends with the entire police department, and he's playing the distraught husband. Of course they're not. Savannah was heading up to Glimmer Lake. Her husband said something about a book club?"

"They don't meet tonight," Val said. "Maybe she was coming up to talk to me. Or see Josh. Maybe she knows where he is."

"As far as Bridger PD is concerned, Savannah Anderson was a happy wife. They don't know anything about her and Josh, and I haven't shared that with them."

Val poured boiling water into a French press. "Do you think that would make Josh more or less of a suspect?"

"Honestly, I don't have any idea. I'm with you. I think the husband is dirty."

A ball of anxiety sat in Val's chest. This was why Josh was worried about Savannah. It was her husband. "Is anyone looking out for her? Does she have police protection? If he tried to kill her and no one suspects him—"

"I know they have a guard at the hospital, but I don't know how to warn them about Anderson."

Val pressed the coffee down. "Tell them about the affair?"

Sully raised his eyebrows. "And how do I know about that exactly? Did Savannah confide in me? A guy she hardly knows?"

Val opened her mouth. Closed it. Hmmm.

"Just... tell them you heard rumors up here. They got into a big fight last week at the coffee shop."

Sully's eyes sparked. "Oh yeah?"

"Yeah. And when Anderson took off, he was driving Savannah's car. She had to wait for a ride. Maybe say someone overheard them fighting about an affair."

Sully nodded thoughtfully. "That's a possibility."

"I'm afraid for her." Val brought two mugs out for the coffee. "Someone tried to kill her once. And if it's who we think it is, he could try again."

"I know why you're worried, but staging an accident is a lot different than going after her directly. I don't think she's in any danger in the hospital." Sully reached for the coffee. "I'll do what I can, but I can't make any promises. Are you sure you have no idea where Josh is?"

She sighed. "I wish I did."

"Well, here's hoping Savannah Anderson pulls through," he said. "Otherwise ten grand is going to be the least of your ex's problems."

ROBIN AND MONICA drove over hours later. Val had ignored

most of the calls coming in from concerned family and friends, but they just showed up with wine and cake.

Because they were brilliant.

"I can't believe he would do this," Robin said. "Not Josh."

"He's not that stupid," Monica said. "Or that mean. Unfortunately, Bridger PD is not the most open-minded police department. Remember those arson cases that Gil was assigned years ago?"

"Vaguely."

"It's when he was doing his stint as the fire investigator and he was assigned to a warehouse in Bridger. He knew it was arson, but the Bridger chief of police knew the owner, so they didn't do anything about it. It's a total boys' club down there."

Robin cut a piece of cake. "So if Americano Asshole has made friends with them—"

"He could literally commit murder and they'd probably look the other way."

"I think he tried," Val said. "Poor Savannah."

"Can Sully do anything?"

"I don't know how jurisdiction works in cases like this where she's in one city but the possible crime happened in another," Val said. "But he thinks Anderson is involved too. He's going to try to do something just to get Savannah some protection."

"Good." Monica poured three glasses of wine. "This whole situation is crazy. Josh is missing and he's getting blamed for all this stuff, and we don't even know if he's okay."

"And my boys have gone from worrying about their dad to not being able to decide if he's a criminal." Val rubbed her eyes and felt her phone start buzzing again. "And my phone will not shut up!" She reached for it and looked at the screen. "Huh."

"Who is it?" Robin froze. "Is it Josh?"

"It's West." Val touched the number to call him back. "Hey. I didn't expect to hear from you. Did you see the news?"

"Yeah. You know he was probably banging that lady, right?"

"I know." She rubbed her temple. "Trust me, I know."

"He's a fucking mess, Val. And the police were here. Again. I'm sorry, but you gotta grab Josh's stuff. I need it out of here."

Fuuuuuuck. "What am I supposed to do with it?"

"Keep it in your garage. Get a storage unit. Something. But I can't keep having the police come round here every time something else comes up with that guy. I got three employees with records and one on probation. Every time a cop pulls into the garage, they all freak out. These guys are trying to keep their nose clean. They don't need the stress, you know?"

She felt the headache building. "Okay. I get it. It's just... a lot."

"Just figure it out by the end of the week, okay? I'll loan you the truck."

"Yeah, I can do that." Maybe her mom and dad could keep the toolbox in their garage. She didn't have room in her own tiny space, and she didn't want to broach the subject with Jackson at the moment. "I can come down to Bridger tomorrow."

"I can go with you," Robin whispered. "I'll see if Mark can help."

"We'll get it taken care of," Val said. "Sorry about this, West."

"I wish I could help more, but..."

"I know." Val hung up the phone. She got it. Josh was her mess to deal with.

CHAPTER 16

*W*est met Val, Robin, and Mark early the next morning at the garage. "Where's your cute friend?"

Val took off her sunglasses. "What? We're not cute enough for you?"

He cracked a smile. "Never gonna complain about seeing your pretty face around the garage. Sorry about this."

"Stop apologizing," Val said, taking a long drink of her coffee. "Josh isn't your problem."

West sighed. "Yeah, I know. But he shouldn't be yours either."

"Whatever." She put her sunglasses back on. "It is what it is. We'll take care of it."

"You have a space to put it?"

Mark raised his hand. "If you have a tow truck we can borrow, it can stay in our garage for a while."

West nodded. "Just go through it and make sure all his junk is in there. Maybe box up any of the personal stuff. Tape up the drawers for transport. It's not going a few

162

miles this time, it's heading up that mountain. You have boxes?"

"We brought some." She patted his rock-hard shoulder. "Thanks, West."

Val and Robin followed West around the back of the garage and toward the three storage units on the alley. It was exactly where Robin had seen the ghost when they'd been visiting before. Mark followed them in his truck.

"I wonder if I'll be able to call anyone back here," Robin said quietly. "Might as well give it a try."

"Did you bring your sketch pad?"

"Yeah. Learned that lesson."

West was unlocking the heavy lock on the metal storage barn. "Can you believe people? I had to get a brand-new lock for this two weeks ago."

Val frowned. "Did someone break in?"

"Yeah. Snapped the lock and cleaned this unit out."

"What did they get?" Val looked at the shipping containers on either side, both of which had the same padlocks. "Just the middle unit?"

West grimaced. "I have a feeling they knew what they wanted. Both my snowmobiles, can you believe it? And that trailer I carried them on. I was so pissed. That's like thirty grand worth of equipment."

"Shit." Val watched the heavy door swing open. "Did you have insurance on 'em?"

"Yeah. I already filed a claim, but they're dragging their feet. Probably won't have a new set of sleds until next winter. And I was planning a trip in a few weekends with the guys."

"People are assholes."

West grinned. "Yeah, they are." He waved at the giant red

toolbox that contained Josh's gear. It was sitting on one wall with several smaller pieces next to it. "There it is."

"We can take the smaller pieces in Mark's truck."

"Okay, I'll send a guy back to help load them up."

"Thanks, West."

He was a good guy. He didn't deserve to get dragged into Josh's crap. The more she thought about Jackson's anger the night before, the more resentment she felt toward Josh and his unwillingness to grow up. At what point were you not just negligent but hurting your kids by not being an adult? She was so used to always being the grown-up that she didn't notice, but Jackson and Andy deserved more.

She deserved more.

Robin and Mark were already getting boxes from the back of the truck.

"Okay," Mark said. "Where do we start?"

"We'll have to go through each box. If it's anything that looks like it could break—any of the smaller tools or sensors—then let's box 'em up. Try to keep each drawer in a separate box if we can manage. That'll make life easier when Josh has to put it back together." Val didn't give her fear a voice. Josh *would* be back. This was all a misunderstanding and he was going to sort his life out and this was going to be a wake-up call to get his shit straight.

Mark narrowed his eyes and watched Robin. "Is she trying to summon someone?"

"Yeah. There was an old guy back here she talked to once, and it sounded like he'd seen Josh. She couldn't get him back when she tried the second time."

"Oh, that was here?" Mark opened a drawer where a neat row of screwdrivers lived. He carefully lifted the plastic case and put it in the first box. "You know, Josh's life was always messy as hell, but his toolbox..."

"I know. He saved all his adult instincts to keep his work space organized. The rest of his life was a disaster." She glanced at Mark. "Hey, do you mind if I give it a listen?"

Mark glanced at her hands. "Sure thing." He stepped back and leaned against the far wall. "Let me know if you're feeling sick or anything."

"Thanks. I'm looking for personal items more than tools." Val removed her gloves and started on one end of the long red toolbox. She moved her hands over the surface, closing her eyes as bits and pieces of Josh's life drifted over her. She caught snatches of conversations and more than a few flirtations.

Drawer by drawer, she examined the chest, rolling each drawer out and scanning the contents for anything that looked more personal than professional.

A lighter he'd swiped off his boss.

The bandanna he wore under cars. Lots of feelings associated with that, but nothing very clear. Everything from amusement to exhaustion to frustration.

"You getting anything?"

"Lots." Val ran her hands along the surface. "But nothing that seems relevant."

It was the smallest drawer she was gearing up for. That was the bottom drawer on the right riser where Val remembered Josh keeping his keys, his wallet, and other personal items while he was at work. It was locked when he kept his stuff in there, but she was hoping he'd left it open.

No such luck.

"Mark, you any good at picking locks?"

He walked over and looked at the lock. "Hmm."

"Any ideas?"

He cocked his head. "How concerned are you about damaging the toolbox?"

"Not very. I'm the one keeping it from getting confiscated. He's not allowed to be too pissed at me."

Mark squatted down so the drawer was in front of his face. "So if this is like most toolbox locks, it has a little metal hook that you have to turn to open it."

"Okay..."

Mark started opening drawers until he found one with a Sawzall. "Let me see if we can get this open." He slid the reciprocating saw blade through the space at the top of the drawer, flipped it on, and within a few minutes a metal piece went *clunk* and the drawer slid open. It was a bit mangled, but Val didn't care.

"Nice work."

"Thanks." Mark put the Sawzall away. "You know he didn't hurt that lady, right?"

"I don't think so, but how much do I really know the man anymore?" She opened the drawer. "We've been divorced for ages. He has a new girlfriend—"

"But you were married to him way longer," Mark said. "You knew Josh. You know him. He's a big kid, but he's not a bad guy."

"Sure." Val was skeptical. The small drawer wasn't full of secrets, but there was an envelope of receipts she was careful not to throw away, and behind that...

"Of course." Val rolled her eyes. Who else other than Josh would keep a Ziploc bag of fresh condoms in his toolbox?

Mark bit back a smile. "Well, it's definitely a personal item."

"Yeah." She pulled the bag out, trying not to wince. "Oh, this is so gross." She reached her hand in and felt the foil packets, hoping to get some insight—

Savannah.

In the store holding her hand.

"We can't let anyone see us."

She was excited. He was excited.

More.

He cared. There was a tight feeling around his heart.

Why was she married to him?

That guy...

Bad news.

"Val!"

She jerked back into her own mind, her hand clutched around the strip of condoms Josh and Savannah had bought at the drug store. "How long?"

"Not too long," Mark said, "but your eyes rolled back and you looked like you might fall over."

"That's normal." She could feel the nausea starting to build. "I think that's all I can do right now."

"Did you get anything?"

"Yeah." Val nodded. "A surprise. He cared about her. Savannah. He really cared about her."

"About Savannah Anderson?"

"Yeah." She could feel the nausea starting to rise.

"Hey, Val?" Robin called her from outside the storage unit.

"Let me..." She pointed toward the alley. "You mind if I take a break?"

"Go for it," Mark said. "I'll keep going here. Walk it off. There's some water bottles in the truck."

"Thanks."

"Robin?" Val walked out of the unit and toward the truck.

One of West's younger employees was walking toward the shipping containers. "You need some help back here? I got some free time if you need a hand."

"That would be awesome. My friend is in there checking all the drawers. If you could help him, that would be great." She nodded to the young man and then walked across the alley to the truck where Robin was sitting in the bed with her sketchbook. "Let me get a water."

"I have tea here if you want it." Robin lifted a travel mug.

"Cool." She walked over and leaned against the tailgate, reaching for the mug. "What's up?"

Robin's hand was on her sketchbook and her eyes were locked on something Val couldn't see. "Val, say hi to Harry."

Val turned to the spot where Robin was looking. "Good to meet you, Harry." She glanced at Robin's sketchbook and saw a detailed drawing of an old man with a thick head of hair and a full beard. He was built like a bulldog and wore a pair of dark coveralls.

"Harry here was the owner of the garage before West bought it." Robin paused, clearly listening to something Val couldn't hear. The corner of her mouth turned up in a half smile. "Harry says he bought it right before West bought it."

Val cracked a laugh. "Good one. Is this the guy who thought he saw Josh?"

"Yep." Robin kept her hand on the sketch, anchoring the

spirit to her. "I described Josh, and he said it was definitely him."

"Does he have any idea when?" It was always a little spooky when Robin was part of a conversation Val could only hear a portion of. Her eyes spaced out a little and her features took on an otherworldly quality.

"Not long, he says." Robin's eyes stayed fixed on the spot where the ghost was speaking to her. "He came with his truck. The one with the welder on the side."

"His new truck." Val nodded. "So in the past two years."

"No, Harry says. It was very recent. He came..." Robin frowned. "He took something. A trailer."

Val's eyes went wide. "The snowmobile trailer?"

"Yes. Harry, could it have been a snowmobile trailer?" Robin glanced at Val. "He said something about motorcycles, but I wonder if he was confused. That's common."

Val waited for Robin to listen to Harry. "They were green. The machines were orange and green."

"Bright colors?"

"Yes. Very bright." Robin smiled. "Harry thought they were ugly."

"Neon green and orange would be pretty common for snowmobiles. Makes them visible in snow."

Son of a bitch! Josh had stolen West's snowmobiles and trailer? What on earth was he thinking?

Val gritted her teeth. "He is such a piece of crap! First he sleeps with West's wife, then he steals the man's snowmo-biles? Why on earth would Josh need snowmobiles?" Val wanted to scream.

Mark wandered out of the shipping container. "What's up?"

Robin glanced at Mark, then back at the ghost. "Thanks, Harry. No, I think that's all." Robin smiled. "Sure. We'll come back. You always hang around here?" She nodded. "Okay. I'll see you. Thanks for keeping an eye out."

Mark walked over and put a hand on his wife's knee, rubbing back and forth while she came back to the world of the living. "You have your tea?"

Val handed over the thermos. "Here. My nausea is gone; I'm good."

Robin lifted the mug to her lips and drank. "He was nice. Very certain that Josh was the one who took the trailer. He came, cut through the lock, and hooked right up to them and took off. He kept calling them motorcycles, but it has to have been the snowmobiles."

"So he took West's snowmobiles right before he disappeared. What did he need a couple of snowmobiles for?" Mark looked at Val. "Did he ride a lot?"

Val shrugged. "Not that I know of. Every now and then he'd go if he had a buddy with one, but we never owned them. It wasn't a thing we did. Did he ever go riding with you and Gil?"

Mark narrowed his eyes. "The only time I can remember riding snowmobiles with Josh was when the kids were little. He and Gil and I all went out to that little cabin his family had in the national forest."

"What cabin?" Robin asked. "I don't remember Josh and Val having a cabin."

"We didn't." Val felt like she'd taken off a pair of sunglasses on a cloudy day. "It was his grandparents' place. How could I be so stupid? I forgot about the cabin."

"What cabin?" Robin asked.

Her heart was racing. "Josh's grandparents had this old cabin way out in the middle of nowhere. It was one of those little seasonal towns in the high Sierra. We would go up and stay there pretty often in the summer before the kids were born. It was pretty rough, but it was livable."

"It's *in* the national forest?" Robin asked. "No one can live in the national forest."

"The town is older than the park. That's why they could keep it as long as it stayed in the family." Val felt like laughing. "It's only accessible by fire roads, and there's only twenty or thirty places still standing."

"Are you sure?" Robin looked skeptical. "Josh was never a fan of roughing it if I remember right."

"I think he's spent some time fixing it up. It's got running water and beds. He took the boys fishing up there like five years ago in the summer. No one goes there in the winter because they don't plow the roads and there's nothing up there." She slapped Mark's shoulder. "You can only get there by *snowmobile!*"

"Why would he go there?" Mark said. "Is he trying to hide?"

"Maybe. Or maybe he doesn't even realize people are looking for him. But if Josh wanted to really be alone, that's where he'd go. The cabin is livable in winter. It'd be cold as hell, but it has a stove and a good roof. It's just inaccessible with the roads."

"Which way?" Mark asked. "How far it is?"

"It's remote." Val shook her head. "We've got to get this stuff packed in a hurry and get back to Glimmer Lake. I need to call Sully."

CHAPTER 17

*M*ark was looking at the old hiking maps he kept in his glove compartment on the way back up the hill while Robin drove the truck.

"I'm not positive, but I think we took this road," Mark said. "The town is marked—it says Keane right here—but they show it right on the highway, and it's not. You have to take a fire road a couple of miles back to get to it."

"Do you think we should just rent some machines and go ourselves?" Robin asked. "Will Sully have to arrest Josh if he finds him?"

Mark looked up. "I think the best way out of this is if Sully is the one who brings Josh in, don't you? If he's been back there, he probably has no idea any of this has happened. If Sully is the one to tell him and Josh comes back voluntarily with him, this will all get cleared up faster."

"Okay." Val nodded. "That makes sense. So we just have to convince Sully that this is where Josh is and he's probably been there the whole time."

"I just can't believe he didn't tell you he was going to this remote cabin," Robin said. "How could he not realize the boys would worry? Didn't you say Andy calls him almost every day?"

Robin got out her phone and put her voice mail on speaker to play Josh's call.

"Hey, Val. I know it's late, but this weekend isn't going to work out to take the boys. Shit got complicated at work and —" The phone cut out. "—you can tell them next week I'll be —" Josh's voice dissolved to crackles. "Anyway, it's a lot to think about, so I'm going to need—" More silence. "—could call me I'd actually appreciate it. Okay. Later."

Robin groaned. "Shit. Okay, hearing that, it's entirely possible he did tell you he was going out of town and the reception was just crap."

"If he was driving to the cabin, the signal was probably cutting in and out," Mark said. "Once you get past Highway 67, it's nothing but dead space."

"Which would also explain why he's been radio silent for the past week and a half." Val mentally urged the truck to go faster. "Do you think Sully will buy it?"

"What's to buy?" Mark asked. "This is the most logical explanation by far. Josh taking off to gamble in Vegas with a client's money never made sense. Josh ditching his job and kids to navel-gaze in the woods for a couple of weeks is completely in character."

"True." Val sat back in her seat. "I just hope Sully is willing to follow me out there."

"You?" Mark asked.

"Do you remember how to get there?" Val asked.

"No."

"He's not going to find it without someone who knows

the area." Val just hoped she could remember. It had been a good fifteen years since she'd been out to Keane. She was hoping the landmarks hadn't changed too much.

SULLY WASN'T AS enthusiastic as Val had hoped. "Keane?"

"Yeah. His family has a place up there."

"No one lives in Keane during the winter. The forest service doesn't allow it."

"I don't think they can technically forbid people from going to their own property in the winter. They just don't plow the roads. And since when did people listen to the forest service when it comes to their cabins?"

Val was sitting across the desk in Sully's office. Robin was sitting next to her. Mark was leaning against the wall. It was nearly five o'clock, and everyone other than a lone deputy manning the phones had left the sheriff's building.

Sully glanced at Mark. "You been to this place in winter?"

"Yeah, but it's been a long time. Val's gonna have a better chance of finding it."

"Oh, I know where the town is," Sully said. "I'm just wondering how harebrained you have to be to head up there when the snow comes. It can fall over the roofs of those old places in heavy years."

"It's a two-story cabin," Val said. "Pump house for water. Good stove. With the right supplies, you *could* live up there for a while, especially if you had a snowmobile."

Sully frowned. "And how do you know it was Josh who

took those snowmobiles from his old boss? There's no evidence—"

"I know," Robin said quietly. "I'm... pretty positive it was him."

Sully raised his eyebrows. "Because...?"

Val said, "Who else could have taken them?"

"Literally anyone else who knew they were there," Sully said. "Did West say he suspected Josh?"

"No."

"Did someone see him or his truck?" Sully looked between Robin, Mark, and Val. "Did they tell you?"

Yep. The dead owner of the garage who is hanging around in the alley in ghost form told Robin while we were picking up Josh's tools.

Val opened her mouth, closed it.

Mark cleared his throat.

Val looked at Robin, who had narrowed her eyes on Sully and was pursing her lips.

Sully said, "I'm not real keen on hanging another crime around Josh Mason's neck when there's already police in Bridger who want him for—"

"I can see ghosts," Robin said. "A ghost told me."

Mark let out a breath like he'd been punched in the stomach. Val's eyes went wide.

And Sully stared at Robin.

"The ghost's name is Harry and he's the previous owner of the garage and he hangs out in the back alley behind it." She shifted in her chair, crossing her legs. "I think he maybe died there, but I'm pretty sure it was natural causes. He described a truck that sounded like Josh's that hooked up to the trailer and took off with West's snowmobiles."

Mark cleared his throat. "According to West, the snow-mobiles were stolen the same day that Josh left the voice mail on Val's phone. So we think it was probably him."

Val nodded. "It... um, just seemed like the most logical explanation. To us."

Sully blinked at her. Looked at Robin. Back to Mark. Back to Robin. He swallowed and reached for a pencil on his desk. "The ghost's name is Harry?"

Robin nodded. "Mm-hmm."

"And he was the owner of the garage before West bought it."

"Pretty sure." Robin tapped her fingers on her sensible purse.

Val watched Sully staring at Robin, practically seeing the gears turn in his head.

If there was anyone less likely to make wild claims of seeing the dead, it was Robin Brannon. Robin was the president of the PTA board. She was the organizer of the town's lakeside trash cleanup day. She was the mom who checked her kids' homework every day after school and was the queen of ruthless organization. She jogged every morning. She never paid a bill late, and she recycled in all the correct bins.

She did not see ghosts.

Unless she did.

Sully looked down at his notepad. "What exactly did West say was taken?"

"Two snowmobiles, both about three years old, and a trailer that hooked up to West's truck," Mark said. "Someone came and cut the lockbox on the shipping containers, and I know Josh has a plasma cutter on his work truck, so it's plausible."

"Right." Sully was staring at the notepad, jotting down something and tapping his pen. He looked up at Mark. "And you knew about..."

"Yeah."

"And you're sure—"

"Not even a question."

"Right." Sully glanced at Robin, who was waiting with a polite smile. Then he stared at Val, looked down at her gloved hands folded carefully in her lap, then back to her eyes. "Hey, Robin, when did you start seeing ghosts?"

"None of your business," Val said.

"After my car went in the lake last year," Robin said. "Just popped up like a grey hair. It took a little getting used to."

"Right." Sully was still staring at Val. "I remember. That accident that you and Val and Monica were all in."

"I don't see ghosts," Val said. "In case you were wondering."

Sully narrowed his eyes. "Oh, I'm wondering." He stood abruptly, threw down his pencil, and walked out of the office.

Val watched him walk toward the door, grab his coat from the rack, and head out into the darkening night.

Mark nudged Val's shoulder. "You might want to go talk to him."

Val looked at Robin. "Thanks for that."

Robin smiled innocently. "You're welcome."

VAL MADE sure her gloves were on before she walked outside. She didn't have to be psychic to know Sully was pissed off. He was pacing in the parking lot, rubbing his hands together to keep them warm, and muttering under his breath.

"Sully." Val stopped just outside the office door. "About Josh—"

"I don't..." He spun and walked toward her. "I don't want to talk about Josh right now." His brilliant blue eyes drilled into her. "You hide things, Val."

"I'm not hiding anything important."

His mouth was pressed in a flat line.

"I'm serious," she said. "As soon as I remembered about the cabin, I came here and told you. I'm not trying to hide—"

"Ha!" The laugh did not sound amused. "Right."

"I'm not trying to hide anything about *Josh*, okay?" She walked toward him. "From the beginning, I've thought all these charges were bullshit. There had to be another explanation. This is the explanation. I don't think he has any idea he's a wanted man, and the best outcome in all this—"

"Why do you care?" His breath puffed out in the cold night air. "Seriously, Val, why are you putting yourself out there and going through all this to rescue this man?"

Her mouth fell open. "Do you... Are you implying that I still have feelings for him? What? Are you... jealous? This is seriously your—"

"I'm not jealous." He put his hands on his hips.

"No? Because you're kind of acting like it." She could feel him. He was close enough that his body heat was tangible. "And this is not about me. Or us. Or... whatever it is you're thinking we might—"

"I don't like it when you lie to me, and I feel like you lie to me a lot." He glared at her. "You tell me why that is."

She glared right back. "I have nothing to say to you about this. I'm not a liar."

"Tell me about the accident."

"The accident was ages ago." *And I am never telling you how it changed me.* "And I already told you, I don't see ghosts."

"But you believe Robin?"

"Yes."

"Seriously?"

Val threw her arms out. "It's Robin! Can you imagine a person less likely to make something like that up? She's like... if Martha Stewart and Oprah had a baby who ran an antique shop in Glimmer Lake but also could probably run the entire world if she really had to because she's that organized. Robin Brannon does not make shit up."

Sully was glowering. That was the only word Val could think of. He knew Val was right and he wasn't happy about it, so his face just had this angry and stubborn look.

"Listen, Sully. I believe Robin. One hundred percent. If Robin said the ghost of a three-headed donkey appeared in her front yard and told her the winning lottery numbers, I would go out and play them."

"A three-headed donkey is ridiculous," Sully muttered.

"Clearly, but if Robin said one appeared, all I'd ask is which head was talking to her."

That made him crack a smile.

"I think Josh is out there, Sully." She took a deep breath and let it out. "He's Jackson and Andy's dad. I don't like him very much, but despite what my oldest says right now, they would both be crushed if something happened to him."

He wasn't talking, but he was listening.

"The best outcome to all this is you bringing him in. Not his dumb ass wandering back into town with no clue about what's going on so Bridger PD can ambush him and trick him into saying something incriminating, which is so, so likely. I cannot tell you how likely it is that Josh would say something inadvertently and absolutely screw himself."

Sully sighed. "It's too late to head out there tonight. If you're positive this cabin is where he's hiding out—"

"I'm not positive," Val said. "About anything these days. But it's my best guess, and I can't imagine any other reason he'd take West's snowmobiles. He does genuinely like the man."

"Can you ride?"

"A snowmobile? Yeah. I wouldn't go off-trail, but the fire roads to Keane are actually pretty wide. If we just follow them, it won't be an issue."

He crossed his arms over his chest, but his glare had softened. "We can go tomorrow. You'll be riding with me. I can't have you driving county property, but we can leave in the morning in my truck. Come here to the station at eight. I don't want to leave until it warms up a little. It won't take more than an hour to drive up there and another hour to drive in if there are tracks. We should be able to get there and back in a day."

"We haven't had a heavy enough snow to cover the trail since he went up. I think there will be tracks. If there aren't tracks on the fire road, then he's probably not in Keane."

"I am taking you along *only* because you know the way to the cabin. Once we're there, I'll determine how this is gonna go."

"Thank you, Sully." She saw Robin and Mark open the station door. "I'll be here tomorrow, dressed for trail riding."

"Okay." He still didn't look happy, but Val would take it.

As long as it got Josh back into civilization and got all this mess straightened out, she wasn't going to complain.

"Thank you. Seriously."

He eyed her. "You sure you can't see ghosts?"

"Very sure." She smiled. "Trust me, if I saw ghosts, I'd be even crankier than I am now."

He eyed her gloved hands again. "Uh-huh."

"Seriously." She backed away and walked toward Robin and Mark. "Okay. Tomorrow morning. I'll be here and I'll bring lunch."

"And coffee."

"And coffee." She gave him a thumbs-up. "Good to know you got your priorities in line."

CHAPTER 18

*J*ackson's arms were crossed over his chest. "I don't understand why you're going."

Val threw her snow parka on top of her backpack. "Because he's your father."

"He's not your husband anymore." Jackson's face was mutinous. "You said you divorced him so you wouldn't have to deal with his shit anymore. Because you wanted the best thing for us. You and me and Andy."

"One, I don't think I used those exact words, okay? And two, you think the best thing for all of us is your dad ends up in jail?"

Jackson shrugged. "Doesn't matter to me."

Val stepped closer and glanced over her shoulder. "Do you think it matters to Andy?"

"He's young, and he's going to realize when he's older—"

"What?" She put her hand on Jackson's cheek. "That his dad is unreliable? That's he's not a very good person? You don't think he realizes that already?"

Jackson looked away.

"He knows it, Jack. And he loves your dad anyway. That says nothing about your dad and everything about your brother. And don't lie—I know you love your dad too. Don't pretend like all the time you've ever spent with him was shit. He loves you guys, and you've had a lot of good memories with him."

"Just being there for the fun stuff—"

"Isn't enough." She squeezed his shoulder. "I know that. We all do. But that doesn't mean he belongs in jail. Or caught in the middle of a situation he has no idea how he fell into. The cops in Bridger are setting him up, and it's not right."

"It's not your job to fix it. You don't have to do everything yourself. Let Dad clean up his own mess for once."

"He's going to have to after this, and I'm not doing this on my own. Sully and I are going together. Sully is the one who's going to decide what to do once he talks to your dad. Once we find him"—she raised her hands—"I'm out of it. Your dad is on his own. I'll have done my part. But I can't just act like he's a stranger." She put her arms around Jackson and hugged him tight. "Without your dad, I don't have you and Andy. And don't you know I'd walk through fire for my babies?"

Jackson hugged her back hard. "We're not babies anymore."

She leaned back and kissed his cheek. "You are *always* my babies. Always. Even when you need to shave." She tapped his chin. "You need to shave, by the way."

Jackson rubbed his chin. "I've been thinking about growing my beard out."

She rubbed the thin stubble. "Up to you. But your dad's beard didn't really grow in until he was twenty-five or so. Just warning you. It was really patchy and kind of gross until his late twenties."

"Thanks." He didn't look very thankful. "So you're going up to the cabin with Sheriff Sully?"

"Yep."

"He likes you."

Val nodded. "He's a nice guy. I like him too."

Jackson gave her his "I'm not stupid" look. "No, Mom. He *likes* you. Like... you know."

Oh. Right. "Uh—"

"He's a good guy. That's all I'm saying." Jackson shrugged. "He seems cool."

"Okay." She picked up her backpack. "Cool. I... don't know what to do with that information."

"Whatever. It's not like you don't know already." He rolled his eyes. "As soon as Andy wakes up, I'll drive us over to Grandma and Grandpa's, okay?"

"I should be back by tonight, but just in case—"

"I know. I was gonna help Grandpa with the woodpile anyway."

Val walked to the door. "Good. Make sure Andy does some work too. Even if you have to force his nose out of a book."

"Okay." Jackson held the door as Val grabbed her jacket and walked to the truck.

"We're taking Sully's truck up there. It's heavier."

"Good call. I think they were tearing down that house with the red roof right by the road, by the way. So make sure you don't miss the turnoff."

"I'll look for the horse-crossing sign. Is that still there?"

"I think so." Jackson waved. "Be careful."

"I will." Val walked to her truck and hopped in, glad Jackson had turned it on to warm it up before he decided to lecture her.

She put her phone in the charging cradle and tapped Monica's number.

"Good morning." Monica cleared her throat. "I hear you're going up to the cabin with Sheriff Hot Stuff today. I'm praying you get trapped in a snowstorm and have to huddle together for warmth."

Val rolled her eyes. "Thanks. That sounds needlessly dangerous. You're the best."

"You're welcome. What's up?"

"One, thank you for filling in at the café for me. I cannot tell you how awesome you are for that. I think Ramon and Honey were about to stage a mutiny."

"I might lead it. I like working there. It's fun."

Val smiled. "It is, isn't it?"

"You did a good thing there."

"You make me feel warm and fuzzy inside." Or was she just hungry? "My real reason for calling is to ask if your boys enjoy lecturing you about your life? Is this a stage? Are they going to grow out of it?"

"Oh God no. I love my boys like crazy, but when it comes to their mom, they're the worst mansplainers on the planet. They have endless opinions about my life."

She winced. "So this isn't just a phase?"

"Afraid not. I'm hoping once they have their own kids, they'll realize I'm not as clueless as they seem to think I am."

Great. So all she had to do was wait ten years for Jackson to grow up, get a job, get married, and father children.

Val realized something and felt her stomach drop. "Monica, do you realize our children are nearly the age we were when we started having kids?"

"Girl, you've got ten years. How do you think I feel? I was eighteen when I started having babies! Every one of my kids is already older than I was when I started. Which I am very happy about, obviously. Gil and I were lucky idiots."

"You were not idiots. You *were* lucky."

"We were kind of idiots. Anyway, be safe today. I had the dream about blood on the snow again last night, which feels more ominous today."

"I'll be careful." She thought about the boys chopping wood. "I might tell Jackson and Andy to leave the woodpile for another day though."

Monica groaned. "I feel useless that I'm not getting anything more than the blood and the snow. Blood and snow and ski tracks. It's coming every night now, which means whatever is going to happen is going to happen soon."

"Call me if you get anything else."

"Trust me, I'm napping as much as I can. I haven't been this well rested since before I had kids."

"Love you," Val said. "Bye."

"Bye."

She swung by the coffee shop to grab the packed sandwiches Ramon had made for the day, then she drove to the sheriff's office on the edge of town. She saw Sully's truck, various county vehicles, and a familiar blue BMW in the parking lot.

What the hell? What was Americano Asshole doing here?

Val walked up to the porch just as Sully and Allan Anderson were walking out.

"I know you know more about Mason than you're letting on," Anderson said. "Do you know who I am? You don't want to cross me, Sullivan. If you think I couldn't have your job if I wanted it—"

"Do you want my job?" Sully put his sunglasses on, tipped his hat down on his forehead, and turned his mirrored stare onto Anderson. He was about six inches taller than the blond man, so Anderson was forced to look up.

"You want my job?" Sully had the edge of a smile on his face. "You think you could handle my job, Mr. Anderson?"

Americano Asshole puffed his chest. "I know you think you're the big man here, but—"

"What I am," Sully said, "is a public servant to the people of this county, Mr. Anderson. Now that includes your wife, who was the victim in an accident that falls under my jurisdiction. I realize you're not happy about my investigation so far, but if you think I'm going to rush the highway patrol investigators just because it's inconvenient for your insurance claim, you're very mistaken."

Val had to admit it was delicious to watch.

Anderson's face was red. "The real police in Bridger City already told me what happened to my wife's car, Sheriff. I don't need—"

"It's interesting that they think they know what happened when your wife's Mercedes has been at the Central Division warehouse in Fresno for the past two days." Sully slid one arm into his coat. "I realize you'd like to... conclude this process as quickly as possible, but we're going to have to wait for the full accident-investigation team to finish their report before I release anything or anyone from suspicion." Sully straightened his jacket and stuffed his hands in the pockets, nodding at Val over Anderson's shoulder. "Now, if there isn't anything else, I have work to do."

Anderson turned and spotted her. "You."

Val leaned against her truck, keeping her hands in her pocket. "Hey, cheapskate."

"I know you were at my house." Anderson's face twisted in rage as he stalked toward her. "And you talked to Steve Garcia. I know you talked to my wife. I know who your ex-husband is, and I ought to—"

"What?" Val leaned forward and got in his face. "Sorry, what are you going to do to me?" She pointed her finger an inch from his nose and wiggled it around, delighting in his curled lip. "I'm not your poor wife, asshole. You don't intimidate me. I've dealt with toddlers more intimidating than you are."

His smile was twisted. "You have no idea who you're dealing with."

Val laughed. "City boy, I drink your type's tears with my coffee in the morning." She looked over Anderson's shoulder. "You ready to go, Sully?"

A wicked light glowed in Anderson's eyes. "You know where he is."

"I've cooperated with the police," Val said. "I have no idea what you're talking about."

"You know." Anderson smiled wider. "Good."

Val shrugged. "No idea what you're talking about." She waved her fingers. "Don't you have someplace to be? Maybe you need to iron your underwear, because I think your panties got a little twisted."

"Val, don't tease the nice man." Sully sidled over to Val and stretched his arm along the bed of her truck. "Anderson,

I've told you I have work to do. You can leave now. And don't even think about harassing Josh Mason's ex-wife or children. If my deputies see you anywhere near town today, I'm gonna give them permission to escort you out of town."

He raised his chin. "I own a business here."

"Well, it's a good thing you have partners, because they're gonna have to take care of things for a while." Sully nodded toward his car. "Go on. Get out of here. I have people of my own I can call."

Anderson curled his lip and backed away from Val. "You're making the wrong enemies, Sheriff."

"Probably. I'm kind of crap at sucking up to rich people though." Sully heaved a sigh. "Good thing I'm independently wealthy."

"Sure you are." Anderson walked to his car, pulling out his phone and putting it to his ear as he unlocked his BMW and slid inside.

Val looked up at Sully as Anderson drove away. "Are you?"

"What? Bad at sucking up to rich people? Yeah. I'm really lucky no one ever runs against me for sheriff, because I'm shit at campaigning. Of course, this is literally the lowest-paying sheriff's position in the entire state, so I don't think anyone other than me really wants the job."

"No, are you independently wealthy?"

He shrugged. "I mean, it depends on what you call wealthy."

Val waited, completely unsatisfied with that answer.

"I retired from LAPD with full benefits and I have a second job here." He shrugged. "I have some money to mess with and I'm good at picking stocks."

"No kidding?"

He reached for her backpack. "It's not a big deal."

"Can you teach me about picking stocks?" Not that she had any extra money to play with. Val was planning on working until she died. She'd probably be yelling at customers from a wheelchair when she was ninety.

"I could." The corner of his mouth turned up as they walked to his truck. "Or you could go out on a date with me and we could casually trade stock tips over drinks."

"That sounds so sexy and cosmopolitan." She hopped in the passenger side of his pickup.

He threw her backpack onto the back bench of the truck, adjusted something on the shotgun rack in the rear window, and slammed the door closed. "That's me, Valerie. Cosmopolitan as fuck."

CHAPTER 19

*T*he road to Keane twisted and wound through the forest, climbing mountains and dipping through valleys blanketed by snow. The temperature dropped ten degrees as they drove higher and deeper into the Sierras.

Glimmer Lake, as high and mountainous as it was, sat on the very edge of a massive mountain range that was mostly inaccessible. It was easy to forget how dense the wilderness could be. An hour after they left the sheriff's office, the road narrowed and eventually came to a stop in a high berm of snow.

There was a wide spot in the forest where a ranger cabin stood and the plows turned around. Two vehicles were sitting in the small parking area, a white service truck with a trailer attached and an older blue pickup that had seen a few winters. The truck bed and trailer were both covered and tied down with heavy tarps, as if the owner expected to be gone for some time.

"Bingo." Val nodded. "He's here. That's his truck."

"Where's the other snowmobile?" The tarp on the trailer was too flat to be covering another machine.

"You know what? It's probably sitting in his garage or something super obvious that Rachel just didn't think to mention."

Sully pulled out his phone. "Can't call her now." He held it up. "No signal."

"Me either." She pointed at the metal gate bordering the road. "Check that out."

Beyond the gate, cutting through the dense white wilderness, were various tracks from snow machines. There was a wide tractor-like track and narrower ski tracks.

"Looks like more than one sled has been through here." Sully took off his sunglasses and squinted into the glare. "I'll get our machine off the trailer. Why don't you see if there are any notices posted at the ranger's cabin?"

"Okay." Val hopped out of the truck and immediately zipped up her parka. She was wearing her snow pants, high boots, and heavy snow gear with multiple layers underneath. Being in the snow was one thing, whipping through frozen air on the back of a snowmobile was a whole other level of cold.

She walked over to the small cabin and surveyed the notices posted on the glass case outside. All the normal warnings about staying on trails and plowed roads.

Hunting in any season is not permitted in the national forest. Firearms are not allowed.

Day use of SNO-PARKS requires a permit available at the Sugar Pine Ranger Station.

Access to Keane is limited to residents only and not advised during winter months.

Not advised but not forbidden.

"Valerie?"

"There's nothing here," she said. "Just the general stuff." She peeked into Josh's truck, but nothing seemed out of place. "Josh's truck looks normal too." Val headed back to the sheriff's pickup. Sully had already unloaded the snowmobile and strapped her backpack onto the cargo area. "The notice at the ranger station says access to Keane is limited to residents and not advised during winter."

Sully nodded at the multiple tracks heading off the fire road. "Looks like no one is paying attention to that."

"It's way more than one," Val said. "There've been people coming and going for a while. That blue truck belongs to someone."

"If there's someone up there," Sully said, "that means Josh could have a proper alibi." He rubbed his hands together. "That would make life a lot simpler."

"Agreed." She looked up, but the sky was grey and heavy. "Are we going to get snow?"

Sully frowned. "The forecast said that storm isn't coming until tomorrow, but those clouds and my ankle aren't making me feel very optimistic."

"You have a bad ankle?"

"Broken and dislocated about fifteen years ago." He lifted his left knee. "Pins and plates and all that shit. Hurts every fucking winter."

"Good times." She blew warm air on her hands and reached for the goggles she'd borrowed from Jackson. "We should go."

"Yeah." He threw his leg over the snowmobile and patted the back. "Hop on. You ridden on the back of one of these before?"

"Yep." She zipped her parka up to her neck, put on her goggles, and tucked her chin in her collar. "Is your hat going to stay on?"

"It better." Sully started up the engine, and Val wrapped her arms around his middle, trying to keep as close as possible to his body.

It wasn't just because he was warm and his body was hard with muscle. Keeping close on a bike or a snowmobile was safer. Of course, cuddling up to Sully felt pretty nice too.

They started down the trail, and within minutes the wind was biting her cheeks and making her wish she'd borrowed one of Jackson's ski masks along with his goggles. She'd manage. Sully was taking most of the cold; she was huddling behind him while trying to keep an eye on the trail to look for markers.

He slowed down when they reached a split in the fire road. Tracks led in both directions, but heavier tracks led to the left. The way was still pretty clear, and the road was wide enough for two vehicles to pass.

"Which way?" Sully asked.

Val looked around and saw the top of a large granite rock protruding into the sky. She pointed left. "That way."

"Got it."

"Watch for a horse-crossing sign in a couple of minutes," she yelled over the engine. "You're going to make a sharp left there and head into the forest. There might be a sign, but there might not be."

"Okay!"

She kept her face to the left, keeping her eyes peeled for the sign. When she saw it, she tapped his shoulder and pointed.

Sully nodded without speaking and veered into the forest, following a trail that had already been cut through three feet of fresh snow. The ground beneath them was hard with packed snow and ice. It had been an average winter and the base layer was a couple of feet thick, but soft snow piled up a few feet under the trees.

Once they turned off the fire road, there was really only one trail to follow, a narrow, one-lane track that was enough for a couple of snowmobiles or a single vehicle. The forest was utterly quiet except for the churn of the engine beneath her and the wind whipping by.

Val tucked her face into Sully's shoulder and held him tight around the waist. She felt him tense when the first flakes of snow started to fall.

Dammit.

"We're almost there!" she said.

"Good."

The first cabin she saw was a tidy cottage with a bright blue roof, completely boarded up for winter; it was clearly uninhabited. The small settlement was arranged in a loop that circled a stand of giant sequoia trees growing halfway up a rising hill. The oldest cabins were in the bottom of the hollow while newer cabins—and by newer, she meant seventy years old instead of a hundred—climbed up the hill.

"Keep going to the left." Val pointed. "Look for a two-story with a green roof."

"I'm just looking for smoke."

"Good call." Val looked up and saw three lines of wood smoke curling into the sky. "He's got neighbors."

The snowmobile slowed. "I can't believe people winter over here."

"I can't believe your hat actually stayed on."

He turned and winked at her. "It wouldn't dare fall off. It knows it's on duty."

Val shook her head and tried to fight back a smile. "I don't know anyone who would stay up here all winter. But a week now and then with the right supplies?" She shrugged. "It'd be all right."

"Yeah."

They skimmed over the snow as the trail curved around and Josh's cabin came into Val's sight. "There it is."

Sure enough, a heavy plume of smoke curled from the stone chimney that rose over the green metal roof. The cabin was covered in redwood shingles and granite stone. A narrow porch wrapped around the entire structure and a pump house rose next to it, painted a deep brick red. The second story was narrow. If Val remembered correctly, there was a sleeping loft upstairs, and that was about it.

Heavy ropes ran between the front porch and the pump house, the outhouse and the shed, a precaution against storms and darkness.

When they parked the machine, she heard the heavy thunk of someone chopping wood behind the house.

Sully was looking at the sky. Flakes were falling faster and thicker. "We're gonna get snowed on."

"Did we bring a tarp?"

"It's got a cover." He still looked grim. "Can't lie, Val. Was hoping this was going to be a quick trip to pick up your ex and I'd be in my bed by nighttime. This is not looking good."

"I thought the same thing, but at least we're not in the middle of nowhere." She looked around. Clear signs of human activity marked many of the cabins despite the heavy snow. Snowshoes and skis hung outside under porches. Fresh woodpiles were abundant, and snowmobile tracks led to at least a third of the houses. "And we're not alone up here."

"Do any of these places have phone lines?"

"Unless something has changed, I don't think so."

"What a relic." Sully unfurled the snowmobile cover, keeping one eye on the sky and the other scanning the area. "Josh Mason!" he yelled. "Owens County Sheriff's Department!"

The sound of chopping wood stilled. "What's that?"

Val heard Josh's voice faintly from behind the house. "Josh, it's Val and Sully."

"Val?" The sound of fast footsteps and Josh appeared from behind the redwood-shingled cabin. He looked between Val and Sully with wide eyes, his breath puffing out in the frigid air. "What are you doing up here? Are the boys okay?"

"The boys are fine." Val looked up. "Maybe we should go inside."

Sully had his hands planted in his coat pockets and his hat pulled low over his eyes. He didn't take his eyes off Josh. "Mason, you know anything about the Andersons?"

Josh's mouth dropped open. "Uh... well, I mean—"

"Let's go inside." Val tugged Sully's sleeve. "Come on. The temperature's dropping already."

Josh looked up. "This storm is going to be pretty heavy."

"According to whom?" Sully said.

Josh nodded down the road. "According to Bill. He's kind of the unofficial mayor of the town during the winter. He's up here the most."

"Uh-huh." Sully hadn't moved.

"It's cold," Val said, glaring at the two men who were staring at each other like two roosters sizing up an opponent. "I'm going inside."

VAL HAD a kettle of water bubbling on the wood stove a few minutes later. Sully and Josh maneuvered around each other in the small living area, taking seats on opposite couches with a worn storage chest sitting between them.

"So I guess you got my message," Josh said. "Sorry I had to cancel on the boys, but—"

"Oh for fuck's sake, Josh." Val turned and put her hands on her hips. "The boys are the least of your problems. Your message cut out. No one knew where you were. We've been looking for a week and a half."

He frowned, his handsome face the picture of confusion. "But I left you a message—"

"That got cut off."

"And I left a note for West," Josh said. "At the garage when I took the trailer."

Val and Sully exchanged a look.

Josh looked between them in confusion. "Are you telling me West didn't get my note?"

"Where'd you leave it?"

"In the mail slot with an apology for not asking—I was kinda crazy to get out of town—and a couple hundred in cash because I had to cut the lock."

Val sighed and sat on the old orange couch next to Sully and rubbed her temple. "Josh, no one got your note. No one realized you were up here. The police have been looking for you for over a week now—"

"The police?" His eyes went wide. "Oh shit! Because of the trailer and the snowmobiles? West thinks I stole them? I'm just, like, renting them. He told me ages ago I could if I wanted to. I didn't have time to ask, but—"

"No, the police are looking for you because Allan Anderson accused you of stealing ten grand from him and taking off."

Josh shook his head. "That asshole."

Sully finally spoke. "Bridger PD put out a warrant for your arrest last week."

Josh jumped up and started pacing, rubbing his hands along his jeans. "That fucking asshole."

"How do you know Savannah Anderson?" Sully asked.

Josh stopped and turned around. "Savannah's not involved in this."

Val pressed her fingers against her forehead and said, "Josh, I know you're sleeping with her."

"It's not—!" He grabbed the back of his hair. "Savannah's not... she's not involved in this. Anderson is just pissed because..."

Sully watched him. "Because what?"

"I told him how much it was going to be to fix his car and he was pissed. He thought I was trying to pull one over on him. All I told him was the God's honest truth. I don't bullshit about that. Then he told me I was going to fix his car for cost only or he was going to report me to my boss even though Anderson is the one who approached me about working on the side."

"Did he give you any money?" Sully asked.

"No!" Josh threw his hands out. "Nothing. He didn't give me jack shit. I told him what parts to order and he ordered them. Or at least that's what he said."

"Where does Savannah come in?" Val asked.

He let out a breath. "Come on, Val. You don't really want to know about me and—"

"I am not asking because I'm jealous or something dumb like that," Val said. "I'm asking because she's in the hospital in Bridger right now, and that's part of the reason the police want to talk to you."

Josh's face drained of color. "Tell me what the hell is going on. Right now."

CHAPTER 20

*F*at flakes were falling outside, and heavy wind was starting to buffet the old house. Val poured coffee for everyone. They sat around the woodstove, keeping warm as the temperature continued to drop.

"This place is safe during storms," Josh said. "I come up here at least once a year."

"I didn't know that. Why don't you ever bring the boys?"

Josh shrugged. "It's kind of my thinking place."

"You think?"

Josh didn't look amused. "Ha ha."

Sully asked, "So what are you thinking about these days?"

He didn't say anything.

"Something to do with Savannah Anderson?"

He took a deep breath. "Are you sure she's going to be okay?"

"She'll be fine as long as she's in the hospital," Sully said. "But if you aren't the one who tampered with her brakes—"

"I would never fucking do that," he said. "If anyone did anything to hurt her, it was that asshole she's married to."

"Why do you think that?" Val agreed with him, but prying information out of Josh was proving to be harder than expected.

"If she's in danger from her husband, she hasn't told anyone about it," Sully said. "She hasn't accused him. There's no evidence of domestic abuse."

"That's not the way he works," Josh said. "He just... controls her. Everything about her. What she wears. What she drives. He won't let her get a job."

"What is your relationship to Savannah Anderson?" Sully said. "And just to be clear, you've been up here for the past ten days?"

"Yeah." He furrowed his eyebrows and mentally calculated. "Yeah. Ten days. I think. What day is it?"

"And people in town will be able to confirm that you've been here the whole time?" Sully asked again.

"Yeah. Uh..." He bit his lip. "Bill's here. Helen and Rick were here a couple of days ago. I had a beer over at their place." He rubbed his hands on his pants. "I've been doing some work to the place. Trying to make it a little less of a bachelor pad and more... comfortable."

Val examined the embarrassed, awkward expression on Josh's face. "If Savannah wanted to come?"

He bent over, rubbing his hands in his hair. "Listen, Val. I know you think I'm a piece of shit—"

"Oh, I don't think it. I know it."

"But Savannah—"

"Is married." Val set her coffee down.

"Told me she loved me." He cleared his throat and stared at his shoes. "She told me... she loved me. And she wanted to leave Allan."

Oh, that poor woman. "And you took off?"

"I needed to think." He rose and paced in front of the fire. "I don't know... I mean, she's not in a good place, so I don't know—"

"She's married, Josh. I know that doesn't mean much to you, but try to think what it looks like to your kids. You're sleeping with this woman who is married, and you still have a girlfriend living in your house and sleeping in your bed. Did you completely forget about Rachel?"

"No!" He looked up. "I'm *going* to break up with her, but I was waiting for the lease to run out on our place because my name is on it and I don't want her to take off and leave me stuck with half the rent."

"You idiot." Val rubbed a hand over her eyes. "You actually think that's a reasonable position to take, don't you?"

"Steve is gonna fire me. You think I can afford—"

"You are lying to one woman so she won't break up with you and leave you financially screwed," Val said. "You're basically stealing from her. And cheating on her with another woman who tells you she loves you, and then you take off to the woods." She groaned. "I can't believe you."

"You know, not all of us come from families with money, Val. You're so self-righteous, but you never had to—"

"Never had to what? Pay my own way? Pay to raise your kids? Pay for all the school stuff and all the groceries and all the—"

"Just to be clear." Sully rose and put his hands out, separating Val and Josh, who were nearly nose to nose. He pointed at Josh. "You've been here for ten days and you have a solid alibi? You never took any money from Anderson?"

"No." Josh shrugged. "I mean, you can look at my bank

account. I didn't take anything. I've got five hundred bucks in there until I get my last check from Luxury Pro."

"Good. I'll do that when we get back." Sully walked toward the front door.

"Sully, it's a full out snowstorm out there," Val said. "You can't go outside."

He turned in the narrow entryway. "Then where can I go to get away from you two?"

Josh pointed up. "Loft upstairs. The chimney goes straight through, so it's warm."

"Great." Sully clapped and pointed to both of them. "Feel free to resume this argument you've obviously had a dozen times."

Sully walked up the narrow stairs that came off the kitchen and disappeared onto the second floor.

Val turned to Josh. "Tell me why Savannah Anderson is any different than any of the hundred women you've screwed around with over the past eighteen years."

Josh took a deep breath and let it out slowly. "Because I think maybe I'm in love with her too."

"Like you said you were in love with me? Or Rachel? Or Tracey? Or... Sarah?" She rolled her eyes. "Seriously, do you ever think about not being led around by your dick? Give it a try, just for shits and giggles sometime, okay? Because your oldest son—"

"This isn't about Jackson and Andy," Josh said. "This is you being offended because you like being offended."

Val felt like screaming. "This is me being pissed off because I am trying to raise two men to *not be like you!*" She wanted to take the log by the woodstove and bash his head in with it. "It's not fun and games anymore. You're forty-four years old! Grow the hell up! Just try to think about someone other than yourself for once in your life and—"

"I am! I'm thinking about Savannah!" He sat on the couch. "If it wasn't snowing out there, I would be on a snowmobile, heading back to town and then driving to the hospital right now. Do you understand me? I am in love with her. She is trapped in that marriage and she wants out. She told me she did."

Val took a deep breath. "When?"

"What?"

"When did she tell you she wanted out?" She held out her hand. "What were you wearing? Were you holding anything? A wallet? A phone?"

"What are you talking about?" Josh reached for something in his back pocket. "You want my wallet?"

"Is there anything from Savannah in here?"

"I guess..." Josh took out a slip of folded paper that looked well-worn and handed it to her.

Val grabbed it and took off her right glove, letting the feel of the pink paper sink into her skin. She closed her eyes and felt the memories rising through the cloud from her antianxiety meds.

"...my phone number."

"You're giving me your phone number?" He slipped a small piece of paper into his wallet. "Is that safe?"

"He won't know. I won't program your number in. It'll just be random. Or you can block it so he can't see." Her voice was worried. "Call me so I have your number though."

"If you want to leave, you should just—"

"It's not that easy," she said. "He tied up all the money I had access to in the ski resort. He said it was because my credit

is so good, but now all he'll do is give me an allowance, and it's never enough."

"If you got a divorce—"

"He'd find a way to screw me," Savannah said. "I'm working on a way to get a good lawyer, but until I have enough cash..."

Val dropped the paper on the storage chest and blinked. She closed her eyes and put a hand out. "Get me some water. No ice."

"What were you doing?"

"Just get me some water, will you?"

She kept her eyes closed, but she heard him walking to the kitchen and filling a glass from the jug of purified water on the stove. He walked back and put the cool glass in her hand.

"What was that?"

"That was me making sure you're telling the truth." She opened her eyes and sipped the water. "You are."

Josh still looked confused. "But what—"

"Don't ask," Val said quietly. "In recognition of all the favors you have never done for me, I am asking for this one thing. Don't. Ask."

Josh nodded silently. "Yes, we were having an affair. But she wasn't just a fuck."

"I can see that."

"I'm really worried about her."

Val nodded. "Then as soon as this storm lets up, we're going to head down the mountain and you and Sully are going to the police in Bridger and you are going to tell them everything. And you're not going to worry about Rachel breaking up with you if you tell the truth. Because she deserves to not be lied to."

Josh nodded. "Okay."

"And then you're going to man up and figure out how to support Savannah as she tries to get out of a marriage to a certified asshole who maybe tried to kill her."

"Do you really think he was trying to kill her?"

"I don't know, but either way, tampering with anyone's brakes ought to land you in jail."

"Agreed." He frowned. "Are you feeling okay?"

"I want to lie down," she said. "Can we turn off the lights in here so I can chill for a little?"

"Sure." Josh walked around, lowering the oil lamps in the corners of the room. "I'll let Sully know you're taking a break."

"Sure. Whatever."

"You guys are together, right?"

"No. We're not... Never mind. It's none of your business."

"Okay." Josh closed the shutters over the windows, shutting out the swirling snow coming down. "I think he's a pretty good guy though."

"Josh, just shut up. Never speak of this again."

VAL WOKE some time later to a soft brush of fingers over her forehead. She opened her eyes, and Sully was crouching next to her.

"You should sit." She cleared the roughness from her throat. "You don't want to put pressure on that ankle."

"It's okay. Just stiff."

"Is it still snowing?"

Sully nodded. "I think we're stuck here for the night."

Val groaned. "Of all the things I wanted, this was not it."

"Same." Sully sat on the edge of the storage chest, playing with the edge of his beard. "You sure you're not still hung up on your ex?"

Her eyebrows went up. "That argument before? What did it sound like to you?"

"You were both bitching at each other. I don't know—"

"No, I was nagging him. Like a mother. That's basically what Josh is at this point. That's what he'd turned himself into by the end of our marriage. He's like a giant, irresponsible child. I constantly want him to do better for our boys' sake, and he constantly manages to fuck things up."

"You know you can't make yourself responsible for your boys' relationship with their dad, right? It's going to be... whatever it is, but it's not on you. It's on him."

"I know that. I do. But they have one father. I love my parents so much, and when life went to shit, they were the only ones there for me. I just don't want them to regret things later, you know? And I tell myself that it's Josh's responsibility to plan things with them, but he never takes responsibility for anything. Nothing is ever his fault. And I don't want them to ever feel like they're to blame for his... lack."

Sully narrowed his eyes. "I don't think they would. They have a really great mom. I'm just saying that you can probably relax a little. I think your boys are gonna be okay."

She smiled. "I will worry about them until they're old men. Maybe longer. But to answer your question, no. I am really not hung up on my ex. He's like a third child. Try to imagine how unsexy it would be to be married to a person like that."

"Yeah." He frowned. "Pretty unsexy."

"Exactly." She tugged on his beard. "I like grown men."

His eyebrows went up. "Any grown men?"

"One in particular right now."

Sully leaned over slowly and then ran his lips, whisper-soft, over her temple, tracing the arch of her cheekbone until his mouth met hers. His lips were warm, and the tickle of his beard against her skin made goose bumps rise all over her body.

His mouth moved over hers with slow, deliberate thoroughness, reminding Val of how he'd made love to her. Every inch, he'd explored. Every curve and every angle. It had been the first time she'd had sex in ages, and Sully had been very, very thorough.

He drew his mouth away. "Tell me what changed after the accident last year."

She kept her fingers on the warm skin of his neck, languid and unguarded in the shadows thrown by the fire. He was using his kissing skills to interrogate her, and dammit if she didn't admire that a little.

Well, fuck it. Josh practically knew, and she trusted Sully a lot more than Josh.

"I touch things."

"Like what?"

She sighed. "Things. Not people. Objects. Hats. Clothes. Wallets. Phones. Anything people are attached to."

"And what happens?" His fingers brushed along her temple, playing with the soft hair.

"I see things." Val arched her back and felt Sully's hand

run from her knee up to her hip. "Hear things. Like little bits of a movie scene. Or a conversation in another room."

"Have you ever done it to me?"

Val froze and forced her eyes to his. "Not much."

His eyebrows went up. "But some?"

"Just about this case. I honestly try to avoid seeing anything. It's really not a pleasant ability."

His hand curled around her knee. "What did you read of mine?"

"Your hat."

He frowned. "My hat?"

"That's how I knew they weren't looking for Josh. That they thought he was gambling in Vegas and had just taken off."

"Huh." He cocked his head. "And that's it?"

"Yeah. I really..." She sat up. "I know this probably kills anything we might have possibly have relationship-wise." She sighed. "Not that we were in a relationship, but we were kinda—"

"I know what you mean, Val."

"I'm just saying who wants to be with someone who can know things like that? I mean, it's weird enough being naked in front of someone, but knowing that I can kind of look into your head—"

"Do you?" Sully sat up straight and put his hands on his knees. "Do you look into my head? Other than the time you just mentioned?"

"No. And it's not your head. Not really. It's more like memories and images... I really don't like seeing all this stuff." She raised her hands, which were still encased in her thin black gloves. "Why do you think I wear these? *All the time.*"

"Is it just your hands?"

"No, but they seem to be the most sensitive."

"Does it come and go or is it always—"

"I take, um..." She shifted on the couch. "I take antianxiety meds. It kind of... dulls it. A little. The pills create kind of a buffer. Without them, even the tiniest brush can trigger something. With them, I have to sit with an object for a little bit."

"Okay." He didn't appear to think she was crazy. So far. "Who knows about this besides me and your friends?"

"Robin's husband Mark knows. My boys do *not*. I kind of told Josh, but I can almost guarantee that he's going to find a way to forget I ever said anything like that. He's not a man who enjoys the mysterious."

Sully sat and looked at her for a long time.

Val stared back. "Do you believe me?"

He shrugged. "It's you. If you told me a three-headed donkey built this cabin, I'd believe you."

Val didn't try to stop her smile. "Thanks."

CHAPTER 21

*H*alfway down the mountain, Monica woke with a gasp. She saw the snow swirling in giant gusts outside her window and reached for the dream journal she kept by the bed.

Blood on the snow. She scribbled her thoughts as fast as she could scratch them down.

Blood. Bright red...

Bright red meant daytime. The sun was out, but it was cloudy. The snow wasn't hurting her eyes. It happened during the daytime on an overcast day.

She glanced outside. It was still dark, but would the storm pass completely? Would the sun break through the clouds?

Blood on the snow.

Wait, there was a foot. Footprints. And ski tracks.

Ski tracks? No, the snow was too churned up.

Snowmobile tracks.

A spatter of blood across the snow.

Fine spatter.

It wasn't a gush.

High impact. Spray. A gun?

She could hear the whoosh in the air now. A shot cracking through ice-laden air. Cold and clear.

Crack!

Hot breaths huffing out.

Have to get back.

Back to the cabin.

"Have to get back." Monica's eyes went wide when the scene in her mind's eye pulled back and she saw it all. She reached for the phone and called Robin's mobile number.

"Monica, what's wrong?"

"The cabin." She tried to keep her words steady, but they tumbled over each other like water rushing down a stream. "The blood is at the cabin. In the snow. Shots. Someone is firing. Shooting. That kind of firing. They're firing on Josh and it hits him and it's at the cabin and it's happening today."

"Mark." Robin said her husband's name louder. "Mark! We have to get up to Keane. We have to leave now."

VAL AND SULLY spent the night of the storm in the sleeping loft over the main room of the cabin, curled up in blankets on a mattress they'd rolled out on the floor, cuddling through the night. It was the first time Val had really slept with someone other than one of her kids since she'd gotten divorced, and it was a lot more relaxing than she'd anticipated.

Of course, it helped that Sully was like a giant furnace and she was freezing cold.

Josh slept in the living room below them on the couch by

the woodstove, waking up during the night to keep the fire going.

It snowed through the night, only stopping about five or so that morning. Looking out from the small window on the second floor, Val saw at least a foot of new powder on the ground.

"It's beautiful." She sat near the window, wrapped in a heavy quilt she'd dragged from the pallet.

Sully sat next to her. "It's going to be a bitch getting out of here."

"Yep." She turned and brushed a kiss over his lips. "You know, Monica said she was going to pray that we got snowed in together."

"Did she mean for us to be snowed in with your ex-husband?"

"I don't think she was really thinking that part through." The delicious smell of bacon rose up the stairs. "He's making breakfast. It's one of the few things he's actually good at. We should take advantage."

He slipped a hand under her shirt. "I wanted to last night, but it felt like the wrong time."

"You think?" She didn't wiggle away while he explored the sensitive skin along her belly and the curve at the small of her back.

"When we get home, I want you to come over." He bent and moved his lips over her neck, kissing and licking the skin just below her ear. "I'll make it worth your while."

Val couldn't believe that confessing her weird psychic power hadn't turned the man off. "I'll have to think about it."

"Okay." He kissed up her neck and across her cheek before he captured her mouth. "You won't regret it." He paused and pulled away. "I mean that. You've got a good life. A good family. A good business. I don't want to take anything from that. You've worked too hard. But maybe think about how I could add something. How being with me could add something to your life."

Val blinked. "I've never thought about it that way."

"Fair enough." He leaned back on the pallet and stretched his arms over his head. "Being with people who always take is exhausting. I've been there. But that's not the kind of person I am."

"Good."

His smile was slow and sweet. "I like you, Valerie Costa."

"I like you too."

"Good." He rolled up and dropped one more kiss on her lips. "That's not a bad place to start."

Sully rose and reached for the blue jeans he'd been wearing the day before under his snow pants. He tugged them on over his base layer and heavy socks. "Okay. Let's go convince your ex-husband to share his bacon and follow us down the mountain."

THEY WALKED DOWNSTAIRS and sat at the table, which was already set.

"This looks good," Val said. "Thanks."

"Help yourself. Eggs and bacon are on the stove. There's some biscuits too." Josh was drinking a cup of coffee by the fireplace, and he looked fresh and ready for a fancy outdoor-gear company's modeling shoot. He'd shaved and his hair was brushed neatly. He was wearing a clean undershirt and a blue-and-green flannel. His jeans were the exact right amount of worn, and he looked like he'd slept for a solid twelve hours.

He looked up, and Val was surprised to see the look of resolve on his face. "I'm going to straighten things out, okay?"

Sully nodded. "Sounds good."

"I'll follow you back down the mountain. I've done all the work I need to here. I mean, this place is completely livable and the water pump is working again. That was the main reason I came up." He walked over and poured more coffee. "What are the full charges against me?"

Sully filled a plate and sat down at the table. "As of right now, there's one warrant standing, and that's for the criminal theft of the ten thousand. Which you say never happened, so you'll have to deal with that. As of right now, it's his word against yours."

"But won't he have to show that he withdrew that money or something like that?"

"Yes. But he may have done that and then put it in a safe for all we know."

"Damn." Josh took a swig of coffee. "I mean, I've never stolen anything in my life."

"Unfortunately, you just admitted to us that you stole West's snowmobiles and trailer," Val said. "Where's the other one, by the way?"

"I left it in the garage back at the house."

"Figures," Val muttered. "So unless West suddenly found the note—"

"I did leave him one. It's probably sitting in a pile of mail. If it's not a bill, he has a tendency to ignore it."

Sully said, "The more serious issue is that Bridger PD

will want to talk to you regarding Savannah's accident. The good news is that if I can connect with this Bill guy and he can confirm you've been here all week—"

"Which he can. But he's usually not awake until ten or so."

"If I can confirm your alibi with Bill," Sully continued, "then the charges against you for Savannah's accident aren't going to be an issue. You'll still have to deal with the theft and the snowmobiles though."

Josh nodded. "I can handle that." He looked at Val. "And I'm calling Rachel as soon as we get back in range. I'm letting her know that it's over and I want her to move out as soon as she can." He shrugged. "She already moved a lot of stuff to her friend's house, I think."

Val nodded. "Very adult of you."

"So we have a plan." Josh nodded. "I should go out and get more wood. Get the path to the shed dug out so we can get the sleds out."

Val stood. "I'll clean up the house and the breakfast dishes, Sully can go talk to Bill, and you get shoveling then." She was feeling optimistic. They ought to be back in Glimmer Lake before noon as long as the path wasn't too snowed over. Even with that, the machines were designed for fresh powder, so they'd be able to get out.

Val started clearing the table while Sully and Josh went outside. She turned on the old radio and managed to find a country station to play while she worked. She washed the dishes and set them in the drying rack. She poured the bacon grease into a can near the stove and wiped down the table.

The cabin was basic but comfortable, and Val tried to imagine Savannah Anderson living there or even visiting. It was light-years away from her fancy house in Pheasant Creek, but it was possible the woman had never wanted that to begin with. It was possible that was all Americano Asshole.

She walked upstairs and shook out the blankets, folding them and storing them in the cedar chest. Then she rolled up the mattress and propped it in the corner near the other mattresses and sleeping bags.

If you brought a bed up to the second floor, you could make it a proper bedroom. Of course, just the mattresses and pillows were pretty comfortable too. She was tempted to ask Josh if she could bring the boys up for camping in the summer, but she hesitated to ask him. She hated owing him anything. Even a favor.

She fluffed all the pillows before she put them in storage tubs, then she headed down the stairs to see how the guys were doing.

She had grabbed another cup of coffee and was just peeking out the front window when she heard the crack.

What?

Val threw on her coat and stuffed her feet in boots, throwing open the door. Sully was running toward the house.

"Back!" He waved a hand and pointed to her. "Get back in the house!"

"Was that a tree branch?"

"Get back in the house!"

"Where's Josh?" Val's eyes swept the yard. "What's—?"

The crack came again, but this time Val knew exactly what it was.

A rifle.

"Josh?" She didn't leave the porch, but she scooted close to the house. "Josh?"

"Get in the house!" Sully was running, halfway crouched, ducking behind trees as he made his way toward the shed. "I've got Josh; get in the damn house, Valerie!"

Val backed toward the front door, but she still couldn't see Josh. "Where is he?"

Sully ran toward the shed, and another crack broke through the air, making a puff of snow rise just past Sully's feet.

"Sully!"

He bent down and lifted something from the snow. It was Josh's prone body.

Val's heart stopped. *No.* Sully was running across the clearing, exposed to God and whoever was shooting at the house.

"Get in the house." Sully grunted, hoisting Josh over his shoulder. "He's not dead."

Her heart started beating when he reached the steps. She cleared the doorway as Sully came barreling through the front door.

"He's bleeding," Val said.

"I think it's just a graze." Sully laid Josh down on the couch. The left side of his head was covered in blood, but his color was fine and he groaned a little when Sully moved him.

"Son of a bitch." Sully stretched his shoulder back. "That man isn't a lightweight."

"Get me a kitchen towel." Val was already cleaning the side of Josh's face with a handful of paper towels.

Sully was right. The bullet had grazed his temple and ear, but it hadn't struck his skull. Heads just bled a lot. She put a hand on the wound and held the paper towel to his head. "Josh, can you hear me?"

"The shed door is open and the sleds are out." Sully walked back with a wet towel in his hand. "He was walking back to the house when I heard the shot. He turned and the second one hit his temple. Would have gotten his head if he hadn't moved."

"Who the hell is shooting at us?" Val asked.

Sully's eyebrows went up. "I can think of one person who doesn't really want this guy found. And he doesn't have much love for me or you either."

"Americano Asshole?" Val was incredulous. "He's *shooting* at us?" She knew the guy was an asshole, but this really went beyond.

"He tried to kill his wife. Is shooting us really out of the realm of possibility here, Val?"

"I'm just saying he doesn't seem like the type."

Sully laughed hard. "Know what he got that gold medal in?"

"Sharpshooting?" Another shot fired and Val heard glass break upstairs.

"He's a gold-medal biathlete," Sully said. "You know that weird racing thing where they cross-country ski and then target shoot?"

"Are you kidding me?"

"I wish I was." Sully stood and moved an armoire in front of a window, shoving the piece of furniture like it was made of cardboard.

Val pictured Anderson's precise haircut and cold eyes. He was ruthless and full of himself. And apparently he was shooting at them.

"How did he even find us?"

"He must have followed us yesterday and put the pieces together when he saw the signs for Keane."

"So he skied in and decided to shoot us?"

Another shot and another window broken upstairs.

"I don't know how he found us, but we're sitting ducks in this house." Sully shoved a bookcase in front of another window. "He found a position somewhere on that hill and he's got a line of sight directly into this clearing."

"So what do we do?"

With all the windows on the ground floor blocked by either furniture or the porch overhang, Sully began to pace. "We can't get to the snowmobiles. Even if we could reach them without getting shot, that road is wide open. We'd be riding away and our backs would be exposed."

Val knew that calling for help wasn't an option. "So we're stuck here?"

"No." Sully shook his head. "There's got to be a way."

"Anderson planned this perfectly. We don't have any mobile phone reception out here. We're isolated. He could—"

"Listen to me." Sully turned to face her. "Panic is useless right now, so don't go there. The television lies; criminal masterminds are fiction. Criminals are mostly pretty dumb. This guy"—he was still pacing—"is dumb and *arrogant*. Sadly, the only gun I have is a shotgun, and that's going to do fuck-all when we have a gunman working at that distance, so I'm taking ideas now."

Josh mumbled, "Bill has a full gun safe." His eyes flickered open. "Is Anderson actually shooting at us?"

"Pretty sure he is, Mason."

Josh muttered, "It was a really bad idea to come up here."

Val was holding the towel to his head, but she really

wanted to hit him. "If you hadn't decided to sleep with a sociopath's wife, it would probably be a fine idea. Unfortunately—"

"I really need to keep my dick in my pants." Josh blinked and sat up. "That burns like a mother. I got it." He held the towel to his head and searched for Sully. "Bill," he said. "He has a small arsenal in his house. But you're going to have to go across the road and through the village. I can show you where—"

"I know where Bill lives, remember? I was over there this morning to confirm your alibi. We had coffee."

"Right." Josh snapped his fingers. "He has a radio too. He might be able to call for help."

Sully took a deep breath and put his hands on his hips. "So I need to get to Bill's house without letting the sharp-shooting biathlete know where I'm going. Any ideas?"

Josh frowned. "Run fast?"

"Right." Sully looked out the door. "Run fast."

CHAPTER 22

*al hid on a corner of the porch, waiting for Sully's signal. She had her supplies piled next to her, and she was holding her breath.

She looked at Sully, who nodded and gave her a thumbs-up.

Val turned and tossed a bright blue hat from the corner of the porch toward the shed just as Sully took off toward the shelter of the trees in the other direction.

A rifle shot cracked the air and a puff of snow rose from the bank by the shed. Val looked over her shoulder and saw Sully, already under the shelter of the pines and moving silently through the scattered cabins in the village.

"Is he out?" Josh called from the house.

"Yeah." Where was that asshole perched? The shots were being fired from an angle, based on the way the snow was flying. "Where is this guy?"

"Up the hill somewhere," Josh said. "Get inside. You're making me nervous out there."

"I don't think he can see past the porch roof," Val said. "So he has to be pretty high."

"We could always just make a break for the snowmobiles and try to outrun him."

"Didn't you hear Sully? The entire road is open. We'd be sitting ducks." Val walked back in the house and tried to watch Sully through the trees. But the man was already out of sight. "How's your head?"

"It hurts, but I don't feel light-headed or anything." Josh walked to the kitchen, put the bloody towel in the sink, then grabbed a fresh one. "Just have a massive headache."

"This guy is screwing himself," Val said. "He's shooting at a law-enforcement officer."

"He doesn't have any choice, does he? He counted on pinning Savannah's accident on me. If I have an alibi up here, the suspicion is going to turn to him in a heartbeat."

"That means he's desperate." Val peeked out the window. She thought she heard snowmobiles and prayed no random recreational vehicles would get caught up in this mess. "Desperate men are even more dangerous."

"What does he think is going to be the end game here?" Josh said. "That's what I don't get. If we're dead up in the cabin, it's obviously not an accident. Sully's a sheriff. They're going to come looking for him and—"

"I hear engines," Val's eyes widened. "Those are definitely snowmobiles. Fuck." She walked out to the porch, planning to wave off whoever was stupid enough drive through Keane, only to see two snowmobiles carrying three familiar figures.

"Oh shit." She crossed her arms and tried to wave them

away, immediately recognizing Robin and Mark's ski jackets. "Go back!"

The sleds surged forward, eating up the ground between the road and the house until—

Crack!

A bullet went through the front of Mark's sled. He pulled it to the side and tumbled off.

"What the hell?"

"Get in the house!" Val was screaming.

Crack!

Another puff of snow and someone screamed.

"In the house!"

All three figures were in the snow, scrambling through the fresh fallen powder between the road and the porch.

Crack!

"Thank God this asshole is out of practice," muttered Val.

Monica was the first to make it onto the porch. Robin was behind a tree, her breath coming in clouded bursts.

"Robin, just jump toward the porch."

"Blood on the snow." Monica panted. "Is Josh—?"

"Grazed him. He's only grazed."

"There was no way to warn you." Monica crawled through the front door as Mark sheltered behind the shed and Robin shook behind a tree.

Val waved at them to get their attention.

"Okay," she said in a low voice. "I'm going to distract him—"

"Don't you dare!" Robin hissed. "Val—"

"Just wait." She reached for another hat from the basket by the door. "When I toss it, run."

She threw the hat toward the tipped sleds in the front of the house.

Crack!

Robin dove onto the porch and Mark ran from the shed. Both of them ducked into the house and into each other's arms as Val slammed the door shut.

"Hey." She let out a relieved breath. "Welcome to Keane."

THEY WERE DRINKING coffee while Val watched the back of the cabin, hoping to see a sign of Sully coming through the trees.

"So you've been up here the whole time?" Monica was talking to Josh. "Just hanging out?"

"I was doing some repairs to the water pump and trying to fix the place up a little. I had no idea about the police or Savannah's accident or any of that."

"It said on the news this morning that she was in stable condition at the hospital," Monica said. "So that's good news."

Robin had lost all her inhibitions in the terror of gunfire. "There are so many ghosts up here. You all don't even realize." She was looking out the windows.

Josh went pale. "In the house?"

She looked at him, looked at Val. "Uh... no. Not in the house. Of course not."

Judging by Robin's expression, there were definitely ghosts in the house.

That wasn't necessarily a bad thing. There was a spirit in

Robin's antique shop. She was friendly, just sad. Val had felt the cool gust of wind in the shop at times, but the ghost had never bothered her.

"The dream woke me up in the middle of the night," Monica said. "During the storm. I got a lot more than I had before. I could see the cabin. I could see Josh lying in the snow. I'm so sorry, but we had no idea how to get ahold of you."

Mark said, "She called us and we left as soon as the light came up. Borrowed our neighbors' snowmobiles. Told them it was an emergency."

"We got the sleds up here fast and it wasn't hard to find the village," Robin said. "When we pulled into Keane, we thought it was going to be a fast visit. We thought we could just grab you guys and get out of here."

Val sighed. "Yeah, Sully and I thought we'd be home by lunch yesterday."

"Where is Sully?" Mark asked.

"There's an old man on the other side of the settlement," Josh said. "Bill has rifles and a radio."

"Sully was going to try to call for help and get something better suited for the situation than a shotgun." Val nodded to the shotgun propped near the door. "He left that one with us just in case."

"Hate guns." Monica shuddered. "But I'm glad Sully knows how to use them."

Mark was looking out the windows. "Who the hell is this Anderson guy?"

"Apparently he's a gold-medal biathlete."

"What's a—?"

"Ohh," Robin said. "I know what you're talking about. The ski-and-shoot thing?"

"Yes. Cross-country skiing and sharpshooting."

Mark frowned. "Well, he's uniquely dangerous, isn't he?"

"I know, right? Why couldn't Josh have slept with a snowboarder's wife?"

Josh was sulking. "I feel like you guys are kinda victim blaming here."

Mark nodded. "Yeah. We are." He stood up and began to pace around the cabin. "Where is this guy shooting from? I don't like sitting and waiting in this house."

"Somewhere up the hill," Val said. "But I can't tell where."

Mark was looking at the long skis hanging on the wall. "Do you have boots for these?"

Josh frowned. "Uh, yeah. In one of the closets, I think. That stuff is really old though."

Robin said, "You have got to be kidding."

"You'd rather just sit here?"

"I'd rather wait for Sully to call the sheriff's department."

"We don't know if he can even reach them," Mark said. "You want to wait here for this guy to get closer and shoot us?"

Val was very afraid that's exactly what would happen. After all, like Josh had said, Anderson had to be desperate. He'd hatched a perfect plan that depended on Josh being a deadbeat and skipping town, not isolating himself in a remote cabin for two weeks where he had the luck to have an alibi.

Monica and Robin were looking at Val. She crossed her arms. "I don't know what the right thing to do is. Monica, you have anything?"

Monica shook her head. "Nothing more than the dream I had. Sorry."

"Don't apologize." Val paced in front of the windows, hoping to catch a glimpse of Sully through the trees. The cabin had felt full with three people inside. With five, it was darn near claustrophobic. "Sully is going to come back pretty soon. Let's not do anything before he returns with better weapons."

"Fine." Mark was scanning the hills behind the house. "I'm going upstairs."

"I think he broke a couple of the windows up there, so he can see in," Val said. "Be careful."

"If he can see in, then maybe I can see him." Mark looked around. "Are there any binoculars around here?"

Josh pointed to the closet. "Some in the cupboard under the stairs. My grandma liked to bird-watch."

Mark went to pull out the binoculars and Val tossed him a dark coat that was hanging on the hooks near the door. "Don't be visible."

"Got it." Mark started upstairs, creeping when he got to the top of the loft.

Robin paced in front of the fireplace. "I'm going to put more wood on," she said. "It's cold."

"Just keep in mind that pile is all we have without going outside," Val said. "We were planning on leaving, but then Josh got shot."

"Right." Robin put a log on the fire, her head angled toward the loft upstairs where Mark was crawling around.

Monica walked over to where Val was standing near the rear windows. "Anything?"

"No." She glanced up. "I have to admit, I'm with Mark.

There's six of us and one of him. Odds are in our favor if we move out."

"Any place we move, we put someone at risk." Monica glanced at the sofa. "And Josh can't run. Not like that."

Mark spoke from above in a steady voice. "I see him."

"What do you see?" Val asked. "Everyone quiet."

The cabin fell silent.

"He's on a ridge above the houses. White suit. Like... it's one of those full snowsuits in white. He's wearing goggles. I caught the shine off them."

Val tried to picture the ridge Mark was talking about, but she couldn't. "Landmarks?"

"He's parked behind an outcropping that looks a little like Jabba the Hutt."

"Oh shit," Val said. "I think I know where that is."

Robin's eyes went wide. "You do?"

"It's a rock that looks like Jabba. Once you see it, you can't unsee it." She squeezed her eyes shut. "I can't remember how to get there. I'm completely blanking." She caught a flicker of movement in the trees and spotted Sully sheltering behind a large cedar. "Sully's back. Mark, do you see Anderson moving?"

"He's just looking through some binoculars. The rifle's up right now."

"Maybe he doesn't see Sully."

"Shit. No, rifle's down."

"Just now?"

"Yeah."

Val leaned out the door and shouted, "Sully, run right now!"

Without a second of hesitation, he bolted from the trees

and made for the porch. By the time the shot rang out, he was under the eaves.

He was panting hard. "You know something I don't?"

"Mark is upstairs and can see him. Anderson saw you, but he'd barely lowered his rifle. Hadn't had time to aim."

Sully's eyebrows went up. "Mark?"

"Long story."

"So you told me to run on a guess?"

"It was an educated gamble."

He muttered, "Same damn thing" under his breath as he walked into the house. Once inside, he pulled a revolver from his waist and unhooked the camouflage bag over his shoulder.

"Bill had two rifles I could use, but he didn't have much ammunition." He glared at the three women. "Why the hell are Monica and Robin here?"

Monica said, "I had a vision of Josh getting shot at the cabin. Unfortunately, by the time we got up here, it had already happened."

"Visions?" Sully's eyebrows went up. "Ghosts and tele— whatever Valerie can do with her hands—and now visions?"

"Unfortunately, they're not always very useful," Monica said. "They get clearer the closer to the event, but that doesn't always give me much time. In fairness, if you'd been in mobile phone range, we could have avoided all this."

Mark's voice rang out. "It's weird, but you get used to it, Sully."

The sheriff was slowly shaking his head. "Mark, you still have eyes on the shooter?"

"I think so. He's behind Jabba now. I think he's on skis. Pretty sure I saw his poles sticking out from behind the rock."

"He's on skis," Sully muttered. "Fucking Olympic sharp-shooter on skis."

"I say we try to take him," Monica said. "There are six of us."

"Forget it," Sully said. He looked at Val. "I managed to get a message to my deputy in Glimmer Lake. He's got to find some machines, but as soon as he does, he'll be up here."

"Where is he getting snowmobiles?"

"I don't know."

"So you don't know when he's coming?"

"He's a resourceful kid. And he's going to alert the forest service. Technically we're on federal land, and those rangers don't mess around."

"So we're just supposed to wait until they get here?" Val said. "Anderson almost picked off Mark, Robin, and Monica while they were riding in. Who's to say he wouldn't be able to shoot any help before they could get to us?"

"What are you saying? You want to mount an assault up the mountain when there's a sniper out there?"

Val looked around. Robin nodded at her. Monica did too. "I'm saying that you have three resources here that you don't normally have. And one of them might come in more handy than you realize." Val turned to Robin. "What do you say?"

Robin was wary. "I don't know any of the people around here. They probably wouldn't listen to me. You want me to call Bethany?"

"Do you think you can?"

Sully asked, "Call who?"

"We're pretty far from Glimmer Lake, but I can try." Robin glanced at Monica. "Help me find some paper and a pencil."

Josh said, "I think there's some in the kitchen."

Sully crossed his arms. "What's she going to do?"

Val stood next to "There's a ghost that's kind of attached to Robin. A girl. She usually hangs out around the lake, but she might be able to call her here."

"I've never tried this far from the lake before." Robin found a blank paper in a kitchen drawer and immediately began to sketch.

Mark called from upstairs. "Honey, you need me?"

Monica moved next to Robin. "I've got her, Mark."

Val whispered, "Headaches. She gets really bad headaches after. Sometimes nausea."

"And you?"

"More nausea than headaches, but it depends on how long I'm in a vision."

"I don't seem to have any side effects from visions," Monica said. "But they almost always come in dreams, so I'm asleep."

"She's here." Robin smiled. "Hey, Bethany. How are you?"

CHAPTER 23

There was a long silence while Robin listened to the ghost.

"Aren't you cold?" She wore an absent smile. "We're okay, but we're wondering if you might be able to help us."

Another silence.

"Yes, that's the one." Robin frowned. Apparently Bethany had a lot to say. "I didn't realize you'd seen him before." She nodded. "Yes. We need a path to get to him without him being able to see us... Yes, we have the loud machines." Robin glanced at Sully. "Bethany really hates snowmobiles. She says horses are much better."

"Horses might get cold in this weather," Sully said. "But I'll keep that in mind."

Robin smiled. "She knows you're an authority figure. She calls you the ranger."

The corner of Sully's mouth turned up. "Oh yeah?"

Robin laughed a little. "You're trying to bargain now?" Another silence. "Okay, I'll ask." She turned to Sully.

"Bethany wants to know if you can make them stop riding snowmobiles at the snow park on the west side of the dam."

Val smiled. "She wants a favor?"

Robin shrugged. "Hey, she's a smart kid. We want a favor from her..."

Sully said, "I can't guarantee anything, but I'll see what I can do. If the snowmobiles are bothering her, I'll try to get them off those trails." He looked at Robin. "I'm insane."

"You're not insane."

"She says she'd appreciate it." Robin's eyes flew to the door and then back to Val. "She's out."

"Is she still wearing a nightgown?" Monica asked.

"Yes. She makes me cold just looking at her." Robin shivered. "No matter what time of the year, she's always in that old-fashioned nightgown with bare feet."

Monica patted her shoulder and stood. "I'll make you some tea. Do you have aspirin in your purse?"

"Yes."

"I'll get it."

Sully leaned against the wall. "I just made a bargain with a ghost child."

"I promise you're not crazy," Val said. "But I completely understand if you feel that way."

Josh was drifting in and out of sleep. "Robin, did you say you can see ghosts?"

Robin put a hand on his forehead. "No, honey, you're just dreaming. Go back to sleep."

"Okay." He closed his eyes again and threw an arm over Robin's legs.

"Yeah, no." She carefully removed his arm and stood. "That man is going to be very confused when he wakes up."

"Join the club." Sully was pacing in front of the fire. "We can't take the sleds. They're way too loud. If we want to surprise him, we're going to have to hike."

"What about snow shoes?" Robin asked. "I saw more than a few pairs hanging on cabins around here."

"I brought a pair myself," Sully said. "But that's only one set."

"Look in the cupboard," Mark said from above. "There was an old set in the back. They might be a little ratty, but better than nothing."

Robin said, "If Bethany comes back with a path that will keep us hidden, we might be able to snag some snowshoes off porches in the village."

Val nodded. "Snowshoes it is." She glanced at the rifle bag. "And guns."

"Forget it," Sully said.

"I'm a good shot!" Val said. "I went shooting all the time with my dad."

"Rifle?"

"No. Handgun."

Sully nodded. "I guess you can handle the revolver."

"I'm a good shot," Robin said. "Ask Mark."

"She's better than me, and I'm pretty good," Mark said. "Plus she's fast."

"Mark has better eyes than me though," Robin said. "So does Val."

Sully took a deep breath. "And I hate any of you being involved in this."

"I have to go," Robin said. "If Bethany is going to guide us, I have to be there."

"And I can shoot," Val said.

"And if I had a radio, I'd stay here and spot for you." Mark creeped down the stairs and stretched his arms up and out. "But we don't have a radio, so I think more people is better. Plus Robin's not going out there without me."

Monica raised her hand. "I have no desire to face danger of any kind, and I'm a piss-poor shot."

"Good." Sully nodded. "You get to stay and make sure this numbskull doesn't do anything stupid."

Monica saluted. "You got it."

A chilled breeze drifted through the cabin.

"Bethany's back." Robin looked at Sully. "And she found us a path."

SULLY, Val, Mark, and Robin took turns slipping off the porch and into the trees. Sully went first, holding a rifle, then Robin followed with another. After her, Val crept out with the revolver, then Mark with a shotgun.

"This way?" Val crouched behind the neighbor's shed. She wiggled her feet, adjusting the old snowshoes she'd strapped on in the house.

"We're going to curve around the village," Robin said, "before we start climbing up. Bethany says there's an old road that leads to the river. We can take that and then climb the hill behind the ridge." She frowned, staring into space. "It's steep, but she says it'll keep us out of sight."

"Good." Sully slid along the back of the shed and peeked out before he waved at Robin. "You lead the way, but stay behind as many houses as you can."

The four moved in silence, ducking behind cabins and

shuffling along narrow trails between houses. There were a few fences and more than one tree line.

Val stopped trying to figure out which direction they were heading and simply followed Sully's lead. Every time they had to cross a clear patch of snow, Robin would wait, Sully would go first, then the rest of them would follow.

"I feel like we have to be getting close to the ridge." Mark was panting behind her. They'd found a fourth pair of snow-shoes for him, but they were really old and kind of rusty. Val tried not to wince every time the joints creaked.

Speaking of joints creaking...

"Sully, how's your ankle?"

"I'm doing okay. It hurts like a bitch, but it hasn't frozen up."

"Robin, how's your knee?"

"Sore," Robin said. "Mark, you okay?"

"Surprisingly, all my joints are intact."

"At least there's one of us."

"Two," Val said. "My complete lack of athletic abilities is finally coming in handy during middle age. I have zero sports-related injuries."

"Lucky."

Val could only see one cabin left before the trees grew even denser. "I think we're almost there, and I haven't heard anything from above, so I'm feeling positive."

Once they cleared the last house, they walked along a downward path for a few hundred feet before Robin stopped and looked up to her right.

"Are you kidding?" She looked back at the rest of them. "We have to climb up here."

Oh fuck. "That's pretty steep."

"I know."

Sully and Mark were panting hard.

"I'm too old for this shit," Sully said.

"I need to jog more." Mark looked at Robin. "You're right, okay? I'm going to start running with you again."

"It's this," Val said, "or going back to the cabin and waiting like sitting ducks for someone to maybe come help who maybe doesn't get shot."

Robin bent over and did a couple of shallow squats. "Okay. I can do this."

"Let's go." Val started up the hill. She was walking sideways, taking her time and trying to stay as silent as possible.

Am I too old to pick up yoga?

Probably should do some cardio too.

Dammit, I should have peed before we left the cabin.

She was wearing too many layers to duck behind a tree. Plus she might literally freeze something important.

Bladder, don't fail me now!

She leaned against a tree halfway up the hill and looked behind her. Sully and Robin were nearly caught up to her. Mark was trailing behind.

The snow muffled the sound of everything, swallowing their breathless pants and dampening the crunch of ice beneath their feet.

"Bethany says he's right above us," Robin whispered. "But he hasn't looked this way. If we stay quiet, we should be able to sneak up on him."

Sully nodded and pointed to the top of the hill. While Val caught her breath, he kept hiking, finding his footing with surprising grace for a large man.

Robin made a clicking sound with her tongue that sounded

like a squirrel as she reached the top of the hill and ducked down under a rise of granite. Everyone followed her and crouched down in the snow, letting their breath return to normal.

Sully was the first to peek his head up. He took off his dark Stetson and put on a white beanie he'd found at the cabin. Keeping the rifle in both hands, he slowly rose and looked over the edge of the rocks. He scanned the area thoroughly, then crouched back down.

Sully found a blank patch of snow and clearly diagrammed where they were and where Anderson was in relation.

Mark pointed to the wide spot between the two points. "How far?" he whispered.

"Twenty yards," Sully said under his breath. "This is the going to be the hard part."

"Trees?" Val asked.

Sully marked a line of Xs on the far side of the Jabba rock where Anderson was camped.

"He's not expecting us." Mark pointed to himself, then to the trees past the Jabba rock. "I'll run. He won't have time to aim."

"We don't know what weapons he has," Robin said.

Sully nodded to her. "Ask Bethany."

Robin let out a breath and closed her eyes. She opened them and looked around. "She's not here."

Sully frowned. "You can't call her?"

"Not without my drawing pad."

"It's not like a button you push," Val said. She grabbed the beanie from Sully and poked her head over the rocks before anyone could stop her.

The Americano Asshole was leaning over the rocks, his rifle aimed at the cabin below. His back was tense.

Val ducked back. "He's totally focused on something below. If we rush him now—"

"Wait." Sully held up a hand. His eyes went wide. "Do you hear it?"

Val waited and caught the faint edge of a sound growing louder.

"Snowmobiles," Mark said. "They're coming."

"And riding straight into his sights," Robin said. "We have to move now."

Mark said, "I'm going to run behind him and into the trees. I have the shotgun if he tries to follow me. As soon as he turns—"

"I'll announce myself and give him a chance to surrender," Sully said. "He has to know he's out of options at this point."

"What?" Val asked. "You're going to—"

"Go." Robin kissed Mark. "I love you."

Mark rose and slid over the rocks without missing a beat, the shotgun slung over his back. Sully and Val stood and everything happened at once.

Americano Asshole squeezed off a shot as Mark yelled, "Hey, you dick!" and ran toward the trees.

Sully stood and shouted, "Allan Anderson, you're under arrest. Put down your weapon!" He aimed the rifle at Anderson while Val jumped to the side and rolled a few feet from Sully before she rose and pointed the revolver at the man who was swinging around—rifle still up—and pointing it at Sully.

They stood frozen, staring at each other, both men with the other in their sights.

"Anderson," Sully said, "put the rifle down."

"Why?" The man asked it so casually Val almost blinked. "I can kill you faster than you can pull the trigger."

"Then I'll shoot you," Val said. "And I won't hesitate."

"Are you sure? After all, you were married to that lowlife Mason for years. It doesn't speak well of your reflexes."

Sully stepped forward, his aim never wavering. "I called my deputy, Anderson. He called the forest service. They have your name. They know what you did. It's over. There is no escaping this. You can't outrun them."

"I don't plan on outrunning them," Anderson said. "I plan on killing you and then skiing away. It's really quite simple."

Mark stepped out from behind the trees, his shotgun pointed at Anderson. "Shoot any of them and you'll be an ugly-ass corpse. That I promise you."

The steady smile on Anderson's face wavered for the first time.

Robin stood and pointed another rifle at him. "Shoot any of my friends and I'll put a bullet between your eyes," she said quietly. "I won't miss."

"Four against one," Val said. "I'm assuming that math isn't too much for you."

Anderson moved so quickly Val almost didn't register the barrel of his rifle swinging away from Sully and toward her. Her finger tightened on the trigger just as a loud shot rang out next to her.

Anderson jerked back, and a red flower bloomed on his right shoulder. He dropped the rifle and fell to the snow.

"Mark, grab his gun!" Sully ran to the supine man. "Allan Anderson, you're under arrest. Don't talk, because you'll just piss me off." Sully flipped the man over and slapped cuffs on him.

"You shot me." Anderson didn't even look angry. He looked offended, as if it was just bad manners to stain his fancy ski suit with a bloodstain. "Do you know who I am?"

"You've got to be kidding me," Val said. "This guy is delusional." She tore off her own glove and reached for Anderson's thin, Gore-Tex glove he'd been wearing to shoot. She took it off his hand and held it in her palm. "Wow. There's a lot on these."

Val closed her eyes and let the images come. For once, she actually wanted to see the world through someone else's eyes. "Someone dropped him off early this morning. Just when the sun was coming up. Tan SUV of some kind. Maybe a Land Cruiser?"

Mark said, "Sounds like one of his partners at the resort."

"The friend knew what he was planning to do." Val closed her eyes and let herself fall into the scene.

What are you going to do?

Get rid of the problem. No one is going to miss him, Charles.

The plan was crystal clear in his mind. Surprisingly simple, really. Kill the mechanic. Kill the sheriff and the ex-wife. Hide the bodies. Ski down to Mason's truck and drive it down the mountain, parking it somewhere near Bridger so it looked like Mason was nearby and responsible for Savannah's accident.

By the time the bodies were found in the spring—if they

ever were—the case would be cold. His friends in the department would never suspect he was part of it.

"He was planning on killing all three of us." Val pulled away and felt an immediate wave of nausea. "You, me, and Josh. He didn't think anyone else would be up here. He was going to hide our bodies."

"Who was the other man?"

"Charles." She swallowed hard to fight the nausea. "He knew Anderson was going after Josh. He didn't realize we'd be with him."

Sully said, "I'll tell Francis to start looking for a guy named Charles who owns a tan Land Cruiser." He turned Anderson over on his side. "Sounds like you had an accomplice, buddy! Wonder how long it'll take him to give you up for a sweet deal?"

Anderson was on his side, staring at Val with wide eyes. "How did you know that?"

Val used his glove to tap his cheek and fought to retain her breakfast. "Oh, Americano Asshole, don't you know who I am? I'm your friendly neighborhood psychic." She winked. "And I'm gonna know all your secrets. Every. Single. One."

She didn't think he could look any paler, but he could. He actually could.

CHAPTER 24

They took the easy way down the hill, pushing Anderson in front of them. The man didn't have snowshoes, and he kept falling into drifts and having to be lifted out. Mark was carrying the sharpshooter's backpack and skis. Robin was carrying a shotgun and a rifle. Sully had two rifles.

Val had wisely handed the revolver back to Sully. Anderson was still pissing her off, and she didn't quite trust herself not to put a bullet in his butt. Which would have been illegal. He already had one legally allowed bullet in him from Sully's gun. Another one would be overkill.

Literally.

Sully shouted to the forest rangers as soon as they got near; a man and a woman in olive-green uniforms and heavy winter hats trudged toward them through the snow.

"Sully." The man spotted the blood on Anderson's shoulder. "Carol, bring the first aid kit!"

"Good to see you, Cartwright." Sully kept Anderson in

his grip, partly to keep the man standing. "Thanks for the assist."

"We got the call from Francis and got up here as quickly as possible." The ranger frowned as a medic examined Anderson and began pressing gauze to the wound under his snowsuit. "Is this who was shooting from that ridge?"

"Sure is."

"We need to get him in blankets and down the hill," the medic said. "I can get the bleeding under control, but I don't want him going into shock."

Sully watched the rangers take Anderson away. "The bullet went in and out."

Cartwright nodded briskly. "We were getting a sled ready for Josh Mason, but we'll take Anderson down first."

"He aimed a rifle at me, so don't take your eyes off him."

"Yeah, he shot at us too, so I don't think you need to worry. Francis should be waiting at the plowed road with the ambulance."

Mark asked, "Did he hit anyone? That last shot, I mean."

Cartwright shook his head. "Grazed a machine, but that's it. Moving targets are far harder to hit than most target shooters realize. I'll call my guys back. They were hiking up to find out where the shots were coming from." He walked away, talking quietly into a radio that crackled on his shoulder.

The female ranger was nearly as tall as Sully. She was eyeing Robin and Mark. "These firearms belong to you?"

Robin and Mark exchanged a glance. "Uh..."

Sully said, "They were an emergency procurement from a local resident after Josh Mason was shot."

She shook her head. "Dammit, Bill. I told him he could have a shotgun to scare off bears. *One* shotgun."

Robin said, "Technically, it says *discharging* a weapon on forest service land is a crime. But, uh, we didn't actually discharge any of these. Sully was the only one who shot anyone."

Val could only think: *Only because I didn't get the chance.*

"Can Bill get a pass this time?" Sully asked quietly. "He had them secured and asked for my badge before he handed anything over."

She sighed. "At least he's being responsible." She turned her back and started walking toward the clearing. "I saw nothing. Take them back and tell him I do not want to see them again."

"Thanks. Just to let you know, we're looking for an accomplice. First name Charles. He drives a tan Land Cruiser."

"I'll get the word out to our people." She nodded at them. "Let us know what else we can do to assist. I'm going to catch up with Cartwright unless you need anything else."

"We're good," Sully said.

They continued toward the cabin, passing a couple of houses, one of which had two sets of eyes peering out.

"Now they look," Val muttered.

"Oh, come on," Robin said. "They were probably scared to death, not knowing what was going on."

Val waved. "I hope they enjoyed the show."

Monica was waiting on the porch. She waved when she saw them. "Look! The cavalry came!"

"How's Josh?" Val asked.

"Still sleeping. His head already stopped bleeding. The medic says he won't even need to go to the hospital if he doesn't want to."

Sully said, "Considering Bridger PD still has a warrant out for his arrest, that's probably a good thing."

The clearing in front of the cabin was a bustle of snow machines of all kinds, one that looked like a mini-tractor, three that looked like long sleds, and another with a person-sized trailer on the back where they were strapping Allan Anderson in. His wrists has been bound in front of him, and he was strapped down with a heavy blanket wrapped tightly around his body.

Val glanced at her friends gathering on the front porch and slipped away to watch Americano Asshole, who was slowly getting paler by the minute.

"He going to be healthy enough to get thrown in jail?" Val asked the ranger securing the ropes.

"Oh yeah. But we need to get him down the hill and into the hospital before he goes into shock. He hasn't lost too much blood, but the doctors will want to rule out internal bleeding." The young man stepped away from the snowmobile to speak to his superior, and Val crouched down next to Anderson.

"Hear that, Anderson?" Val leaned forward. "*Internal* bleeding. The gift that might still be giving."

His lips barely moved. "How did you know... all those things?"

Val leaned closer. "You know how."

"Impossible."

"I'm going to head to your house, Anderson. Maybe head to your garage. I'll be able to get in. Your wife will probably make me coffee." She slid a bare finger down the line of his cheek. "And I'll know all your secrets, Allan. Every single one."

His expression wavered between rage and fear. "I don't believe you. It's a trick."

"Keep telling yourself that," she said. "You're going to go to jail. For attempted murder of Savannah and Josh. You just couldn't handle her leaving you, huh?"

"She's nothing without me. She was a backwoods—"

"Was it her leaving you, or was it the money?" Val asked.

His eyes flickered.

"Huh. So more about the money. Interesting. Well, looks like *she'll* be the owner of that fancy ski resort soon enough."

The ranger walked back. "I'm ready to go. Ma'am, can you please step away from the sled?"

"Sure thing." She handed him a free coffee card. "Come by Misfit Coffee in Glimmer Lake. Next coffee's on me."

The young man grinned. "Cool. Might get a bear claw too."

"They're to die for, right?" Val winked at Anderson and mouthed, *To die for.*

"Yeah, they're something else." He started the machine and within minutes, the first aid sled and two other snowmobiles with forest service rangers were headed back to the main road.

Cartwright walked up to Val. "You're Mason's wife?"

"Oh God no," she said. "Ex-wife. We have two boys together. That's why I've been trying to find him."

"Ah." He glanced at Sully. "You have an interesting group of friends."

Val pulled out another free coffee card. "I know. They're

awesome. Come by Misfit Coffee sometime when you're at the lake. I'll hook you and your guys up with some free drinks, okay?"

"I will." He stuck the card in his pocket and nodded. "Thanks. Take care."

"Thank you!" She waved as the last of the rangers scattered.

When she turned, Sully was already loading Josh onto the back of his snowmobile. "Probably best if I get this guy back to the sheriff's department as soon as possible." He patted Josh's shoulder a little harder than was necessary. "We have a lot of paperwork to start filling out."

Josh curled his lip. "Paperwork?"

"So much." He looked at Val. "You good getting home with the other guys?"

She looked at Robin, Monica, and Mark standing on the porch. "Yeah. I'll be fine."

Sully looked like he wanted to say something else, but he shut his mouth, nodded, and started the snowmobile.

Val walked back to the porch. "We better get this place locked up and ready to be empty," she said. "It may be a while before Josh is back."

MARK AND ROBIN dropped Val off in the parking lot of the sheriff's department just in time to see her parents pulling in next to her truck with two familiar dark heads in the back seat. Andy burst out of the car and ran toward her.

"You found him! Dad called and he said you found him!"

Andy threw himself at Val, wrapping his arms hard around her middle. "How did you find him?"

"It wasn't just me." Val hugged Andy and kept her eyes on Jackson, who was hanging back. "Sheriff Sully helped. Robin and Mark and Monica helped. It was a group effort." She rubbed the top of his head. "Kid, remind me to get you a haircut."

Andy laughed. "Dad said he didn't do any of that stuff on the news, which makes sense because he was up at the cabin for a long time. I forgot about that place. We haven't gone for so long and we never go in winter, so I didn't think about it, but if he was there the whole time then the police can't even say anything, right?"

"Take a breath, kiddo." Val kissed his cheek. "Why don't you go inside? I'm sure your dad is dying to see you."

"Oh my gosh, right?" Andy's face lit up. "Okay." He looked around for Vincent and Marie. "Grandma, Grandpa, I'm gonna go inside."

"I'll go with you." Vincent put a hand on Andy's shoulder and steered him toward the stairs. "Quite a story he's going to have, huh?"

"Totally."

Val turned to Jackson as Andy and her dad walked into the sheriff's department. She held her arms out. "Hug. Now."

Jackson rolled his eyes, but he walked into her arms. "You're not the cool mom if you hug. You know that, right?"

"I do not care about being the cool mom." Val wrapped her arms around her tall boy. "Go easy on him. I know you're mad, but take a breath."

"I know."

"None of us are perfect," Val said. "And hopefully, this will be a lesson learned."

"He's kind of old for that, don't you think?"

"Hey." She leaned back. "You're never too old to stop learning." She tweaked his ear. "Aren't you the one who told me I didn't have to do everything myself?"

"Yeah." His cheeks flushed a little.

"So you should have seen me asking for help the past couple of days. I was asking for help all over the place. Sully, Robin, Mark, random forestry personnel..."

"Very funny, Mom."

"Seriously." She didn't know if Josh had told the boys about Anderson trying to kill them, so she figured she'd wait and see. The less the boys knew about that, the better, in her opinion. "Go on." She pushed him toward the doors. "Go see your dad. Try not to lecture him too much. He's had a rough day."

Val watched Jackson follow Andy and her dad up the stairs and into the sheriff's department, slouching as he walked. Val leaned against her truck and took a deep breath.

Marie slid an arm around her waist. "Random forestry personnel?"

"Savannah Anderson's husband tracked us up there and tried to take a few shots at us from a distance."

Marie's arm tightened around Val. "And?"

"Sully arrested him. Josh has a graze on his temple, but he'll be okay. The medics checked him out."

"So that man really did try to kill that sweet girl?"

"Yep."

Marie shook her head. "My heart hurts for the world, Valerie Jean."

"Just don't let it hurt for Allan Anderson," Val said. "He'll probably get off with a slap on the wrist because he didn't actually succeed in killing anyone."

Marie shook her head. "I'm just glad that you're safe, Josh is safe, and that woman isn't going to be in danger anymore."

Sully walked out of the office, shrugging into his jacket as he donned his hat and scanned the parking lot. He spotted Val and his gaze stopped.

She raised a hand and waved. "Hey."

Without a word, he walked over to Val and Marie.

"Mrs. Costa." He tipped his hat. "Val."

"I just realized Josh's truck is still up by the ranger station in Keane."

"Yeah. He gave me his keys. I'll have a couple of deputies head up there in the morning to pick it up. I called Bridger PD and filled them in. Mason is on the phone with his snow-mobile buddy right now. I guess he did find the envelope with the money. It was in a pile of mail they thought was junk."

"Crazy."

"I know. Anyway, Bridger PD agreed he could drive down with me in the morning to officially turn himself in."

"He still has to go through all that stuff?"

"The warrant doesn't just disappear because everyone figures out the person making the complaint is a criminal. He's going to have to go through the process."

"And tonight?"

Sully shrugged. "He could sleep here at the station."

Val grimaced. "Or... on my couch." She sighed. "Ugh." She couldn't leave Josh to sleep on a broken couch or in a cell. Her boys would never forgive her.

Marie put her hand on Val's shoulder. "Why doesn't he sleep in our guest room?" She smiled. "It's Josh. He may be a bit of a headache, but he's Jackson and Andy's father. At the end of the day, he's still family, but you don't have to do everything. Dad and I will take him tonight."

Marie walked into the sheriff's office, giving Val a curious look as Sully leaned on the truck next to her.

"What does that look mean?" Sully asked.

"It means she's getting ideas."

"About?"

"Us."

"Good." He handed Val his hat.

She took it, frowning. "Why are you giving me your hat?"

He wiggled his fingers. "I figured you could do your thing. Get the scoop on what's going on with your ex."

Val didn't take her gloves off, but she smiled. "You're giving me your hat so I can 'do my thing'?"

"I figured it was more efficient for you to just... see what happened in there instead of me explaining everything."

She fingered the brim of his hat. "Tempting. But no."

"No?"

She smiled. "I don't need to know everything. I don't want to know everything. I trust you to tell me the important stuff."

He angled his shoulders toward her, his arms crossed on his chest. "You mean that?"

"Definitely." She wiggled her fingers. "You really think I like having this ability?"

"I figured you might have trouble trusting people," Sully said. "I imagine a lot of what people say versus what they're really doing or thinking doesn't match up."

She was shocked that he recognized it. Few people brought that aspect of her power up. "Yeah. I do have trouble trusting people," Val said. "But not you."

The corner of his mouth turned up. "No?"

"No. You don't hide much. When you want something, you say so."

He nodded. "Good."

She handed him his hat. "Who you are on the outside matches up with the inside," Val said. "As far as I can tell."

"I'm too lazy to lie." Sully put his hat on his head and angled the brim over his eyes. "Lying takes a lot of energy."

"So it won't bother you? Really?"

"Your thing?" He raised an eyebrow. "I mean, it might get annoying around Christmas and birthdays. Don't push it."

Val smiled. "I won't."

"Good."

Sully's broad shoulder was right there and Val was tired, so she leaned her head on it. It felt nice. Solid and warm.

"...maybe think about how I could add something. How being with me could add something to your life."

Val smiled. "I like you, Sully Wescott."

"I like you too, Valerie Costa. Want to go out?"

"Yeah. I think I do."

CHAPTER 25

Two days after the shooting in Keane, Val watched on the news as Savannah Anderson left the hospital with Josh at her side. Andy and Jackson were sitting next to Val on the couch, eating popcorn and waiting for the news to end so they could switch to watching *Friends*.

Because apparently that was cool again?

Jackson said, "You think this one will last?"

"She looks nice," Andy said. "Her smile is really pretty."

And visible, Val thought. That was a definite change. Savannah Anderson might have looked like she was still recovering, but she also looked like a new woman. There was a brightness in her face and the smile she aimed at Josh...

"I really hope he doesn't mess this up," Val said.

Jackson muttered, "Well, it's Josh, so who knows?"

Her oldest had taken to calling his father by his given name. Val honestly wasn't sure what to think about it, but she decided that since Jackson was the more responsible of the two of them, he could call his father what he wanted.

"I think she'll be nice," Andy said.

Of course you do. Val brushed Andy's hair back from his forehead. "She seems like a nice person to me. I hope your dad is good for her."

"Rachel was nice too," Jackson said. "And so was Carrie. And Jess. And Melanie. I forget the one before Melanie, but Sarah—"

"He gets it." Val put a hand on Jackson's arm. "Just leave it, Jack."

"Just saying."

Hearing Jackson's bitterness about Josh's relationships made what she wanted to bring up even harder. Sully had asked her out on a date that weekend. While she knew that she didn't have the same history as Josh—

"Mom, you should be the one getting a boyfriend," Jackson said. "You deserve someone nice taking you out."

Val blinked. *Huh?*

"Yeah," Andy said. "Oscar's mom got married again, and his stepdad is so cool and he goes to all Oscar's robotics competitions. Oscar's on the robotics team."

Jackson said, "I just think you should have someone nice. You never go out or anything unless it's with Robin and Monica. You should go out with someone fun."

"*If* I get a boyfriend... or even date anyone, it'll be because... I don't know. They're nice and responsible." God, how boring did she sound? "And fun. Um... I might be going out with someone this weekend." She shifted in her seat and picked up the remote. "*Friends*, right?"

"What?" Andy's eyes were wide. "You have a date this weekend?"

Jackson had a sneaky smile on his face. "I know who it is."

Andy was nearly screeching. "Who? Did she tell you? Who is it?"

Jackson smacked the back of Andy's head. "Dude, calm down. You know."

"Jack, don't hit your brother." Val was trying to ignore them and scrolling through the episodes. "Okay, I never watched this show. What episode are you on?"

"She's totally trying to avoid the conversation."

"I still don't know who you're talking about," Andy said. "Jack, tell me!"

Jackson leaned over and whispered in his ear. Andy's mouth formed a small O. "Is it Sheriff Sully?"

Jackson's smile was bordering on smug. Val tossed the remote at him. "You think you're so smart."

"Is it?" Andy was nearly jumping. "Are you going out with Sheriff Sully? That's so cool!"

Val felt like her face had to be the color of Andy's red sweatshirt. "It's just a date. We're going out to dinner. It's not a big deal."

"Sure." Jackson started an episode. "Whatever you say, Mom."

"Sheriff Sully is cool, and he has a really awesome truck!" Andy had a huge smile on his face. "He'll be a great boyfriend. I saw him open the car door for you like Grandpa Vincent always says we should do."

"You do that for anyone," Val said. "To be polite and helpful."

"But that's totally a boyfriend thing, right?"

Jackson shot Andy a killer look. "Dude. Be cool."

"Andy, please do not tell all your friends at school that

Sully is my boyfriend, okay?" She mussed his hair. "We're not jumping into anything. We're just going on a date."

"Okay." Andy tried his best to be calm. "That's cool."

"Yeah." She turned her attention to the sitcom on the television. "He's nice."

Four months later…

AT THE END of the day, Allan Anderson got far more than a slap on the wrist. The district attorney was newly elected and more than happy to make an example of the privileged domestic abuser who'd cut his wife's brake lines, tried to frame her lover, and then shot at law enforcement.

There was a slight media flurry for a month or so, with reporters coming in and out of Bridger City and Glimmer Lake. The story of the former Olympian, the beautiful and sad wife, and her dangerously handsome lover made for attractive cable-news fodder. Val had to shut the door on reporters more than one time, but after a month or so—by the time the real legal ramifications started to roll in—things had calmed down.

"Mom!" Andy barreled into Misfit after school. "Dad says he's taking us up to the cabin with Savannah this weekend! Can we go?"

"Of course." Val exchanged a look with JoJo, who was getting ready to shut down the espresso machine. "Sounds like fun. Is there still a little snow up there?"

"I think so."

JoJo leaned over the counter. "What can I get you?"

Andy smiled innocently. "Double espresso?"

JoJo looked at Val with a dubious expression on their face.

"Not on your life," Val said. "You and caffeine? Think again, kid."

Andy sighed dramatically. "Vanilla cream frappé, please."

"Coming right up." JoJo poured milk into the blender and chatted with Andy, who yammered about his day at school like the ray of sunshine he was.

Since the accident, Josh hadn't missed a weekend with the boys. He'd even taken them to Las Vegas for a boys' weekend the month before. Val didn't know if he was turning over a new leaf, feeling guilty for almost half-orphaning them with his bullshit, or taking cues from Savannah, who seemed to love having the kids around. But either way, Andy was ecstatic, Jackson was begrudgingly civil, and Val had a few weekends to herself.

Jackson slunk into the coffee shop a few minutes after Andy did, staring at his phone and avoiding Val's eyes.

Uh-oh.

"What's up?" she asked. It was finals week, which meant he'd only had one class that day and he'd had the rest of the day free. "Did your final go okay?"

Jackson looked up as if he'd just registered where he was. "Oh. Hey, Mom. Yeah, it went fine."

Val leaned on the counter. "What's up?"

Val didn't need to be psychic to see his internal debate.

Should I tell her?

She won't let up until I do.

She won't get it.

Parents are such a pain in the ass.

"Just tell me what's going on," Val said. "And I'll make you a macchiato."

Andy's head swung around. "How come he gets coffee?"

"Because he's seventeen now and much taller than me, so I'm actively trying to stunt his growth." Val scanned her son. He was being cagey. He was fidgeting with his left wrist. He was...

Val's eyes went wide when she spotted the familiar bandage.

Her baby was tattooed.

Tattooed.

She snapped her fingers. "Come here."

Jackson groaned. "Mom, it's not a big deal."

"Nah-uh." She slapped her hand on the counter. "Come. *Here.*"

He sighed. "It's not like you don't have a ton of them! You just got two more—"

"I am forty-six!" She pointed to her chest. "You are *seventeen*! How did you get this? Did you go to someone unlicensed? Jack, so help me—"

"We drove to Nevada, okay!" Jackson sighed. "After the final. We just barely got back, okay? I drove to a place on the state line and got it. It was a regular tattoo parlor, okay? It had a bunch of reviews online. It was clean and I watched them unwrap the needles and it was totally safe, okay?"

Val wasn't happy. Even though she'd done literally the same thing when she was sixteen. "Give me your wrist."

Andy and JoJo were watching from the side in horror as Jackson approached his irate mother.

So help her, if her oldest child had marred the perfect

skin she had created *in her own womb* with a cartoon character, girl's name, or any of the stupid shit that teenage boys—

"See?" Jackson pulled up his sleeve and unpeeled the bandage. "It's not a big deal."

Val looked at the honeycomb-looking structures inked in fine lines on her son's skin. "What is it?"

"It's the chemical structure of dopamine and serotonin," Jackson said. "Mood-regulating hormones."

She looked up. "That's... cool? Why?"

Jackson stared at the tattoo. "To remind me that moods are really just chemicals that come and go. Happy. Sad. Angry. They're just chemicals in my brain. They don't get to decide my life or make my decisions." He looked up. "Think. Don't just feel."

Oh, her proud, determined kid. Val lifted his wrist and kissed just to the side of the healing skin. "You need both, kid. Head and heart."

He smiled. "That'll be my next one then."

Val groaned. "He's already an addict."

"Hey." He pointed at her. "Takes one to know one."

The bell over the door rang again, and Val re-covered Jackson's healing tattoo with the bandage. "Talk to me tonight about how to take care of it, okay? Do *not* use Neosporin."

"Okay." He bounced on his heels. "Do I get my macchiato?"

"No."

"Mom!"

"Fine." She nodded to the side. "Now shoo."

Val smiled at Robin and Monica, who were walking toward the counter. "You guys know we're closed, right?"

JoJo laughed as they pulled another shot of espresso. "Right."

Val looked at them. "You know, we flip that sign over every afternoon and no one ever pays attention to it."

"To be fair"—JoJo scrunched up their nose—"we keep making coffee for all the stragglers."

"It's like feeding bears," Val whispered.

"I heard that!" Monica dropped her purse on a table and took out a folder. "We are here for business reasons, Ms. Costa."

"Do you have the contract for Russell House?"

"Yep!" Monica grinned. "You ready to sign?"

"Is it the same as what Phil looked over last week?" Val was going out on a limb and setting up a coffee stand at Russell House like Monica and Robin had been pestering her to do, but she wasn't doing it without someone smarter going over the contract.

"Yep," Robin said. "We had our guy look at it, and Phil gave it his stamp of approval too. We're both covered, and you'll technically be renting space from us, so the insurance stuff will be taken care of like we'd already detailed in the previous contract."

"Cool." She reached for a pen.

It had taken a good amount of legal finagling to make sure everything lined up and both Russell House and Misfit Mountain Coffee Company were covered and insured and happily independent, legally speaking. Now that all the details were out of the way, Val was starting to feel excited. Eve would be managing the new stand, and JoJo would be taking over as head barista at the main shop. Eve was excited about the promotion and the profit sharing idea Val had dreamed up. JoJo was excited about the raise.

And Val?

Val was... still busy.

She had her boys and her parents. She had the coffee shop and a new stand at the fancy-schmancy boutique hotel on the shores of Glimmer Lake, which would need to be up and running in only a few weeks.

She continued to take her antianxiety meds and felt like she was finally gaining control over the psychometry—she'd finally done some research into her gift—that had become a part of her life. It was starting to feel less like a curse and more like a superpower.

That's what her newest tattoos were about. She glanced down at the lightning-like branches inked from her inner arms down onto her wrists. The ends of the lightning ended under the fine black gloves that had become her signature fashion accessory.

This power wasn't going away, so Val was claiming it. It was hers, and she wasn't going to hide it from the people she loved.

Well, maybe her boys. For now. The last thing they needed was a complex about how much their mom could spy on them.

Not that she did. Much.

"Hey, boss!" Ramon called from the kitchen. "I'm finished cleaning up back here. I'm heading out."

"Good man." Val took a breath and quickly signed her name. "Tell Honey I said hi." Just another day in the coffee shop. Minding her business. Opening a second location.

Ramon said, "She's making bear claws tomorrow morning."

Monica caught Val's eye. "Save me one, or I will break your wrist."

Val blinked. "Um, a little violent over a bear claw, don't you think?"

Robin shrugged. "I mean, it's one of Honey's..."

To be fair, Honey didn't make bear claws every week. It was more a once-a-month thing because they were so huge and took so much work.

The bell rang again, and Val looked up from leaving her signature on the papers spread across the table. This time it was Sully walking through the door.

"Wow," he said. "Someone plan a party and not invite me?"

Monica said, "Honey's making bear claws tomorrow morning."

"Oh shit." Sully's eyes went wide. "What time do you open?"

"For Pete's sake, they're just pastries, people."

"I don't know who Pete is," Sully said, "but he doesn't make bear claws like Honey."

"Bye, all!" Ramon waved at the crowd and disappeared into the back.

Val put the cap back on her pen. "Okay, there is officially another branch of Misfit Mountain Coffee Company."

A cheer went up from Sully, JoJo, Robin, Monica, and the boys.

Sully's smile was wide and generous. "That's awesome." He looked at Monica and Robin. "So I'm gonna be able to get decent coffee up at Russell House when I have to come break up the fights there, huh?"

"Ha ha." Monica rolled her eyes. "That was one guy who brought a flask to a business retreat. It's not exactly Chaco's bar up there."

"I don't blame him for the flask," Robin said quietly. "Who does trust falls in the snow?"

"We did warn that manager about the slush," Monica said. "She overruled us."

Jackson walked over to Sully. "Hey, check out my new ink."

Sully glanced at Val, who nodded, before he looked at Jackson's arm. "That's cool. Science stuff, huh?"

"Yeah."

He was good with her boys. Sully hadn't spent a ton of time around Jackson and Andy yet. They were keeping things pretty casual for now. But when he did run into them, Andy was his usual bursting ray of sunshine and Jackson played it cool, but Val could tell he liked having Sully's opinion on things.

She put her copies of the contract in the folder Monica brought and stared at it, thinking about everything that had changed in the past year.

New business.

New perspective.

New man in her life.

She looked up to see Robin and Monica smiling at her.

Some things never changed. Some things didn't need to.

She stared at the two greatest friends in the world.

Love you, she mouthed.

Monica blew her a kiss and Robin mouthed, *Love you more.*

Val was still staring at the folder with her shiny new contracts when Sully sidled up next to her and leaned down. "So can a hardworking law-enforcement officer get some coffee this time of day, or am I out of luck?"

"I don't know. Did you bring your own mug?"

Sully gave Val the secret smile she loved. "Of course."

He'd taken to leaving hidden messages on his coffee cup. Well, hidden to everyone but Val. Sometimes the images she saw when she touched his coffee cup were sweet. Sometimes they cracked her up. She slipped off her right glove and reached for his silver travel mug, letting the metal warm in her hand as the image became clear.

As soon as Val saw the memory on Sully's mug, she burst out laughing so loudly she clapped a hand over her mouth.

There was Sully, freshly showered and dressed only with a bath towel around his waist, shaking his hips in front of his foggy mirror to Sophie B. Hawkins's "Damn, I Wish I Was Your Lover," and singing into his travel mug like it was a microphone.

"Val?" Robin looked up with a curious expression, but Val couldn't stop laughing. There were tears running down her cheeks.

Before she could slip away, Sully pinched her ass and cleared his throat. "Jeez, Valerie, get a handle on yourself. All I asked for was some coffee."

She shook her head and walked behind the counter, still wiping her eyes.

Robin and Monica were watching her with amused expressions. Jackson was rolling his eyes, and Andy was listening intently to whatever JoJo was talking about. Probably some new meme on YouTube.

Sun poured through the windows, and Val took off her gloves, pressing both her hands to the counter behind the register.

It was warm. The counter shouted memories of laughter and frustration and yelling and singing. Voice after voice of employees she adored, customers she cherished, and the cacophony of love that filled her life.

She poured Sully's coffee and added cream to the brim before she looked around the business and life she'd built.

In a world where she'd never fit in, she'd somehow managed to build a family like no other. Silence? Who needed it?

Her coffee cup runneth over.

———

THANKS FOR READING SEMI-PSYCHIC LIFE! I hope you enjoyed Val's story. **Monica's book is coming in August 2020 and you can preorder it now**, but turn the page if you want your first look at the synopsis of PSYCHIC DREAMS.

FIRST LOOK: PSYCHIC DREAMS

Coming August 2020!
Available for preorder now.

It's been three years since Monica Velasquez lost the love of her life to a sudden and devastating heart attack. She's held her family together and picked herself up with the love and help of her two best friends. Now the kids have moved out, and Monica has a new business, a new wardrobe, and a new vision for the future.

As in, *actual* psychic visions. Dreams that manifest in reality. Monica still isn't sure why or how it happened, but she's been seeing everything from unexpected visitors to visions of fire and destruction.

Separating psychic premonitions from morbid imagination is proving harder than she expected, and Monica starts feeling the heat—or is it a hot flash?—when the town's new fire inspector grows suspicious of her accurate and anonymous tips.

Is their town about to feel the burn of a serial arsonist, or can Monica, Robin, and Val figure out the dangerous secret smoldering at the heart of Glimmer Lake?

Psychic Dreams is a standalone paranormal women's fiction novel in the Glimmer Lake series by USA Today best seller Elizabeth Hunter, author of the Elemental Mysteries and the Irin Chronicles.

Order today for delivery on your e-reader in August 2020.

Sign up for my newsletter for all the latest updates or visit ElizabethHunterWrites.com for information about my books.

ACKNOWLEDGMENTS

First of all, because this book was published during the COVID-19 pandemic, I would like to thank all the people around the world working in essential jobs:

The nurses, doctors, and scientists finding answers and treating the sick.

But also the postal carriers, the grocery clerks, the agricultural workers, the truck drivers, the warehouse personnel, and all the countless men and women around the world who make our lives possible. Thank you for all your hard work.

We are stronger together.

You know, when I wrote *Semi-Psychic Life*, finding reasons for Val to wear gloves seemed like a challenge. In a few short months, she became an early adopter.

It's not often that the things that are most important in life come into such stark focus. Food. Home. Safety. Health.

Coffee. (Kidding, but not really.) For that reason, I want to thank all the essential workers above.

I also want to thank my family. My husband and son are so crucial to my mental well-being, I doubt they realize how much of their love and care go into every book I write. When you read about an awesome boyfriend or husband, or a funny and (generally) great teenager, you're seeing a little bit of them. David and Colin, I absolutely adore you both. You make my life so rich.

To my readers, who buy my books and (an even bigger compliment) talk about them to their friends and family, I love and appreciate you so much. People often thank me for writing books, but a novelist isn't going to make much of an impact (or an income!) without readers. My readers are the absolute best, and I love to brag about them, especially all the fabulous Hunters in Hunters' Haven.

To the administrators of my reader group, Hannah, Meg, Tiffany, Danielle, and Fiona, you are wonderful and I owe you so many rounds of your favorite adult beverages. Someday, my friends. Someday.

To my wonderful Jenn and Gen, I miss you. Oh, I miss you. Video chats are not nearly enough. I'm in the office completely alone now, except for the dogs, and they are way harsher than they look. Don't let the cute furry faces fool you. Brutal. Absolutely brutal critics.

To my awesome editing team, Amy Cissell at **Cissell Ink** and Anne and Linda at **Victory Editing**. You guys are amazing and I'm so sorry that I will never spell grey with an "a" like a proper American but it just looks wrong—wrong, I tell you! Please forward all complaints to my father and the British schooling system.

Author's Note: *Also, they didn't edit these acknowledgements because I always leave them to the very end, so if there are typos (which there probably are) it's all on me.*

To my fabulous cover artists at **Damonza**, thank you for always making my book covers so eye-catching and gorgeous. The covers for Glimmer Lake defied every expectation.

To all the folks at **Social Butterfly PR**, but especially to **Emily Kidman**, thank you for your love, faith, and the numerous and frequent reminders that are necessary to keep me on track. (Seriously, I have no idea what I'm supposed to be doing to promote this book. For the love of toilet paper, Emily, please text me and remind me what to do.)

To the wonderful ladies of the Paranormal Women's Fiction Fab 13, I want to give love, kudos, and shoutouts! **Michelle M. Pillow, Mandy Roth, Jana DeLeon, KF Breene, Shannon Mayer, Darynda Jones, Eve Langlais, Robyn Peterman, Kristin Painter, Deanna Chase, Denise Grover Swank, and Christine Bell.** You are a consortium of awesome, and I don't know why you agreed to let me hang out with the cool kids, but I'm so glad you did.

Cheers, everyone! Stay home and stay safe. We'll get through this together, and I'll see you online.

EH

ABOUT THE AUTHOR

ELIZABETH HUNTER is a *USA Today* and international best-selling author of romance, contemporary fantasy, and paranormal mystery. Based in Central California, she travels extensively to write fantasy fiction exploring world mythologies, history, and the universal bonds of love, friendship, and family. She has published over thirty works of fiction and sold over a million books worldwide. She is the author of Love Stories on 7th and Main, the Elemental Legacy series, the Irin Chronicles, the Cambio Springs Mysteries, and other works of fiction.

ElizabethHunterWrites.com

Night's Reckoning

Dawn Caravan

(Summer 2020)

The Irin Chronicles

The Scribe

The Singer

The Secret

The Staff and the Blade

The Silent

The Storm

The Seeker

Linx & Bogie Mysteries

A Ghost in the Glamour

A Bogie in the Boat